Murder to the Max

Murder to the Max

Paul Chmielewski

iUniverse, Inc.
New York Lincoln Shanghai

Murder to the Max

All Rights Reserved © 2003 by Paul Chmielewski

No part of this book may be reproduced or transmitted in any form or by any means, graphic, electronic, or mechanical, including photocopying, recording, taping, or by any information storage retrieval system, without the written permission of the publisher.

iUniverse, Inc.

For information address:
iUniverse, Inc.
2021 Pine Lake Road, Suite 100
Lincoln, NE 68512
www.iuniverse.com

ISBN: 0-595-29936-9

Printed in the United States of America

This book is for my wife, Patty—with love.

Acknowledgements

The author wishes to acknowledge the invaluable assistance of the following people; Denise Hurd, Linda White, Sue Galli, Holly Hurd, Chuck Tice, Carol Sigler, Bev Piskorski, Alice Kowalczyk, and Lissa.

Chapter 1

▼

"Excuse me!" I said, interrupting the irate woman screaming into the phone. "Exactly why are you calling me an asshole? Bob West is your stylist and he's the one who stood you up."

"Well you own the salon, don't you?" the angry voice asked.

"Yes."

"And you hired him?"

"Yes, but…"

"In my book," she said cutting me short, "that makes you an asshole too."

It was hard to argue with such linear logic.

"I had an important job interview at Ford World Headquarters yesterday," she continued. "And it was crucial my hair look its absolute best."

"Once again, Ms Dunn," I said through slightly clenched teeth. "I'm sorry this happened. If you would like to come in today, I'll color and highlight your hair for free."

"As if!" the woman said snappishly. "No way are you getting off the hook that easy."

I felt my fingers tighten around the phone. "Is that a threat?"

"No," she said "more like a promise. If I don't get the position at Ford, my attorney will sue your ass off."

Sitting alone at the reception desk, I placed the handset gently down in its cradle and glanced at the clock beside it. 9:01 a.m. I'd been at work for less than thirty minutes. It felt like three hours.

My name is Max Snow. I'm the owner of Maxie's Hair Salon, located in South Lyon, Michigan. You can check us out on the second level of the Rolling

Pines Mall; east-wing, center-court, sandwiched comfortably between Victoria's Secret and the always scandalous Fantasy Footwear.

I arrived at the salon that morning about eight, found an inch of water on the floor of my office, and just knew the day was going to tank from there. Sometime during the night the hot water heater (ever notice how the beasts only act up in the middle of the night?) had loosed its entire seventy-five gallons, flooding the rear of the salon and peeing, through minute cracks, into the Disney Store below. Mall Security had called me at home to report the damage. Seems the famous mouse and friends were not at all pleased with the unexpected shower. Although I'm what might be called "plumbing challenged" I successfully cut off the water to the tank, fielded several more complaints from the clients Bob West had stiffed yesterday, and just as I managed to re-boot the stubborn computer for the third time in ten minutes, the electrical power in the mall blinked out.

With the power down, the phone was blissfully silent so I took the opportunity to try and track down Andra Martin; my business partner, salon manager, and cracker-jack solver of all problems therein. She was scheduled to start work at eight that morning and had an almost anal quirk about showing up on time. I used my cell phone to call Andra's cell, house, and pager. No luck. My fourth call was to the apartment of her best friend, and the salon's assistant manager, Carly Fox, a green eyed, auburn haired twenty-four-year old who'd been tight with Andra since the third grade.

"Hey Foxy," I said when she picked up. "You got a line on Andra? I can't seem to find her."

"What do you mean you can't find her? She's not there?"

"Nope."

"Well, where could she be? It's after nine."

"I was kind of hoping you'd know. Did you see her last night?"

"She stopped by after work," Fox said. "We did pizza and a chick-flick. She left for home about ten."

"Are you sure that's where she was heading?"

"She said she was. Did you call her house?"

"Of course. All I get is a recorded message saying the line's being checked for trouble."

"How about her pager?"

"Yep."

"And her cell phone?"

"Well, duh."

"Sorry," Fox said. "Do you want me to come in and help out?"

I considered the offer briefly, but declined. Fox was dealing with her own problems. She had recently dumped a guy she'd dated for a little under a month, but Mr. Macho was having trouble with rejection and wouldn't back off.

"I don't mind," Fox said. "I could be there in twenty minutes."

"Thanks honey, but it's your day off. I can handle things until Andra shows up. And Gwen the wonder receptionist should be here any minute."

"Okay," Fox said. "But tell our missing girl to call me as soon as she comes in."

"Right."

"You promise?"

"Yes, Fox, I promise."

The moment I hit disconnect, the phone signaled an incoming call.

"Max Snow."

"Max, it's Riff."

Linda Riff is a friend, client and police lieutenant for the city of Southfield.

"Hey Riff, what's shakin'?"

"Did you hear about the fire?"

"Fire?" I repeated. "What fire?"

"Hold on a second, Max."

While I waited, my mind swung back to the overdue salon manager, and by the time Riff came back on the line a minute later, a strong sense of anxiety had tightened my chest.

"I'm calling from Andra Martin's home, Max. There was a fire here last night. Both she and her mother died of smoke inhalation."

The blunt statement rocked me like a shot to the head, and I stared blankly through the salon's double-glass doors into the dark hallway.

"Max? You still there?"

I nodded in answer to her question as a swarm of white dots orbited my head like mini satellites. A second later I realized I was holding my breath and when I exhaled in a gush, a round of deep-seated coughs racked my chest.

"Are you sure?" I asked, my voice sounding raw and anxious.

"I know how you must feel, Max," Riff said, "but I need your help. Andra's sister just showed up here and she's going to need some support. Is there a family member I could call...someone she's close to?"

"There is no other family," I answered automatically. "Except for a stepbrother, but he's a big time doper and the family doesn't have much contact with him."

"Well then, how about you?" Riff asked. "Think you can handle it?"

"Yeah," I heard myself say although a big part of me wanted to scream "forget it". "Be there in twenty minutes."

Before leaving, I wrote a note for Gwen instructing her to cancel my appointments for that day and to contact the plumbers about the leaky water tank. I would have liked to write more, or wait and explain what was going down but I couldn't sit still. And I hated the thought that Jessica Martin was facing that grizzly death scene all alone.

Driving to the house in Southfield, my thoughts were a jumbled mess. How could Andra let herself die in a stupid house fire? She was young and agile. And there were plenty of doors and windows in the house for crissake. Why didn't they get out?

Andra had first entered my life as a client four years ago, and despite an age difference of almost two decades, we became instant friends. Our first meeting felt like destiny; it was that comfortable and both of us thought we might have done this friendship thing before. This time around, things were purely platonic but not because I wasn't attracted. Andra was a living doll and surprisingly, at the tender age of twenty-three, one of the most mature women I had ever known. But the rapport we shared was more like big brother-little sister, and wasn't complicated by the hassles and insecurities that a physical relationship can bring. We simply enjoyed each other's company.

Two years ago when I hit the state lottery for twelve million, I exited the hair biz, thinking two decades of anything was more than enough. Andra had a different idea, and after seeing that a life of decadent leisure might possibly lead to my early demise (okay, so I have an addictive personality), she suggested we open a salon together. Six months after we agreed on a partnership, "Maxie's" opened in the mall, and mostly because of Andra's over-the-top organizational skills and boundless enthusiasm, the salon was an instant success.

Half a block from the still smoldering house, I pulled to the curb and parked. Did I want to do this? Not even. My usual way of dealing with a crisis was to ignore it and hope it went away, or step back in the wings and let somebody else take charge. Not exactly what you'd call a mature attitude for a forty-two year old man, but when something works, I tend to stay with it.

I got out of the car and walked toward the house, marveling at the selective damage the fire had caused. The fatal flames had blackened only the left side of the ranch-style home. The right side, although slightly smoke damaged, remained practically untouched. Yellow police tape surrounded the area. When I ducked under it, a gruff looking uniformed officer came over to ask my business.

A few minutes later, Riff emerged from the house and walked over to me. I had known this bright, attractive woman for several years. She was a good cop and I admired her ability to maintain a sense of compassion despite serving twenty years on a busy metropolitan police force. Dressed casually in khakis, loafers, and button down gray fleece sweatshirt, she gave me a half-smile but the ice-blue eyes reflected her grim mood.

"What the hell happened here, Riff?"

"Fire started in the mother's bedroom," she answered and glanced back at the house. "As far as we can tell, Lila Martin had been drinking and fell asleep with a cigarette in her hand. Arson found an empty pint of whisky in bed with her."

We locked eyes as my stunned brain processed the information.

"Andra was probably overcome by smoke when she entered her mother's room," Riff said, answering my next question before I could ask. "Her body was found on the floor beside the bed."

A knot of tension twisted my stomach as I tried not to look at the house.

"Jessica Martin told me her mom had a problem with alcohol," Riff said. "Know anything about that?"

"Yeah," I said. "It was a big problem. Started when her husband was gunned down three years ago."

Riff gave me a palms-up.

"He saw some guy being mugged behind a building in downtown Detroit, tried to help, and got two .45 caliber slugs in the gut for his trouble. The way Andra told it, Lila drank herself to sleep practically every night after that, sometimes with a burning cigarette in her hand."

"Is that why Andra still lived at home?"

I nodded, my brain tinged with the irony. "She was afraid her mom was going to burn the house down."

Four cops in dark blue jumpsuits exited single-file from the house, and Riff went to speak to a woman who seemed to be heading up the team.

Waiting for her to return, I tried in vain to understand how this tragedy could have happened. There must have been smoke detectors in the house. The ever-efficient Andra would never neglect something so important, given her mom's history. Plus they owned a poodle. Wouldn't Muffin have smelled smoke and warned them?

By the time Riff returned, my emotions were wired and I snapped at her. "Weren't there any fucking smoke detectors?"

"Yeah." she shot back. "Two. Neither had a battery."

I glared at her and felt angry tears leak from my eyes. "That's impossible, Riff. Andra was all about detail."

My friend only shrugged with a cop's detachment.

"What about the dog then?" I said unable to adjust my attitude. "Didn't the damn dog smell the smoke?"

"The dog was locked in its cage in Lila Martin's bedroom."

"What? No…"

"Look, Max," Riff said slipping an arm around my shoulder, "if you want to help Jessica, you're going to have to put your own grief on hold right now."

I leaned into her for support. "I have no idea what to do," I said my voice choked with emotion. "I never faced anything like this before."

"Neither has Jessica Martin," Riff said as we locked eyes. "My advice is to take her home with you tonight. Tomorrow you help her make funeral arrangements."

I must have looked panicky because Riff pulled me closer.

"All you need to do is pick a funeral home, Maxie. The people there will guide you through the process."

To dodge the media hounds, Riff had put Jessica in a police car parked a short distance away. As soon as she stepped out, I was struck like I usually am by the eerie resemblance to her younger sister. Their heights were basically the same give or take an inch, and both had the ultra-slim figure of a fashion model. Only the color and style of their hair truly made one stand out from the other. Jessica is a natural blonde with a shoulder length shag. I had colored Andra's one-length hair a deep chestnut-brown just last week, and it fell almost to the middle of her back.

"God, Jess," I said when the woman's inwardly-focused eyes met mine, "I'm so sorry."

"Take me away from here, Max," she said and hugged me tightly. "Please."

I led her to my car and after checking my mirrors for traffic, pulled away from the curb. As I did, a small knot of gawkers outside the police line caught my attention. There was a familiar face in the crowd, and when I slowed to get a better look, the man I knew only as Kenny turned toward the street. Kenny is a middle-aged, mentally challenged busboy who works in one of the mall restaurants. We met in the Coffee Beanery several weeks ago, and fueled by my undisciplined caffeine consumption, I came on a bit too friendly. After that, he decided we were buddies. And when he began stopping by the salon four or five times a day, I decided he was a pest.

The clock on the dash read eleven-thirty by the time I pulled up to the back door of my house; a large, two-story modern pagoda with an attached garage located on the east-shore of Cradle Lake. Inside, I settled Jessica on the couch in front of the fireplace, handed her my cell phone, and headed for the kitchen. Checking the big double-freezer, I found two unopened pints of Ben and Jerry's best, Chunky Monkey and Cherry Garcia. Scooping some of each into a couple of bowls, I drizzled the tops with hot fudge and after adding a shot of whipped cream, carried them into the living room.

Jessica's expression was bemused when I set the ice cream sundae in front of her.

"When I was a kid," I explained, "my mom told me ice cream soothed the soul. I still use her remedy when I'm feeling down."

Fresh tears filled Jessica's eyes but she wiped them away. "I like your mom," she said trying for a smile. "She's very cool."

I paused with a scoop of ice cream halfway to my mouth. "Oh she's cool all right. Sometimes a little too cool. But she's got a big heart under that pushy exterior."

Jessica spent the next several hours walking the beach in front of my house. I thought about joining her but sensed she needed space. It was my guess she was working out issues connected to the deaths of her mother and sister; issues almost everyone has to face when a family member dies.

At six o'clock, a light rain forced her inside and she stood warming herself by the fireplace.

"Feel like any dinner?" I asked while pulling a veggie frittata and a pan of blueberry muffins from the oven and placing them on a glass bistro table. "I wasn't sure if you'd be in the mood to eat but I didn't know what else to do."

With arms folded, Jessica walked into the kitchen and leaned over the frittata. "Smells great. Guess I am kind of hungry."

She sat in the chair I offered and watched me plate the food.

"You're a very sweet man, Maxie. I can't think of anyone else I'd rather be with tonight."

"Same here," I said resisting the tears that threatened to spill over.

Jessica and I spent most of the next morning making arrangements at the Chapman Funeral Home in Southfield. And although the director there was helpful, it was still one of the hardest things I ever had to do. The worst part for both of us was the coffin showroom.

"As you can see," explained Mr. Chapman, a tall, gaunt faced man with skin the color of aged parchment, "we offer a large selection. This one is called 'Heavenly Slumber'." He stopped and placed a hand almost lovingly on what had to be the top of the line model. "Pure mahogany, hand-tooled by master craftsmen, and lined in grape Gucci silk. It retails for twenty-one-thousand, but if you decide to purchase a set I'm sure we can work out a deal."

"A Gucci silk casket lining?" I thought while gazing into the plush interior. Why not headstones by Tiffany? Martha Stewart burial vaults?

Obituaries for the two women ran the following morning, and the next day was the viewing. I hate that part. Hate the whole box-me-up and show-me-off sideshow, and nobody better ever do that to me. I want to go from wherever I croak, straight to the crematorium. Period. End of story. If people want to have a wake, get buzzed and talk about what a prince or an ass I had been in life, fine. But damn if I'm going to have people staring down at my embalmed corpse critiquing the makeup job.

Andra and her mom were buried on Wednesday and Jessica stayed with me again that night. The last several days had been challenging, and neither of us was ready to go it alone just yet. After dinner, we sat side by side on the couch thinking our own thoughts and watching the flames dance in the double-sided fireplace.

My two-year-old cat Blue, a sleek smoke-gray Oriental, walked into the room and sat tall on his haunches at Jessica's feet. In a fluid motion, he jumped lightly to her lap, pointed his nose to the ceiling, and let out a haunting howl that raised the hair on my arms. When he had finished this macabre performance, the cat composed himself in a compact bundle atop the woman's jean clad thighs and waited to be stroked. Jessica obliged and the sensitive animal purred lustily. An hour later when she went up to bed, Blue was right on her heels.

I stayed up for a while longer, not quite able to shake the image of the two caskets placed head to head, and the mountain of flowers spilling out from behind. Because of injuries Lila Martin had sustained in the fire, her casket had to be closed. Jessica chose to do the same for Andra, and I, for one was relieved. Some people might need to see the body for closure but not me, brother. That's not the way I wanted to remember my friend.

As I sat there staring at the curling flames, my mind replayed an odd comment Linda Riff had made about finding an empty bottle of whisky in Lila Martin's bed; odd because I was positive the woman's drink of choice was vodka. Also playing on my mind was the fact that Kenny had been on the scene the morning after the fire. How weird was that? And finally, why were there no batteries in the smoke detectors? That little detail bothered me the most because it was completely out of character for Andra.

I decided to mention these things to Riff next time I saw her. All I wanted now was to slip between the covers of my waterbed and let sleep try and smooth out the kinks.

At work on Thursday I did my job but was only going through the motions. When Fox, who was supposed to start at ten that morning, hadn't shown up by eleven, I phoned her apartment. There was no answer so I tried her mom's house.

Rita Fox picked up on the second ring.

"Rita, it's Max."

"Oh my God," she said sounding flustered. "I'm so sorry, Max. I was supposed to call and tell you Carly won't be in for a couple of days."

"Why? What's wrong?"

"Her asshole ex-boyfriend tried to break into her apartment last night."

"Is she okay?"

"She's fine—just a little shook. Luckily her brothers stayed with her after the funeral. They were both asleep in the living room when Pete tried to come through a window."

"Did they catch him?"

"No, but the fools chased the bastard a couple of blocks in their bare feet," said Rita Fox with a mother's protective outrage.

"I hope she applied for a restraining order."

"Our attorney drew it up this morning," Rita assured me, "and we filed it with the police immediately after."

I ran tense fingertips over a tight scalp and stared blankly at the floor. "Is there anything I can do, Rita?"

"Thanks, Max but no. Carly will be all right in a day or two. All this has just been too much. You know how close she and Andra were."

There was a pause and I waited for her to continue.

"To tell the truth, I'd always been jealous of the close relationship Carly had with Andra and her mom. I'm sorry about that now. I guess you can never have too many people loving you at the same time."

After hanging up the phone, I stared at my reflection in a mirror and wondered what had happened to my easy and peaceful life. Did the universe suddenly decide things were going too good for me? Thought it was time to whack me up side the head and remind me there was a Yang to every Yin? If so, I had definitely got the message.

At the end of the day I was wiping down my scissors when the door to my private studio opened and Kenny walked in. He was dressed in his usual outfit;

faded jeans, dingy red high-tops and a food splattered white tee shirt only half tucked in. His face is long and horsy; the kind only a mother could love. And perched on top of his mass of salt-and-pepper curls, almost like it had been there from birth, was a pink baseball cap with the words, "Welcome to Aruba" embroidered on the crown.

Sliding uninvited into the styling chair, the busboy eyed me silently in the mirror.

"Hey, Kenny. How you doing?"

"I'm cooool," he said, drawing out the last word. "I am always cool."

I stared at the man, trying in vain to decide if he really was mentally handicapped or if it was some kind of act he was putting on.

"Didn't I see you in Southfield a couple of days ago?" I asked trying to sound casual. "You were standing outside a house that had burned the night before."

The pink cap bobbed up and down.

"Did you know that was Andra Martin's house?"

Kenny tilted his head back and looked at me from beneath the cap's bill.

"You know Andra, Kenny. She was the manager of my salon. The young woman with the long dark hair?"

"I know who Andra is. Sure," said the man slowly. "And that was her house."

The last thing was a statement, not a question.

"I knew the house was burning," he exclaimed with alarm. "Two people were killed in the fire."

Kenny's homely face contorted into a grotesque mask and heavy tears pooled in his eyes. He accepted the box of tissues I offered, pulled out a handful and proceeded to blow his nose like he was playing a trumpet.

What was up with the tears? I asked myself as I watched the man carefully. And how did he *know* Andra's house was burning?

"The police think the fire was an accident," I said, in an attempt to calm him. "Andra's mom was smoking in bed and fell asleep."

Kenny turned slowly in the chair and shook his head. "That was no accident, Max. Andra and her mom were murdered."

The pointed words re-ignited my own lingering sense of doubt but with effort I pushed it away. "I don't know where you got that idea," I said trying to muster up some conviction, "but that's not what happened."

Kenny stood and took a step toward me. "The cops don't know everything," he said as his liquid brown eyes peered deeply into mine. "And if they're not going to investigate Andra's death as a murder, I guess it'll be up to you."

I gaped at the man. "*I'm* going to investigate?"

He nodded.

"Yeah, right."

"Andra told me she loved you, Max," he said as if in explanation. "That makes it your responsibility."

"My responsibility is to trust the police to do their job," I said dismissing the man's loopy supposition, but he wasn't finished yet.

"You'll change your mind," Kenny said backing slowly toward the door. "He won't give you any choice."

"Who won't give me any choice?" I asked. But Kenny slipped out the door without another word.

It was seven o'clock when I stepped out of the mall and into the mid-September evening. The rain that had been threatening to fall earlier in the day was coming down in sheets and as I stepped off the curb, a bone rattling clap of thunder exploded above my head. By the time I climbed into my car, halfway across the lot, I was soaked to the bone and shivering. The wet sky was responsible for the first thing. But the shivering was motivated by pure unchecked grief at the loss of a good friend.

Chapter 2

▼

The rain stayed with me as I exited the expressway and turned onto the gravel road circling Cradle Lake. Cruising slowly around a familiar bend, I spotted the life-sized Buddha statue that marked the entrance to my driveway and turned in. My house is a four thousand square foot wood and stone pagoda sitting fifty yards off the road. It's hugged on three sides by a thick, ragtag forest and shrouded that night by an eerie mist rolling in off the lake. A Detroit area mob boss named Johnny Lott, had the home built approximately three years ago. The first time I ever saw it was on the cover of *Architectural Digest,* and after viewing the five-page spread detailing the home's design, I had fallen in love. Fortunately (for me anyway), Lott didn't get to live in his dream home very long. He was gunned down on the cobblestone driveway less than a year after moving in.

Lott's widow, a Ms. Loretta Lee, former star of stage, video and bachelor party fame, had joined my client list six months earlier. She has a hefty set of boobs with a brain to match; finagled a pre-nup agreement guaranteeing her five million if Johnny died or the marriage crashed. And if she behaved anything like she looked—picture Marilyn Monroe in her prime—Lott got off dirt-cheap.

Two days after her husband was killed, Sweet Loretta, as she was known in the salon, came in to get her hair done for the funeral. When I realized she wasn't exactly suffering over her recent loss, I offered to take what she had always referred to as the "Chink monastery" off her hands. She was delighted, and a week later we signed the deal. I purchased the house and flanking lots for 2.5 million.

Lott had hired the well know Japanese architect, Seigo Nakao to construct the house. Nakao's claim to fame, were the built-in closets and cupboards he ingenuously concealed in almost every home he designed and mine was no exception. I found some by searching, some by accident, but none held as much surprise as the one I literally stumbled across the very first summer I moved in.

It was a steamy night in the middle of June, and I had been asleep for only an hour when an odd sound in my bedroom caused me to sit up and switch on the bedside lamp. Nothing seemed out of order but as I reached to kill the light, a bat flew so close to my face I felt the wind from its wings. It didn't matter that I outweighed the little bugger by a hundred and sixty pounds. My imagination elongated its tiny fangs to the size of steak-knives and told me it was probably a vampire bat, up from South America to suck my blood.

Wrapping the sheet around me like a shroud, and thinking it wouldn't be a bad idea to keep a couple cloves of garlic in the nightstand for protection, I slipped out of bed, crouched low, and opened the nearest set of windows. When I shuffled across the room to open a second set, I tripped on an edge of the sheet, lost my balance, and slammed back-first against the heavily textured west wall. The solid surface behind me seemed to give way and turning, I discovered the shadowy edges of a narrow doorway. Keeping one eye on the bat circling the room, I stood and leaned my weight against the panel. The mechanism securing it released with a soft click and it moved back as if on rollers.

It was pitch-dark inside, so I scuttled over to my nightstand and fished a flashlight out of the drawer. On the way back, I opened two more sets of windows giving "Dracula" every chance to beat it out of there. I didn't want to have to whack the little guy with my tennis racket, but I also didn't want him thinking he could take up residence.

With my heart beating out a drum roll, I stepped through the doorway and blinked as recessed lights flashed on automatically above my head. The hidden space turned out to be a Buddha shrine, the size of a walk-in closet, with polished bamboo walls, a rough stone floor and a foot-tall jade statue of the Buddha sitting atop a carved marble altar. But Buddha wasn't alone on his holy perch. Two out-of-place items flanked him. One was a semiautomatic pistol nestled in a lidless rosewood box. The other a Kevlar vest encased in a clear plastic sleeve.

Directly beneath the altar, two large suitcases sat crying out for some curious soul to come along and look inside. Not wanting to disappoint whoever had placed them there, I hefted one and balanced the butt end on the Buddha's round belly. I remember thinking at the time that the case was exceptionally heavy. I also remember experiencing a kind of tunnel vision when I looked inside; triggered no doubt by the thousands of one hundred dollar bills staring back at me.

My hand shook as I set the first case down, and lifted the other. The weight was similar; its content seemingly identical. Eventually I discovered that packed inside the two cases was roughly four million, all of it in crisp, new bills.

My first reaction was elation. I would be happy to spend Lott's stashed cash. But when my imagination slipped to the other edge of the sword, it sliced my happy mood in two. What if someone else knew about the money? A man in Lott's line of work had to have associates who would kill for a treasure half this size.

Heavy raindrops, drumming against the top of my car woke me from the memory of that dubious find and with some effort, I pushed away the connecting fears. Almost two years had gone by with nobody trying for the money. And odds are it would never happen.

Signaling the garage door, I pulled inside and parked next to my newest toy; a sweet, English racing green Lexus SUV I had bought after seeing a bevy of beauties posing on its hood in last months GQ. The truck is loaded for bear and was very expensive. But I rationalized the knee-jerk purchase by telling myself I would need it to navigate Michigan's snow covered roads during winter.

At the door connecting the garage to the kitchen, I disarmed the security system and walked in. Blue was waiting on the other side, butt up, and head low in a languorous stretch. As I set my keys on the edge of the countertop, he nuzzled his head against the toe of my shoe. I bent to stroke his back but as my fingers made contact, he shot across the room and licked furiously at the spot I had barely touched. Years of living with cats had taught me not to be insulted by this sort of behavior. They have a keen sense of smell and although I washed my hands a hundred times a day, Blue could still scent the hair of people I had worked on.

"Hey, Blueboy," I said as I peeled off my wet jacket and hung it over a chair back. "Catch any mice today?"

The cat eyed me like I was from another planet. The only mice my pampered feline had ever encountered were on the Cartoon Channel.

After popping the lid off a can of Blue's favorite food, I watched the hungry animal devour the tiny cubes of beef in brown gravy. I was hungry too but in no mood to cook, so I whipped up a peanut butter and jelly sandwich, poured a tall glass of milk and headed upstairs to my bedroom.

Just before dawn, I was awakened by ten pounds of cat standing on my chest. And when I opened my eyes, Blue's furry face was only inches from mine.

"It's not time for breakfast," I groaned and pushed him away. Undeterred, the cat sniffed at my ear, moved his cold nose down my cheek, and nipped me lightly on the chin. I sat bolt upright, startling the animal who leapt from the bed and skidded to a stop beside the open door. The bite hadn't been malicious; it was meant to get my attention. And after listening hard for several seconds, I caught the sound of a set of keys hitting the floor below my bedroom. They were my keys. I was sure of it. Every set I ever had its own distinct sound, and since they couldn't have fallen off the kitchen countertop without help, somebody, or something was in the house.

At the door to my bedroom, Blue produced a low growl he usually reserves for dogs on the beach and disappeared down the dark hall. Catching his drift, I slipped silently out of bed and tiptoed to the open doorway. It was difficult to hear anything over my own booming heartbeat but the tread of feet on the stairway was unmistakable.

A strong sense of panic gripped me as I considered what to do. Calling the police was out. There was no phone in the bedroom and even if there was, who would I call? The Cradle Lake police force had only two part-time employees. And the Sheriff's Department or State Police were too far away. Pressed to act, the image of Johnny Lott's gun flashed through my mind. It was still in the shrine room beside the Buddha. The big question was did I actually have the guts to use it? Hiding in the concealed space seemed the better idea and if the intruder entered the bedroom, it would probably be best to have the gun nearby.

At the entrance, I pushed back on the door and felt it click open. Once inside I closed it again and attempted to get my breath under control. When that failed, I tried ordering myself to calm down, a technique that had never worked before. But old habits die hard.

Despite the fact that I was on the verge of hyperventilating, or maybe because of it, I moved towards the altar and the gun. Something inside told me I was going to need it. The same something that knew whoever was in the house had come for Lott's money, and hiding in the little room had made me the proverbial sitting duck.

I killed the lights and a second later realized it would have been smart to have the gun in hand. Regrouping, I felt my way along the bamboo wall until I located the altar and the pistol. Grabbing the unfamiliar weapon with a sweaty hand, it slipped from my grasp and hit the floor with a loud clunk.

At the sound, I froze in place and then moved again when a little voice inside my head ordered me to get a grip. Squatting, I searched the floor near my feet, located the pistol, and aimed it at the door. If anyone tried to enter my dubious sanctuary, I would pull the trigger. The one hitch in my plan? I had no idea if the gun was loaded.

Footsteps entering the bedroom doubled my heart rate. When they stopped immediately outside the shrine room wall, I was sure somebody had finally come to claim Lott's cash.

Placing a thumb on the gun's ridged hammer, I eased it back to the cocked position. Presuming whoever had broken in my house was armed; my single advantage would be to shoot before they did.

I flinched at the echo of the door lock disengaging. When the panel moved inward, I pulled the trigger.

There was a deafening blast as the gun jerked in my hand. I squeezed off a second round and then a third, before a sharp cry of pain made me hold my fire. Straining to catch any movement, I pitched back at the sound of feet running from the room. A few moments later the heavy back door slammed shut with a bang.

My body felt electrified, like I'd just taken a poke from a 220-line. My ears were ringing off the hook and blue-white spots, remnants from the gun's blinding muzzle-flash, sparked before my eyes.

Several minutes passed before I worked up the courage to open the door. As I did, the phone on the main floor rang. At least I thought it did. My ears still echoed faintly from the gunshots.

"Hey, Snowman," a muffled voice said, "it's Riff. I'm heading out to see you, so if you're not up, get up. And how about whipping up one of those feta cheese omelets you're always bragging about? I'm starving, man and in desperate need of strong coffee."

I glanced warily around the room still gripping the gun between both hands. When I finally stepped out, something slick and wet gushed under my bare foot. Jumping back, I stared down at a dark puddle. Even in the inky morning light, I could tell it was blood.

Perched on the edge of my bathroom Jacuzzi, I quickly washed the blood off the bottom of my foot, pulled on jeans and a tee shirt, and carried the weighty cases full of Lott's cash out to the garage. There was no doubt the money was the reason for the break-in but I wasn't about to reveal that little secret if I didn't have to. It would only trigger problems with the IRS. And the four million would be tied up in court for years.

By the time Riff arrived, I had calmed down enough to tell my story. She was all business after that and with the ease of a seasoned professional, called the county sheriff to describe the situation.

Thirty minutes later, an unmarked car parked behind the house and I reiterated my tale to a pair of plainclothes deputies. Both seemed abnormally interested in Johnny Lott's gun, and no matter how many times I repeated my story, they never seemed quite satisfied. I started to feel like I was the criminal, and if Riff hadn't been there I'm sure I would have been arrested for possession of an unregistered firearm.

Through the window, I watched Riff talking to the two detectives. When they finally drove away, she reentered the house and we sat drinking coffee at the kitchen table.

"You're a lucky man, Max," she said, raking me with her cool blue eyes. "Lucky you didn't shoot your dick off with that frickin' gun."

Before she could continue the lecture, a cell phone chirped in her handbag. Following a brief conversation, she looked at me; the lines around her eyes visibly tightened.

"I got to go," she said standing and pushing her chair back. "If I were you, I'd change the code on that fancy security system. And it wouldn't hurt to install some motion detector lights outside either."

"Sounds good. I'll get on it today."

Riff nodded and picked up her bag to leave.

"What about the gun?" I asked as we walked to the door.

"What about it?"

"Will I get it back?"

"Maybe," she said. "After the investigation. Why?"

"Thought I might like to learn to use it."

Riff paused and stared into my eyes for a long moment. "You know anything about guns?"

"Not much," I answered and flashed my most innocent grin. "But I'm willing to learn. You willing to teach me?"

The corners of her mouth lifted in a reluctant smile. "I could do that."

"Where and when?"

"There's an indoor gun range on the corner of Woodward and Lincoln in Royal Oak. Do you know it?"

"Sure."

"Meet me there this afternoon, around five thirty."

"Cool."

"You'll have to apply for a gun permit and take a CCW class. Got anything shady in your past?"

"Ten arrests, no convictions," I replied batting my eyes.

Riff grabbed the handle of the door and jerked it open. "Say that when you apply for your permit, pal and they won't let you carry a water-pistol."

I squared my shoulders and gave her a snappy salute. "I'll be on my best behavior, Lieutenant."

"The gun lesson," Riff said, "will cost you dinner at Melissa's…plus the answers to a few questions about the Martins."

"What kind of questions?"

"The kind I need answers to," she said dismissively. "But they'll keep till this afternoon."

Chapter 3

The first thing I did after Riff left was to change the code on my security system. The instructions in the manual proved intricate and I accidentally set the sensitive little shit off three times. It was probably a wasted effort anyway; given the fact that the detectives investigating the break-in thought my intruder either had access to the code or the smarts to bypass it.

Andra was the only person besides me who knew the security code. My house was her refuge when she needed space from her mom. She had also known about the shrine room and the four million. I told her because I trusted her completely. And I had to tell somebody or bust.

After changing the code, I called Bill Brown, a long time friend, client and the electrical contractor who had wired the salon. We talked for a few minutes about the outside lighting Riff suggested and he promised to have a man out that afternoon.

My second call was to the salon. I wasn't on the book that day, but wanted to touch base in case there were any problems. I knew I should be there, but my heart just wasn't in it. The salon would have to run itself for a while.

When Fox picked up, I felt an instant sense of relief. "Hey girl. Glad you're back."

"You and me both," Fox said. "My mom was making me crazy. She sees Pete in every car that drives down the block."

"Rita told me he tried to break into your apartment."

"Do you believe that? I don't know what the hell I'm going to do."

For a moment I thought about inviting her to stay at my house but decided it wasn't such a good idea. The would-be-thief in the night could return at any time. "How about if we put you up at a motel?"

"No thanks. Motel beds give me the creeps."

"How's that?"

"They don't wash anything but the sheets when people check out, and you couldn't pay me to touch the TV remote. How many times do you think those things ever get cleaned?"

We both laughed and that made it easier to ask my next question. "I know things are crazy for you right now, Foxy, but would you consider taking over as manager of the salon?"

There was a pause as we both thought of Andra.

"Maybe," she teased. "Do I get a raise?"

"Absolutely."

"Wow, that was quick. I must be in a pretty good negotiating position."

"What else would you like?"

"Hmmm, let's see. How about the use of your patio and pool in the summer."

"You already have that," I reminded her.

"Oh yeah. Guess I did spend a lot of time there last summer."

"Yeah, you did. What else?"

She stalled, thinking it over. "How about dinner once in a while at the restaurant of my choice?"

"You got it. But anything over four stars, you leave the tip."

"Deal."

"Does that mean you'll take the job?" I asked.

"I guess so, but…"

"But what?"

"Do I get business cards?"

"Sure, you can have business cards."

"How about a nameplate for my desk? You know, one of those triangular things with gold letters."

"What would you like it to say? 'Queen of the Office'?"

"Queen sounds good. Can we get that in three inch letters?"

Despite the death of two people she loved dearly and the ongoing harassment from her ex-boyfriend, Fox seemed to be coping pretty well. That was more than I could say for myself. You know the TV commercial comparing your brain on drugs to a fried egg? Well, my brain on grief wasn't faring much better. I was having a hell of a time accepting the reality of Andra's death. And depression, usually a rare emotion for me, was knocking hard on my door.

In an attempt to stay focused on the present moment I decided to do a painting, something abstract so I wouldn't have to think too much. Ever since I was a kid, art has been my great escape. I use it liberally, like some people use drugs or alcohol. The buzz is better, and there's no chance of arrest.

Not long after moving in, I had a local construction company fit out two of the four upstairs bedrooms into one big art studio. The hardwood floors had been resurfaced in white marble and the ceilings and trim brightened up with a warm silky cream. Natural light is plentiful. The walls on the second-floor of my home are almost all windows.

Upstairs, I thinned out several primary colors to the consistency of heavy cream, set out a 3x4 foot canvas on the central work table, and parked my butt in a straight-backed chair facing the lake.

I'm an on and off meditater; have been since I took a course in TM at the age of eighteen. It keeps me connected with my spiritual side (I just can't get into the organized religion thing), and it's routine before I begin a new piece of art. Most of the time it helps me center, sometimes I fall asleep, and occasionally, like it did that day, I take a trip to la-la-land, and somehow do the painting while I'm there. I mean, I remember pouring the color on the canvas, tilting the corners so the pigments could intermingle. But how the very recognizable image of the Martin's ranch style house, with its left side engulfed in flames managed to form near the bottom was a complete mystery.

After staring at the scene for what seemed like an hour I was totally creeped out, so I booked from the studio, fit Blue out in his harness, and drove to a lakeside park half-a-mile up the road. The park is a three-acre peninsula owned and maintained by the lake association. It has playground equipment, a sandy beach, and an asphalt running track circling the perimeter. Blue and I were more than half way around when a solitary cyclist came screaming out of nowhere and skidded to a stop beside us.

Still spooked by the previous night's break-in, I tightened my grip on Blue's leash and stared at the rider. He was short, chunky around the middle, wore a baggy, sky-blue running suit with the hood pulled up and a pair of oversized mirrored goggles that reflected the clear sky and surrounding trees.

As if sensing the fight or flight chemicals flooding my brain, the man raised both hands in an "I'm not going to hurt you" gesture. When his lips spread wide in a goofy grin, I suddenly realized who it was.

"Kenny!" I said feeling the tension in my chest slacken a bit. "What the hell are you doing here?"

"Just riding my bike," he answered casually as if our meeting in the private park was not the least bit odd. "Is that your cat? He's pretty. Cum'ere, pretty boy."

To my amazement, the usually reserved cat walked straight up to Kenny, and allowed the man to pet him roughly around the head and neck. Blue's friendly actions to the stranger were as baffling as Kenny's garish attire.

Straightening to face me, Kenny slid the goggles to his forehead and returned my incredulous stare. "Well, Max? Did you change your mind yet?"

"Change my mind about what?"

"You know what," he said accusingly.

I took a deep breath and tried to calm the anger that had retightened my chest. "Look," I growled trying hard to restrain the irritation. "If you know something about the fire at Andra's house, you damn well better tell the cops."

"I don't think so," Kenny replied and gave me an insolent stare. "Crazy people like me don't get a fair shake with the law. Before I even open my mouth, they assume whatever I'm about to say is crap."

I shrugged not knowing how to respond.

"But you could tell them," Kenny said.

"Tell them what?" I shot back. "That the fire wasn't an accident?"

Kenny nodded.

"Then they'd think I was crazy."

We stood there staring each other down. I wanted to tell him his theory was full of shit but I would have been lying. There were things about Andra's death that didn't add up and I was having a hard time buying into the cops' explanation of that night's events.

Kenny shook his head in obvious disapproval, remounted his bike and started back down the trail. "Look me up when you stop kidding yourself," he shouted over his shoulder. "If it's not too late, of course."

As Blue and I watched, Kenny disappeared around a jog in the path. "I hope the son-of-a-bitch falls off his bike," I said as we headed off in the opposite direction. "Maybe he'll whack his head on a rock and forget all about me."

Back home I showered for my date with Riff, ran the electric razor over my afternoon stubble, and after stepping in front of a full length mirror, assessed my forty-two year old body with a critical eye. At just over six feet, I weighed a comfortable hundred-and-sixty-five pounds, and because I'd been working out faithfully the last couple of months, my body was tighter than it had been in years. The beginning of muscle definition in my arms and shoulders had motivated me to continue, and although the long ignored abs still needed work, I was happy with their progress. I'd been wearing my dark brown hair cropped close to my head; a style that suited me well and made the sprinkling of gray around the temples less noticeable. All things considered, I didn't look bad for a guy on the fast track to middle age.

Ten minutes later, I was in front of my closet wondering what to wear to a gun date. It was my first and I didn't want to come off looking too hick or too slick. In the end I chose my favorite black jeans, a cashmere sweater of dusky-plum, Italian loafers I paid way too much for, and a gray tweed sports coat a friend had picked out for me at the Salvation Army. Not exactly an outfit you'd see in GQ but good enough to take me from gun range to restaurant.

The image in my painting still haunted me as I set off for my gun lesson. When I arrived and parked in the asphalt lot surrounding the building, I had absolutely no memory of driving there. My oft-used autopilot had been obliged to once again deliver me safely to my destination. And despite the fact that the rats of depression continued to gnaw away at my usual happy-go-lucky personality, at least the subconscious part of my brain was still in decent working order.

The dashboard clock read 5:15, Riff's red Mustang was nowhere in sight, so I got out, stretched, and decided to wait for her inside. I had always been curious about what goes on in a gun range, and when the automatic doors whooshed open, a quick scan of the store told me I wasn't in Kansas anymore.

Immediately upon entering, I noticed three men in black staring directly at me. All sported what looked like a miniature Uzi in a hip holster and not one looked shy about using it. Intuition told me they were store personnel, and in an odd way, their "you start any shit, we'll finish it" look made me feel comfortable.

Tactical Sports employed a straightforward marketing system; pistols to the right, rifles to the left. Sandwiched between them was clothing and a myriad of hunting accessories. Drawn by a display of handguns running the entire length of one wall, I walked slowly along the showcase, gawking at the different sizes and shapes, and amazed at how creative humans can be when it comes to violence.

As I neared the end of the counter, a woman I guessed to be somewhere in her early thirties smiled at me. She had a sleek cat-like form, lustrous black hair that framed her face like a mane, and a very snug vee-neck tee that drew me like a moth to a flame.

"Good afternoon," she said, her velvety-soft voice a stark contrast to the very macho scenery surrounding us. "Can I show you something today?"

"Sure," I said playfully. "What did you have in mind?"

The woman whose name was Eden, according to her nametag, placed ten manicured fingertips on the counter and leaned forward seductively.

"See anything you like?"

"Oh yeah," I said, as my eyes traveled from her pert breasts and up the soft curve of her neck. "Unfortunately I'm not here to pick up anything."

Eden's matte-red lips pursed in mock disappointment. "Too bad," she purred. "It just so happens I'm free for dinner."

For the briefest of moments my gaze dropped from her eyes to her tight décolleté. "An extremely tempting offer," I said and gave her my hundred-watt smile. "But I'm here to meet a friend who's going to give me my first gun lesson."

"You're a virgin?" Eden asked, and slid me a lopsided grin. "That's a hoot."

"Well somebody has to be," I said, "or you'd never get any new business."

The saleswoman eyed me with amusement. "What's the make and caliber of gun you'll be using?"

"Beats me," I said, and nodded at the gun holstered on her hip. "What kind do you have?"

"This is a .40 caliber Sig," she said as she patted the weapon lovingly. "The size is perfect if you intend to carry concealed. Plus, if you need more firepower it can be converted to a .357 with a simple barrel change."

"Yow," I said. "Kind of scary to think the guy next to me in the mall might be packing that."

"Is it?" Eden said. "Don't you think people have a right to protect themselves?"

"Absolutely. But I've heard a .357 can drop an elephant."

Eden's smiled tightened but remained friendly. "All the more reason to own one. Wouldn't you agree?"

I nodded, thinking it best not to argue the point with such a well-armed woman. "Well thanks for the advice. I'll keep it in mind and ask my friend what she thinks."

"The friend that's teaching you is a woman?"

"Yeah. Her name is Linda Riff. Do you know her?"

"Very well," returned Eden. "And you couldn't ask for a better teacher, Mr....?"

"Max Snow," I answered offering my hand.

"Always happy to meet a friend of Riff's," she said and laid her slim palm against mine. "But I'm jealous she met you before I did."

At the sound of the front door opening, Eden shot a glance over my shoulder and I turned to see Riff looking in our direction.

"Speak of the devil," she whispered as the policewoman who was carrying a leather briefcase in her right hand walked over to join us.

"I see you two have met," Riff said. "Leave it to Max to find the only female employee in the place. Has he tried to charm your pants off yet, Eden?"

"Not yet," the saleswoman teased. "But we've only been talking a few minutes."

"That's usually all it takes," returned Riff as she slipped her arm through mine.

"Don't let her fool you, Eden," I said. "I'm not like that at all. And besides, you're too well-armed."

"No need to worry about this," Eden said and stroked the butt of her gun tenderly. "I never wear it to bed, unless of course, you'd like me to."

"Come on, Romeo," Riff said and pulled me toward the rear of the store. "You're here to learn how to shoot. You already know how to pick up women."

At the entrance to the shooting range, the distinctive pop, pop, pop of muffled gunfire could be heard inside. Riff laid the briefcase on a nearby shelf, opened the top, and after withdrawing two pairs of aviation-type ear-guards complete with microphones, she fit a set on each of us.

"The mikes are sound activated," she said through my earphones. "They're set to screen out anything louder than the human voice. Can you hear me all right?"

"Perfect."

She nodded once, picked up the case and we entered the dimly lit gun range. Inside, three middle-aged black women occupied the first trio of nine shooting stations. As we paused to watch, the woman in number three rapid-fired an entire clip into a downrange paper target, ejected it in a well practiced movement and slapped another one home.

"Hot damn," I said widening my eyes at Riff. "Hope to God I'm never in that babe's gun-sights."

Riff agreed with a nod of her head, led us to the very last station, opened the leather case and lifted out a matt-black semiautomatic.

"This," she said displaying the gun from the palm of her hand, "is a .45 caliber Glock model 30. It's compact, easy to conceal, and packs a hell of a punch."

She laid the gun on the ready shelf, lifted two magazines from the briefcase and after demonstrating how to load eleven rounds into the spring fed clip, she handed the empty one to me. The procedure felt awkward. But when I presented the full rack for her inspection, it felt like I had leapt a giant hurdle.

"The butt on this Glock is short," she said slapping the clip home, "so I like a magazine with an extended floor plate. It gives me something to rest my pinky finger on." She wrapped her hand around the gun butt and displayed the finger placement. "It's also been fitted with an internally mounted LaserMax sighting system, accurate to within an inch-and-a-half of your target."

"Is it complicated to use?"

"Nada. Just push this slide lock to the left, aim the red laser dot at your target and fire away."

Riff returned the gun to the ready-rack and my eyes locked on to it like laser beams. Even with no one holding it, the weapon possessed a lethal aura, and I questioned my desire to learn to shoot. Riff must have sensed my doubts because when I looked up, her expression was serious.

"Cops don't usually encourage people to carry a gun, but in your case I think it's a good idea."

"Why? Because of what happened last night?"

"That," she said, "plus you're the perfect target for any yahoo trying to scam a quick buck."

"What's that suppose to mean?"

"It means you drive expensive cars, live in a big-ass house, and you're always being spotlighted by the local media at fashion shows and celebrity shindigs."

"I don't push the media stuff," I protested. "My staff thinks it's good for the salon's image."

Riff lifted the gun, placed it in my hand and pulled the finger that instantly wrapped around the trigger away.

"But you own the salon," she said pointing my arm downrange. "And it's your name they print in the paper."

She was right of course. The media attention came with the territory. I didn't particularly like it, but I didn't discourage it either.

I shrugged. "So what are you suggesting, Lieutenant? That I give away all my money and go to work in the Sears tool department?"

"Hell no. I love dining at all those expensive restaurants you take me to. Couldn't eat half as good on my salary."

I leaned into her shoulder and met the laughing eyes. "So you're saying I'm just a meal ticket?"

"That," she teased and kissed the air inches from my lips, "and you got a mighty fine butt."

If it wasn't for the gun in my hand, I would have taken Riff in my arms and kissed her. I'd been wanting to for a long time now.

Mimicking my lusty smile, she reached into the briefcase and lifted out a paper target with the outline of a man imprinted in black ink.

"Meet Mr. Silhouette," Riff said as she clipped the target to the automatic slide and sent it speeding downrange; "'your worst enemy'. He's raped your cat, crapped in your pool and now he's coming for you. Stop him…or he's going to take you down."

We spent an hour at the gun range and if I do say so myself, I was pretty good at this shootin' stuff. Years of styling hair had given me a keen eye and a steady hand. By the time we finished, I had fired over one hundred rounds, most of them striking near the center of the chest.

"Sure you haven't done this before?" Riff's voice said inside my headphones.

I winked and felt a strong sense of exhilaration standing next to the exciting woman. Maybe it had something to do with the strength of character it took to do her job. Maybe I was high on gunpowder. Or maybe it was because she's charming, smart, funny, and has a figure that most women would hock their eye-teeth for.

Riff was married when we met three years ago, but her husband had a hard time with her wacky hours and dedication to the job. Last year he decided not to go the distance and they divorced. With that door closed, the lieutenant and I became better friends. We worked out at the Farmington YMCA. Both of us had a passion for the Beatles. And we dined together several times a month. So far, the relationship had not been physical, but if I was reading her cues correctly, that was about to change.

Riff had just finished packing everything away when I pulled her close and kissed her. Initially she seemed surprised, but a moment later she returned the kiss with enthusiasm.

"If that's your way of thanking me for the lesson," she whispered when the kiss ended, "you're welcome. But you still owe me dinner at Melissa's."

Before leaving the shooting range, we stopped briefly to talk with Eden.

"Well, girlfriend," Eden said, as a mischievous grin stretched her full lips. "How did our virgin perform? Is he man enough to handle your firepower?"

Riff smiled at the thinly veiled suggestion and looked me over like a lioness assessing a potential meal. "I'll get back to you on that one. But so far, no complaints."

Melissa's restaurant is located in downtown Royal Oak, a few miles south of the gun range. I pulled into an empty space directly behind the rear entrance, a veritable miracle given the horrendous parking situation in the popular little town.

Inside, the proprietress herself, a charming lady somewhere in her sixties, seated us. Melissa has the figure of a pixie, treats everyone like family, and if she has anything to say about it, you don't leave her establishment hungry. I had called on the way over to reserve our favorite table near the front window. It was slightly apart from the rest of the crowd and had a good view the chic town's eccentric fashion parade.

"How about an appetizer?" Melissa asked after we were seated and a busboy had set up our table.

"What's good tonight?" I asked.

"Everything, as you well know. But the salt-roasted mussels with pimiento dipping sauce will knock your socks off."

I looked at Riff and she nodded.

"And a nice bottle of wine?" Melissa asked.

"Bring us…"

"I know. I know. The Toasted Head Chardonnay. I always keep it in stock for my two favorite customers."

"You're a jewel, Lissa," I said. "If you weren't already married I'd ask you out."

"Ask me anyway," she kidded. "My old man is in Arizona for a month and I could use the action."

After checking out the "catch of the day" on the board behind the bar, Riff and I both decided to go with the blackened catfish. When the wine was delivered and poured, she raised her glass.

"To my outstanding pupil. I had no idea you would be such a quick study."

"Oh, I enjoy learning," I said, "and I'm definitely looking forward to your night school class."

Riff narrowed her eyes and leaned across the table. "Because I'm a cop," she said in a low voice, "I tend to be pushy in bed. Hope you don't mind."

"Mind?" I answered and touched the rim of my glass to hers. "I'm counting on it, babe."

Riff's seductive smile funneled an avalanche of lusty hormones to my groin and for a long moment I toyed with the idea of skipping dinner and going straight to dessert.

"So," I said in an attempt to ignore the pull between my legs. "You were going to ask me something about the Martins?"

"It's probably no big deal," Riff said. "But did Andra mention taking both the TV and VCR in for service before the fire?"

The unexpected question caught me off guard and I went temporarily brain-dead. "No," I finally said. "But that's not too surprising. Andra didn't do much television. Her mom was the big TV freak. Spent hours watching the cable shopping channels. Both sisters joked about Lila spending their inheritance on Swarovski crystal."

I paused to watch a young couple stroll arm-in-arm by the restaurant window. Each had a shaved head; a multitude of facial piercings, and colorful tattoos decorating their scalps. When they noticed me staring, the girl (at least I'm pretty sure it was a girl...their make-up was identical) blew me a kiss.

"Thinking about a new look?" Riff asked running her hand playfully across my hair and fingering the diamond stud in my left earlobe.

"No. Just the thought of a tattoo needle poking me several thousand times is enough to give me nightmares. And as for the bald look," I said rolling my eyes toward the top of my head. "Family genetics will get me there soon enough."

Riff gave me an assessing look. "Wouldn't bother me. In fact, I prefer men without hair. They usually try harder."

I smiled and sipped my wine.

"Now," she said. "What were you saying about Lila Martin collecting jewelry?"

"According to Andra she was into it big-time."

"Did you ever see her collection?"

"Only once. Andra took me into her mom's bedroom and showed me Lila's jewelry box. It was literally overflowing with the stuff. Kind of like a cartoon version of a treasure chest."

"Is that right?" Riff said. "We didn't find anything like that after the fire. Where was the box when you saw it?"

"On top of Lila's dresser."

Riff sat silently for a few moments, the fingertips of her right hand slowly twirling the stem of her wineglass. It was obvious she had switched gears from date to cop.

"Talk to me, Riff," I said searching her eyes for the truth. "Did something weird go down the night of the fire?"

"I'm not sure. But loose ends keep me up at night."

"Well I don't want to aggravate your insomnia, but there are a few questions I can add if you're interested."

Riff relaxed back in her chair and gave me her full attention.

"I keep thinking about the liquor bottle they found in Lila's bed. You said it was whisky but I know for a fact that she only drank vodka."

"Maybe there was no vodka in the house. Alcoholics aren't usually picky."

"This one was."

Riff nodded. "What else?"

"The smoke detectors. Why didn't they have batteries?"

She shrugged. "Ever read the statistics? No batteries. Dead batteries. It happens."

"Andra was a detail person. She would never overlook something that important."

Riff didn't reply but I could tell she was intrigued.

"This last part is the weirdest," I said and took a long, slow sip of my wine before continuing. "Feel free to tell me I'm crazy at any time." During the next few minutes I laid out the story of Kenny and his weird behavior. How I'd seen him outside Andra's house the morning after the fire, his insistence that the deaths were not accidental, the way he showed up in the private park near my house, and before I could chicken out, about the image of the burning house in my painting. "I thought at first that I was losing my mind. But it was there, plain as day. It's there right now and I swear to you, I didn't paint it like that."

With practiced movements, Riff lifted a notepad and pen from her purse. "This Kenny person," she said looking at me from under lowered brows. "You got a last name?"

"No, sorry," I answered.

"How about the restaurant he works in?"

"It's called Litza's, sort of an Americanized Greek place on the third floor."

Riff jotted down the information and returned the pad to her purse.

"I'll check it out tomorrow," she said switching back from cop to seductress. "I'm busy tonight."

In my bed later that evening, the two of us lay spent in each other's arms. Riff's second orgasm had hit her abruptly, almost like an accident, and if satisfaction can be judged by the swell of a woman's nipples, she had enjoyed the hell out of it. Like everything about the woman, her passion was direct and explosive. And being a quick study, I just followed her lead.

The next morning I was up early. And by the time Riff joined me in the kitchen, I was about to slip a feta cheese omelet into the oven.

"Hey, Snowman," she said in a quiet morning voice. "Sleep well?"

"Excellent," I said, and moving behind her, brushed my lips lightly across the base of her neck. "How about you?"

"Like a baby. You're a great cuddler."

She was wearing one of my white silk tee shirts. And my position behind her allowed me to appreciate the pliant nature of the fabric as it clung to the contours of her body. I knew I was supposed to be a gracious host, but the sight of this sexy woman in my kitchen was driving me crazy.

To break the spell I offered her coffee.

"Mmmmm," she replied and sat down at the small round bistro table. "Yes, please."

I poured the steaming hazelnut brew into two cups and sat down beside her.

"What time do you have to be at work today?" I asked, and when our thighs touched beneath the table I hoped it wasn't soon.

"By nine," she answered blowing lightly on her coffee. "And unfortunately I can't be late. The Chief is stopping by and I want to make sure everything in my office is covered. I also want to start looking into what we talked about last night and tell the boys in the lab to recheck everything from the Martin house."

I stared at her, marveling at the way she could slip in and out of police mode. She noticed my interest and cocked her head.

"What?"

"I was just thinking," I said running my hand up the silky inside of her thigh, "how hot you look in my shirt."

Riff's expression didn't change but her eyes sparked with carnal fire.

"How long before that omelet is done?" she asked.

"About fifteen minutes, give or take a few."

"Well," she said pulling the tee shirt off and throwing it across the room. "That sounds just about right."

An hour later, I walked Riff to her car.

"Thanks for breakfast and...everything else," she said as she shot me a look that made me want to start all over. "I mean it, Maxie. I was beginning to think it would never happen again."

"Always happy to assist the police," I said and gave her a salute.

When we reached her car, I opened the driver's side door and Riff slipped into the tan leather seat. "One last thing," she said looking up at me. "Jessica told me Andra kept a journal."

I nodded. "She was constantly writing in the damn thing. Sometimes she'd whip it out in the middle of a conversation and jot down things we said to each other. I never knew whether to be flattered or bothered. Why?"

Riff slid the key home and rolled the engine over. "Thought it might help shed some light on what happened that night. It wasn't in the inventory arson compiled. I checked."

"She always carried it with her," I explained. "It was a small, black notebook, the size of a paperback. She kept it in her purse."

"Interesting," Riff answered as she pushed in the clutch and shifted into first. "We never did find her purse."

Chapter 4

▼

Two days later, I stood alone on my patio staring out at the lake. The afternoon sky was cloud-covered, the water gray and turbulent like my thoughts. I missed Andra and would give anything to see her walk in my door again. Guess I never realized what a large part she played in my life until she was gone. My mind was also on Riff. I hadn't heard word one from her since the morning we had breakfast together.

On Wednesday, I called her office and was intercepted by a surly desk sergeant.

"Something I could help you with?" he asked brusquely. "She's kinda busy."

"No," I answered annoyed at the put off. "Please ask her to call Max Snow."

Riff never did call back that day, leaving me feeling a bit insecure. Was it the sex thing? Even between mature adults, casual sex can be the kiss of death to a great friendship. When it's happening, everything seems cool, or hot, rather. We all have needs. Right? When it's over, and those horny little hormones have abandoned you like rats off a sinking ship, things can, and usually do, look a lot different.

Driving to work early Thursday morning, my monkey mind was busy swinging through the synapse jungle, determined to invent the wildest scenarios about Riff's failure to get in touch. I finally collared the little bastard with what was probably the truth; Riff's job kept her very busy and I was lucky to hear from her as much as I did.

At the mall, I lucked out and got a parking spot close to the entrance. I thought I deserved my own parking place, given the fact that I pay this establishment well over a hundred thousand dollars in rent each year, and that didn't even include security, or the cost of garbage removal. Garbage is serious and expensive shit at the mall. There's a trash compactor half the size of Rhode Island in all four of the ground-level loading docks, and every store has its own access code.

Inside, the halls were teeming with a herd of bullies known as mall walkers. If for some reason you're ever in the mall before the stores open, it's a good idea to give them a wide berth. This crowd is like a gang of bikers without bikes, wearing polyester instead of leather, and if you get in their way, they'll run your ass over without ever looking back. You may think I'm exaggerating, but anybody who's in the mall before 10 a.m. knows who owns the halls at that time of day.

Skirting the rat pack, I jumped on the escalator and rode it up to the second level. After a quick stop at Koffee Konnections where I slammed a double espresso, I felt pumped and ready to leap tall buildings in a single bound.

My salon sits at the end of a short spoke off the mall's center court; a prime location and we were damn lucky to get it. Flanking us to the left is Victoria's Secret with its boudoir motif, intoxicating scents and giant posters in the windows showing Wonderbras at work. On the right is Fantasy Footwear, the only place in town where you can buy beach sandals with six-inch heels, and known throughout the mall as "FMPs Are Us." If you're into bad girl shoes, and judging by the store's phenomenal success, a lot of women are, it's definitely worth the trip. But hold on to your wallet; the two owner-operators are both former strippers, versed in hawking their product and extremely adept at separating you from your hard earned cash.

As I neared the salon, the sight of a striking, bronze-skinned woman sitting behind the reception desk stopped me in my tracks. Even seated, her size was impressive, as was the thick, black hair that fell in waves across her muscular shoulders. "Who the hell is that?" I asked myself as I straightened my shoulders and prepared my best smile. "And where has she been all my life?"

I entered the salon just as the stranger finished writing something in the appointment book.

"You're Max Snow," she said in an intriguing accent I couldn't quite place. "I've been looking forward to meeting you."

We shook hands, and as she stood, I felt the breath catch in my throat. The woman was awesome, all six-feet two inches of her, and everything I could see looked buffed to the max. Exotic features made it difficult to guess her age but who was counting? I was having trouble enough trying not to get lost in the seemingly endless curves barely contained by the snug fitting, lilac-suede suit. Standing before me was my Alpha fantasy; Xena the Warrior Princess dressed by Versace.

The woman studied me intently, and as she did, I felt an almost uncontrollable desire to take her in my arms and kiss her. Good thing I possessed a small amount of self-control. The exquisite beauty looked strong enough to break me in half.

When my lust-fueled fog finally cleared, I realized I was still holding her hand and although reluctant to let it go, decided I should before the moment got awkward.

"And you are…?"

"My name is Zed."

"A pleasure to meet you, Zed. Are you working for us? Or have we been the victims of a hostile Amazon takeover?"

"Nothing so dramatic I assure you," she said in her charming accent. "You needed a temporary receptionist. So here I am."

"Where's Gwen?"

"On her honeymoon," Zed replied, and then graced me with a knee-weakening smile. "She arranged for me to take over."

I suddenly remembered that Gwen had left last Saturday for a month stay in the Caribbean. "I had forgotten all about her going out of town."

"That's why I'm here," the intoxicating beauty said. "To keep track of the details. A busy man like you can't be expected to remember everything."

"You got that right," I said. "Lately I feel lucky to find my way home."

Zed smile was empathetic.

"I am supposed to be here today," I said. "Correct?"

Zed nodded at the appointment book on the desk. "You're booked solid, so I'm glad you showed up. Otherwise I might have had to go hunting for you."

"That doesn't sound so bad," I said. "Maybe we could try it sometime."

Zed didn't reply but a look of amusement lit her dark eyes.

"So how's everything going?" I asked.

"Excellent," replied the creamy voice.

"Everybody here that's supposed to be?"

"Everyone but Bob."

"You've met Bob?" I said curious to see the woman's reaction to the one staff member I found to be irritating as hell.

"Yes," Zed answered and narrowed her eyes slightly. "He enjoys being difficult but I can handle him."

My imagination instantly conjured up a picture of the muscular woman "handling" Bob. I saw her hands clamped tightly around his neck and his feet dangling several inches above the floor.

"I sincerely hope that won't be necessary," Zed said as if commenting on my unspoken thoughts. "I abhor violence."

I started to reply but before I could get the words out, the phone rang and she picked it up.

"Thank you for calling Maxie's. This is Zed. How may I help you?"

While Zed penciled a client's name and phone number in the appointment book, I thought about Fox, and wondered if she was working today. With a feeling of chagrin, I realized I didn't have a clue as to what was going on in my own salon. Turning to the computer on the desk, I punched up the day's employee schedule and ran my finger down the list. Fox's name wasn't on it but when I closed the screen, Zed, who still held the phone to her ear, waved to get my attention. "If you're looking for Fox," she said hand over the mouthpiece, "she's in your office."

As I rounded the wall separating the reception area from the salon, I tried to decide if Zed was a mind reader or just a good guesser. If it was the former, she probably thinks I'm a sex pervert. If it was the latter, I'm inviting her to the casinos first chance I get.

My salon is a long rectangle, with twelve haircutting stations, six on either side. The floor is pink veined marble; the textured walls dove-gray, charcoal and lavender. An island of black on black hood dryers sits dead center of it all. And the entire salon, including the shampoo area, a manicure-pedicure room, the staff break-room and my office, is lit by Art Deco wall sconces and warm, overhead spots.

At the office door, I stood silently watching Fox note something in a business ledger. "Well if it ain't the 'Queen of the Office' hard at work."

"That's what you pay me for," Fox said as she rounded the desk, arms out for a hug. "So that's what you get."

We held each other for a full minute, silently exchanging grief for our lost friend. When she finally looked up at me, her green eyes were magnified through a puddle of tears.

"Shit," she said swiping at her cheeks with the back of a hand. "I promised myself I wouldn't do this at work."

"Don't sweat it, babe. I feel like bawling every minute of every day."

The eyes narrowed, sending tears racing down the curve of her cheeks. "I am so damn pissed at Andra," she said and made a valiant attempt to smile. "We were like, planning to be friends forever."

"Tell me about it," I said and pulled her close. "She promised to play nurse for me when I was an incontinent old fart; said she'd change my diapers and help me spend my money."

Fox laughed softly against my chest and I felt my heart expand two sizes.

"Sign me up for that last thing," she said flashing her signature impish grin. "But I draw the line at diaper duty."

"What? You're not dying to get into my pants."

"Get in em', maybe," she said, palms flat against my chest. "Change em', I don't think so."

Grasping both my hands, Fox sat on the edge of the desk. "So how's life?"

"Excellent! I just met the met the receptionist my dreams are made of."

"Zed is a dream alright," Fox said. "Took over the desk like she'd been doing it forever. The only problem is that she's a magnet for every horny teenage boy in the mall. One look at those boobs and their hormones drag them in."

"Worked for me too."

"Big surprise. I had a bet with the staff you'd start drooling the minute you saw her."

"I do not drool over women, young lady. I just happen to appreciate height and strength in the fair sex more than most men."

"Yeah, right."

"So what's up with the Pete situation?" I said ignoring her eye-roll. "Is he still bothering you?"

"The asshole keeps calling and hanging around my apartment. I phone the police, but they never get there on time."

"There's always my friend Guido. For a fee, he'd be glad to take Mr. Pete for a long ride."

Fox laughed. "I'm not there yet, but give me his number just in case." Walking to a table in the far corner of the office she filled my favorite mug from a steaming, carafe style coffee maker. "Try this new coffee I just picked up," she said. "It's Jamaican Blue Mountain."

She handed me the mug and I took a sip. "Yow," I said wincing at the brew's heavy wine-like body. "Kind of strong isn't it?"

"Yeah. But I think you're going to need it."

"Need it? What do you mean need it?"

Fox looked at me. "Did you check your book today?"

"No. I was more interested in checking out the new receptionist. Why? What's wrong?"

"Nothing's wrong," Fox said but her lips spread in a wide smile. "Only that your first client happens to be your mom."

I stared at her in disbelief. My mom is one great lady and I love her to death. But in her senior years she's morphed into Auntie Mame on steroids.

"Ahh, man," I whined. "I thought she was still in Hawaii with Bud, or Rex, or whatever the name of her latest boyfriend is."

"It was Collin. And he's already ancient history."

"What? Did the champion ball buster crush another set?"

Fox nodded. "Marie told me she caught him trying to cozy up to some young Wahini on Maui. So she left the island without telling him."

"How much you want to bet she canceled his return airline ticket before she took off?" I said.

"She did," Fox said laughing. "She also donated his clothes to the Salvation Army."

"Why didn't you tell me she was back in town? Thought it might be fun to watch me squirm?"

"You bet," she said.

"Well I'm so glad I could entertain you."

Fox shook her head. "Your mom's not Godzilla, Max. She's a sweet old lady."

I shook my head. "You better hope I don't repeat that sweet old lady crack to Marie, because you'll be in big trouble."

Fox flashed a Cheshire cat grin as I exited the office and walked back through the salon to my private studio; a twelve-by-fifteen foot room that separates the salon from the reception area. The studio is equipped with everything I need to do my job, plus it provides my clients complete privacy while they have their hair done.

Closing the door behind me, I sat down in my styling chair and thought about my mother who at the age of sixty-four had already buried two husbands—my father, and Jack Watson, a beer drinking, motorcycling madman, who had coaxed her from her lethargy after dad died.

The cycling seniors had married six months after they met and took off to explore the country in a thirty-five-foot motor home with a Honda Goldwing trailered behind. Personally, I could never understand why anyone would want to drive their damn house down the street, but hey, to each his own.

Marie's marriage to Jack had liberated her in so many ways I was never sure what to expect when she showed up at my door. On her first trip out west she got a tattoo; an arrow shaped tribal symbol done high on the inside of her thigh. After that came an eyelift, a facelift, a neck and tummy tuck, and last year she had her breasts reduced and reshaped. Finally my dear sweet mother, who once had trouble making left turns in a car, drove up my driveway on her very own Honda Goldwing.

Madman Jack died the night of their seventh anniversary. He was out on a beer run and ended up smack in the middle of a multi-vehicle pile-up. While not a wealthy man, he did believe in life insurance. Mom collected death benefits from five different insurance companies.

At three minutes after ten, there was a sharp thump against my studio door, and turning in my chair, I watched the five-foot-five bundle of energy otherwise know as my mom hustle into the room. She looked her usual kick-ass self in jeans, black motorcycle leather, and a pair of scuffed Dr. Martens.

"Marie!" I said in mock disapproval. "What the hell did you do to your hair?"

"My hair?" she said, reaching up to stroke the half-inch of silver-white stubble covering her nicely shaped head. "I had a guy in Hawaii buzz it for me."

"Why?"

"Because it was too damn hot, that's why," she said and her brown eyes blazed with challenge. "If you can go around looking like you're in the freaking military, why can't I?"

I held up my hands. "No need to get your shorts in a knot, lady. I think it's great. You look like Liz Taylor."

Mom turned and glanced at herself in the mirror. "Well," she said and ran her hand across the brush-cut. "When you're right, you're right. I do look damn good, don't I? Just goes to show you what yoga, power walking and fifty-thousand dollars worth of cosmetic surgery can do for a gal my age."

She sat in my chair and I snapped a cape around her neck. "How would you like your hair styled today, madam?"

"Just tune it up, baby boy," she said and gave me the fish-eye in the mirror. "Don't scalp me."

While I trimmed around her ears, the irrepressible Marie Snow enumerated the drawbacks of a two-month summer vacation in Hawaii. The sun was too hot; the ocean too cold; the natives too happy.

"And those damn trade winds never stopped blowing for a second," she said. "I don't think I ate one meal without sand in it."

"You poor thing," I said while clipping the downy hair at the base of her neck. "How you must have suffered."

Mom leaned forward and looked at me over her shoulder, not entirely able to hide her smile. "You should start dyeing your hair, buster. How do you expect to attract a young woman who will have your babies with all that snow up there?"

I shook my head in amused disbelief. We'd been down that road before, many times. "I don't want a young woman, Mom. And in case you forgot, I had a vasectomy ten years ago."

She fixed me with a stare and raised one precisely shaped eyebrow to form a perfect arch.

"You don't know what you're missing, sweetie pie. Having a kid can change your life. It might even help you grow up a little."

I returned her stare with an almost mirror-like expression.

"Oh yeah. Look what it's done for you. Most women your age are taking bus trips to Branson. You're cruising through Alaska on a motorcycle."

Suddenly I became aware of raised voices in the reception area. Holding up a hand to silence Mom's inevitable snappy comeback, I cocked an ear in that direction.

"Leave me alone," I heard Fox say. "I don't want to see you anymore."

"For crissake, Fox," an enraged male voice countered. "How the fuck can you say that? That Andra bitch poisoned your mind."

I grabbed my cell phone and dialed mall security. After the first ring I handed it to my mom. "Tell them to get here fast and to call the real police. There's a restraining order out on this guy. His name is Pete Deville."

Marie nodded and I raced out of my studio. The scene that greeted me as I burst into the reception area would have been comical if it wasn't for the serious nature of the situation. What I saw was a wild Pete Deville, his usually handsome face twisted with rage, his lean wiry muscles struggling in vain against a pair of powerful bronze forearms that encircled him from behind.

"Please calm down, young man," I heard Zed hiss into Pete's ear. "Or I'll be forced to hurt you. Don't doubt that I can."

I didn't doubt it and neither did Pete, who ceased his futile grappling after a final attempt at escape and relaxed. At that moment, two security guards entered the salon and Zed released her prisoner.

The commotion had alerted the people in the salon and in the blink of an eye, the reception room was filled to capacity. There were stylists, customers and additional security personnel, all jockeying for position and asking questions. For several moments the scene was chaos, and in the confusion, Pete saw his chance to escape. Shaking off the distracted guards, he burst through the crowd and sprinted towards the entrance. He made it, but only in time to collide head-on with two South Lyon police officers.

A few minutes later as Pete sat quietly between the two guards; I looked him over with interest and disgust. He was all slicked out in a new set of threads. His hair had been freshly styled and there was a diamond stud in his right earlobe that must have weighed half a carat.

When the police had finished questioning Zed and Fox, they cuffed Pete and led him away. He glared defiantly as he went by and I glared right back. I knew the cops couldn't keep him long on the P.P.O. and I didn't want to give Pete any reason to return and harass the salon. Still, a man's got to do what a man's got to do. So as they walked through the door, I stuck my tongue out at the back of Pete's head.

Chapter 5

▼

Early Sunday morning, I was awakened by the ringing telephone. Half asleep, I picked it up and croaked out a hello.

"Morning, Max."

Recognition of the voice brought me instantly awake.

"What is it with you and these early morning calls, Riff? Seems like you're fond of getting me out of bed."

"Just the opposite actually," she teased. "But I'm a slave to the people and they need me more than you do. Sorry about not returning your calls. I've been swamped."

"No problem," I answered stifling a yawn. "I figured you were tied up. Anything new on Andra's case?"

"You haven't seen today's paper?"

"I'm in bed."

"Well get up, rich boy. And find out what's happening in the world."

"This better be good, Lieutenant. I like to sleep in on Sundays, and this bedroom floor is cold as hell."

"Awww. Poor baby."

Reluctantly, I slid into my robe and started down the wide wood staircase.

"How are you, Ms. Riff?"

"Exhausted," she said and I could hear the stress in her voice. "Been pulling doubles for a week."

"I'm sure the department will give you a big sendoff when you drop dead on the job," I joked. "You know, flag draped casket, all your fellow officers standing at attention, nice shiny badge presented to your relatives."

"Screw you."

I opened the back door, plucked the newspaper off the steps and made my way toward the living area. The first level of my home has a completely open floor plan; almost two thousand square feet of wall-free space. I love the simplicity. Plus it clears up a lot of short-term memory problems. Like when you go from one room to another and ask yourself, "Why the hell did I come in here?" On the main floor I was always in the same room.

Phone in hand, I sat down on my favorite piece of furniture in the world; a softly curving, twelve-foot long, obscenely overstuffed couch covered in raw, oatmeal silk. It's a man's couch, full of bold lines and deep cushions but it holds you like a woman. If it had a connecting kitchen and bath, I could easily spend the rest of my life there.

I spread out the paper on the glass coffee table, and my eyes were immediately drawn to the page one headline. "Southfield House Fire Scene of Double Homicide." I quickly scanned the story picking out the highlights. "New evidence points to arson. Mother and daughter murdered. Vincent Lovejoy, 25, of Madison Heights, questioned in connection with deadly blaze. Investigation ongoing."

Leaning back, I breathed out a long sigh. "So it's true. They were murdered."

"Looks that way."

"God I hate that."

"Join the club," Riff said in a cynical tone. "Now tell me about Lovejoy and Andra."

"I don't know much," I explained. "They'd been going out for a couple of months. I've met him three, maybe four times."

"And," Riff prompted.

"And he seemed like a nice guy."

"Seemed?"

I hesitated, knowing my answer would throw more suspicion on the man. "He started dating Jessica on the sly. When Andra found out, she dumped him."

"And that happened when?" Riff asked.

"A few weeks ago."

"Obviously, Mister Lovejoy didn't go away."

"No," I said thinking about the flowers Vince had sent to Andra almost daily for the last couple of weeks. "But his attempts to win her back were all gifts and apologies. You thinking he's a serious contender?"

When Riff answered, her fatigue was evident. "What I think is that your buddy's in deep shit."

"Why? What have you got on him?"

"A statement from the Martins' next door neighbor. Claims to have seen Lovejoy hanging around the house the night of the murders."

"Outside ain't inside, Lieutenant. And what would his motive be?"

"We can place him inside," Riff said. "The lab boys picked up his prints all over the place. And you just gave me a motive."

I remained silent, knowing that I had just implicated the man in a pair of brutal murders.

"Don't sweat it, Snowman. That's the first place we look."

Her reassurance made me feel better but not much.

"Want to hear about your friend from the mall?"

"You mean Kenny?"

"Kenneth John Dougland is his full name. He's forty-six, lives here in Southfield and has contacted my department several times in the past two years to report...are you ready for this?...crimes in progress."

"Crimes in progress?" I repeated. "How the hell could he know about them?"

"He claims to be psychic."

"Get out of town."

Riff laughed. "According to the report I'm looking at, he's got this split personality thing going on and he thinks one of them is tuned into local crime."

I looked at the phone in my hand to make sure I wasn't dreaming the conversation. "You are shitting me, right?"

"No, I'm not. And there's more to the story."

"Nothing could be that strange."

"Wanna bet?"

When I didn't respond, Riff dropped the second shoe.

"I assume you're familiar with the Dougland Funeral Home chain?"

"Hard not to be. They're the biggest operation in the metro Detroit area."

"Well your friend's father is owner and CEO of the whole shebang."

"What?" Even to me, my voice sounded astonished. "I think I'm about to go into information overload here."

"Save some room," Riff advised, "because I kept the best for last. Dougland wasn't trespassing when you met him in that park. His parents own a house on the west side of Cradle Lake."

"You're serious? Kenny lives on my lake?"

"He stays there occasionally is my understanding," Riff answered. "Most of the time he lives with three other men in a group home. But he does go to the lake twice a week to tend his rose garden."

"His rose garden?"

She chuckled at my surprise. "Apparently."

"How do you know all this, Riff?"

"There's a sheet on Dougland down here. For the rest of it, I called his parents' home. Mothers are usually happy to talk about their children, if you ask in the right way."

When Riff rang off I laid the phone on the coffee table, and began to reread the news story. Halfway through the first paragraph, the phone beside the couch rang.

"Hello."

There was no response.

"Hello?"

As the silence stretched, I glanced over at the caller I.D. The name Jessica Martin was spelled out in green digital letters and beneath it her home phone number.

"Jess, are you there?" I asked gently.

"Oh Max," she sobbed. "Vince murdered my mother and sister and it's all my fault. I only dated him to bug Andra and now…"

"Hold on, Jess," I broke in. "Nobody said Vince was guilty, only that he was being questioned. Sometimes the media stretches a point to make the story more exciting. Let's just wait and see what happens."

There was the sound of muffled crying on the other end of the line, then nothing for a few beats.

"My step-brother Mitchell was here yesterday, looking for money," Jessica said. "I told him he'd get his share of the estate after the will was probated. He got pissed when I wouldn't let him stay the night, but I don't care. That creep doesn't deserve to get one thing from my mother. All he ever did was break her heart."

"Look honey," I said. "Why don't I come over? We can spend the afternoon together, maybe go to lunch."

Her voice on the line sounded tired and thin.

"Thanks, Maxie, but I'd rather be alone for awhile. Hope you don't mind."

"No, of course not. Call if you need me."

I hung up the phone and thought about the tragedy the young woman had gone through in her short life. Her father killed trying to be the Good Samaritan. Her stepbrother whacked out on hard-core drugs. And now the horrific murders of her mother and sister. It was a lot to ask of anyone, and I wondered if she could cope.

I showered, dressed in black jeans and sweatshirt, and was out of the house by ten. The weather was autumn crisp, the skies a clear cobalt blue as I drove into the tiny city of Cradle Lake. The original downtown, established in 1947, was approximately two blocks long. It still retained that cottage-town flavor but you didn't have to look hard to see it was in the process of change. A new group of upscale shops had recently been added. Another was going up across the street from them. For better or worse, growth was inevitable as more people moved into the area.

An hour later I had finished my errands and was walking to the car when the millionaire busboy, Kenny Dougland, popped up in front of me, looking wild eyed.

"Jesus, Kenny." I said almost dropping my packages. "You scared the hell out of me."

"You gotta do something, Max!"

"Chill out, man. The cops are on to Andra's murder just like you wanted."

"No!" shouted Kenny blocking my path. "You gotta do something now before it's too late."

I stepped around the man thinking his personality had split once too often but he followed close behind repeating his plea over and over.

Finally I stopped and turned back. "What are you talking about? Who do I have to help?"

"Andra's sister. At her home. You gotta help her."

"Jessica is fine," I assured him. "I just spoke to her."

His expression looked pained. "What does it take to get through to you? Think I'm playing some kind of game here?"

"No, but…"

"Get over there," he said cutting me off. "If you don't, you'll be sorry."

I unlocked my car, slipped behind the wheel, and dropped my packages onto the seat beside me. After cranking the engine I sat for a moment, listening to the almost silent purr of the Jaguar. I wanted to dismiss Kenny's warning about Jessica, but how could I? The guy had been dead-on about Andra and her mom's murder. I flipped open my phone and punched up Riff's number. When she answered, I described the confrontation with Kenny and Jessica's anxious call that morning.

There was a moment of silence as static crackled across the connection. When it cleared, Riff's tone was decisive. "Head over there, and I'll meet you as soon as I can."

I dialed Jessica's number. Four rings. Five rings. Six.

"Shit."

Forty minutes later, I pulled into Jessica's drive and parked behind her blue compact. At the front door, I rang the bell several times but there was no answer. I knocked loud and hard. Still nothing. My view inside was blocked by closed mini-blinds, so I sprinted to the rear of the house and pounded on the back door. In the answering silence, I sensed something was very wrong.

Grabbing a plastic lawn chair from a nearby brick patio, I placed it under the kitchen window. When I climbed up and looked inside, the sight of Jessica lying still as death on the living room floor chilled my bones. Pulling out my phone, I punched redial. Riff answered on the first ring and I spoke only three words before disconnecting.

"Send an ambulance."

Several good-sized stones lined a flowerbed behind the house. I hefted one, returned to the back door and smashed the windowpane nearest the handle. Reaching in, I flipped the lock. A moment later I was beside the unconscious woman.

Jessica's face felt cool and she seemed to be breathing but the movement of her chest was shallow and erratic.

"Please don't die, Jessie," I said as I slid a pillow under her head. "Help is on the way."

It was then that I spotted the empty bottle of sleeping pills lying beside the unconscious woman. When I picked it up, Jessica's phone call that morning replayed in my head. That she would attempt suicide had never entered my mind, but why I couldn't imagine. The twenty-six-year-old had lost her entire family to violence, and because of a spurious front-page news story, she blamed herself for the deaths of her mother and sister.

Two minutes later, there was the sharp screech of brakes in the driveway and far off in the distance the whine of an ambulance siren. I opened the front door and Riff rushed into the room. Kneeling beside Jessica, she checked for signs of life.

"We've got a pulse," she said, "but not a good one. Hope the paramedics get here fast."

An emergency siren whooped outside the house and within seconds, a trio of techs was in the room. Two uniformed cops followed and as I watched the group gather around Jessica's body, a shudder of guilt ripped through me for not seeing this coming.

Riff spoke to a member of the ambulance team before coming to stand beside me.

"How is she?" I asked.

"I don't know. They think she may have stopped breathing at some point."

Two plain-clothes officers arrived on the scene. After speaking to Riff, they took my statement outside the back door. We finished just as the ambulance was pulling away and I followed it to Beaumont Hospital. An hour later the doctor working on Jessica agreed to talk to me.

"She is out of immediate danger," said Dr. Gosh, a slight, dark-skinned East Indian with a singsong accent, "and that is good. But she has not yet regained consciousness, and I cannot be sure when that might happen. Go home and rest now. The nurse will call when there is any change."

I thanked the doctor and left my name and number at the nurses' station assuring them they could call me at any hour.

On the way home, I stopped at a popular fast-food restaurant. It wasn't my usual fare but I was hungry and wanted something quick and easy. I sat at an orange Formica table slowly eating my burger and fries but not tasting a single bite. Each mindless mouthful followed the next until the food was gone and my hunger was vaguely satisfied. Numb and confused by the recent happenings in my life, I was reluctant to think what might come next. I didn't have long to wait.

One moment I was alone and the next thing I knew, Kenny Dougland was sitting across the table from me. He appeared to be in a somewhat more rational state of mind than he'd been earlier that morning.

"Saw you sitting here," he said. "Is Jessica Martin all right?"

"Why don't you tell me, psychic boy," I spat in frustration. "You seem to know everything else." I wanted to blame this weirdo for all the trouble going down in my life. He was handy and strange enough to be suspect.

Kenny sat quietly, absorbing my anger like someone who's had a lot of practice. When he answered my charge, his voice was laced with melancholy. "People are always mad at me for trying to help. What did you want me to do? Let Jessica die?"

I ground my teeth together and stared across the table. Inwardly I cursed his logic. But how could I argue? Kenny had helped save Jessica's life and I was acting pissed about it.

"Sorry," I said shaking my head. "This whole thing's been too weird."

"Hey, no problem," he replied and gave me a toothy grin. "But what are you going to do now?"

"What do you mean?"

The odd little man glanced around the room before speaking in a whisper. "I mean," he said as he leaned forward across the table, "that I'm tuned into this case. And I thought we could partner up and find out who killed Andra and her mom."

For a moment I was drawn in by the suggestion, but when the full weight of it hit me, I sat back and shook my head. "I'm not joining you in anything. You could be a suspect in the murders for all I know."

Kenny slumped in his chair and mirrored my cynical expression. "So you're just going to what? Sit back, and wait your turn?"

"My turn?" I said. "Who'd want to murder me?"

"I don't know," Kenny answered. "Who'd want to murder Andra and her mother?"

The blunt question stumped me, but I recovered quickly.

"Forget it," I said. "Besides, why do you need my help? You're the big psychic. Don't you already know who did it?"

"No, I don't," Kenny said. "Just like I don't know what the lottery number is going to be this week or if you'll keep losing your hair. I sense things. Sometimes I'm wrong, but not this time."

"Then why the hell didn't you warn Andra?" I demanded.

"The images I get are usually disconnected at first," Kenny shot back. "I don't always know what they mean."

I thought about what Riff had told me concerning this man and shook my head. "Just let the police handle it, Kenny."

As if these last words were a trigger, he stood, turned his back on me, and exited the restaurant.

Driving the deserted stretch of expressway on the way home, my mind went over the day's events. Jessica's call; her attempt at suicide; Kenny's offer to form an alliance. The trio of thoughts had me so hypnotized I never saw the big, black SUV until it sideswiped the driver's side of my car. The surprise hit caused the Jag to careen violently on and off the road's shoulder. Only my frozen grip on the steering wheel kept it from spinning out of control.

When I braked to a stop, Kenny's question at the restaurant rang in my ears. "What are you going to do? Sit back and wait for your turn?"

My turn? Nah. The SUV driver was probably drunk. But a sense of fear gripped me when the black truck, parked barely twenty-five yards ahead, began to creep slowly toward me in reverse.

Instinct told me I didn't want to meet the truck's occupants on that dark and lonely stretch of highway. So after a glance in the mirror and a prayer that nothing vital was damaged on the Jag, I punched the gas and shot up the highway.

For several seconds nothing appeared behind me. A moment later, the truck came barreling out of nowhere and kissed my car's rear end with its monstrous snout. I floored the gas pedal widening the gap but the truck roared back with vengeance pushing and prodding me toward the side of the road. When my wheels caught the soft shoulder, I slid into a sideways spin. The moment I regained control, the truck's cowcatcher-like bumper slammed battering ram style into my door and the world went black.

When I awoke, the first thing I saw was a state police officer hoofing it through the roadside scrub toward my car. He was reporting the scene into a shoulder mike and when he saw me watching him he nodded.

"Are you hurt, sir?" the officer asked through the cracked window.

I looked down at my body and moved my arms and legs to check for damage. Nothing seemed broken. In fact the only pain I could detect was on my left temple. Reaching up, I explored the spot. It must have been where my head connected with the window because there was a goose egg and some tender skin.

"I'm fine," I said and unlocked my seatbelt. "Can I get out?"

"You sure you're all right? I could call EMS."

"No thanks," I said and tried to force a smile. "I just want to get out of here."

The driver's door was stuck fast so I exited the passenger side, rounded the car and felt my heart sink when I checked out the extensive damage.

"What happened?" the cop asked eyeing me intently.

"I'm not sure. An SUV smacked into me about a mile back, and then tried to force me off the road."

The cop turned from me to gaze at a white Corvette that sped west doing at least a hundred miles an hour. He lifted a radio from his belt, spoke into it then returned his attention to me. "Any idea why somebody would want to hurt you?"

I looked at him blankly.

"Maybe you cut him off by mistake," he offered.

"There was no one on the road with me until he showed up."

"Was he driving erratically, like he was drunk?"

"I have no idea," I said feeling the bump on my head throb. "But he was definitely determined."

"Have any enemies?"

"None that would play this rough," I said nodding at my car.

With a hand on my forearm the officer led me to his patrol car, and after settling me in the back seat punched my driver's license number into the onboard computer. When my record checked out clean and he was convinced I wasn't drunk or stoned, he offered to drive me home.

Chapter 6

▼

The next several days passed without incident. Nobody tried to kill me. The wounded thief did not return. And as far as I knew, all my friends were safe and sound. The only bummer was that it was ten o'clock Friday evening and I was still at the salon. You've probably noticed I'm not a workaholic. I was only there because Fox threatened to cut off a favorite body part if I didn't catch up on the paperwork. The government makes it hard on lazy people like me. They're always asking for numbers. I doubted that anybody actually read them but my CPA didn't feel it prudent to test the theory.

Fox had left several things on my desk that needed immediate attention but I was having a difficult time maintaining my focus. Mentally I was scattered. And my brain was not responding with its usual efficiency. Well okay, my brain never operates efficiently when it comes to office work, but that night it was moving slower than usual.

I was still worried about Jessica. The overload of drugs in her system had induced a coma and so far she had remained unresponsive. At Dr. Gosh's suggestion, I visited the hospital as often as possible, but watching someone you love being kept alive by machines is very spooky. I talked to Jessica as if she could hear me, hoping the sound of a familiar voice might pull her back from wherever she was. To tell the truth I'm not sure if it helped her, but it made me feel a whole lot better.

With effort, I forced my mind back to the damn paperwork. The only thing left was to sign the weekly paychecks, and I was just finishing when the chirp of my cell phone startled me. As I reached for it, my heart contracted. I hate when it does that.

"Hello?" I said cautiously. I didn't need any more bad news.

"Max. It's Riff."

"Hey."

"I wanted to bring you up to speed on Jessica's condition."

"Uh huh."

"She woke up from the coma late this afternoon."

"Is she okay?"

"She will be," Riff said, "but she told me a strange story."

I waited, not knowing what to expect.

"Jessica never tried to commit suicide. Her stepbrother pushed his way into her home and forced her to take the drugs. To help finish the job, he shot her up with some heroin."

For a moment I was speechless. But the shock of Mitchell Sanders attempting to kill his only surviving relative was enough to break my silence. "I swear, Riff, if it weren't you telling me this…" I stopped mid-sentence as cold understanding broke through my confusion. "Wait a minute. Are you thinking Mitchell killed his mother and Andra?"

"It's a possibility," Riff said in her no-nonsense cop voice. "He's got a record of domestic violence. Assaulted Lila Martin twice last year, and again a few weeks ago."

"Andra never told me that," I said.

"Well, she reported all three incidents to the police," Riff continued, "but Mrs. Martin refused to press charges."

I sat there shaking my head. "How does anybody decide to murder their entire family?"

"We don't know for sure that he did. But if he tried to off one…" Riff paused and let the sentence hang between us. "We're still checking out Lovejoy's story. He admits to being outside the house that night. Claims he wanted to talk with Andra but no one answered the door."

"What time was that?" I asked.

"Lovejoy says ten, which jives with the neighbors' story."

"And what time was Andra and her mom killed?"

"The coroner says approximately 11 p.m."

I kept my mind quiet. I didn't want to think about what might have happened to the two women in the last hour of their lives.

"Sorry to cut our conversation short, Maxie. But I need to take another call."

I thanked her for filling me in, and before she could ring off, asked her to lunch the next day. She was reluctant to take time out from her work but when I pushed a little, she agreed.

Stepping out of my office into the dimly lit salon, I noticed a familiar form stretched out on the padded bench beneath the hood dryers.

"So you're finally done," said the dreamy accent. "I thought you were going to be at it all night."

"You could have interrupted me anytime," I said offering Zed a hand-up. "I have absolutely no dedication when it comes to business matters."

"I've noticed that," Zed returned playfully.

I smiled at the woman's candor and was rewarded with an answering grin. "Did Fox send you here to keep me on task, or what?"

Zed pushed the thick black hair behind her shoulders. "Actually I was heading for a private club in Detroit. Thought you might like to tag along."

"Can I get anything to eat there?" I asked slipping into my black fleece jacket and snapping off the office lights. "I haven't eaten since four this afternoon and I might start chewing the table legs. Could be embarrassing for you."

Following Zed's direction we arrived at our destination; a windowless, two-story building that looked like it might have been erected when the French controlled Detroit. It sat half-a-dozen blocks from the city's well-policed collection of theaters, sports stadiums, and upscale restaurants that draw people downtown from the suburbs, but way too far into the "hood" to allow me to feel the least bit secure. More than twenty cars were parked in the fenced lot but I had some serious doubts about leaving my new Lexus.

"Don't worry, Max," Zed said. "The people in the area know the club. They won't mess with your truck."

As we stepped into the night, I locked up and set the security alarm. Not that I didn't trust Zed's opinion. I just didn't think offering my truck like chum to Detroit's chop-shop sharks was a good idea.

We approached the brown brick building and stopped before a rusty metal door. It appeared in the dim light to be painted shut, but at Zed's knock, it opened wide enough to allow us to slide inside. Although I had no idea what to expect, the sumptuous décor that met my eyes came as a complete surprise. Four walls of polished satinwood glowed brilliantly under Tiffany-style lamps. A stone fireplace, big enough to house a family of four, blazed away in a far corner, and a mahogany bar so intricately carved in tropical relief that it looked almost alive, curved halfway around a small dance floor.

Impressed as I was by the luxurious surroundings, the thing that really caught my attention was the size of the people filling the place. Every man there was at least six-three, the women only slightly shorter. All looked buffed to the max. And although a few tawny blondes salted the crowd, the majority had bronze skin of varying hues and hair the color of midnight. Leather seemed to be the clothing of choice. I hadn't seen that much cowhide in one place since I'd visited a friend's dairy farm in Minnesota.

It would be hard to miss such unique looking people on the street, and yet with the exception of Zed I had never met anyone like them before. Where did they work? Do their grocery shopping? Get their hair cut?

The expression on Zed's face was pure mischief as she watched my reaction to the crowd. Leaning close she draped an arm around my shoulders and brushed my ear with her lips. "Something you want to ask me about my friends?"

"Yeah," I answered and turned to face her, "What planet are they from? And do they bite?"

"I think you'll find these people exceptionally earthy," Zed answered as her coal-black eyes burned into mine. "And as for biting, well, you should be so lucky."

During the next few hours, I put my problems aside. Something about the atmosphere in the club made me feel safe, so I decided to take advantage of the respite. Zed was clearly a popular figure there and the people that stopped by our table seemed genuinely pleased to meet me. I sampled the house ale. It was dark, full-bodied and magically delicious. After my third glass, I decided, since I was driving, that I had better switch to water.

While still under the influence of that delightful elixir, a lone woman stopped at our table and stared down at me. She was built like the proverbial brick shit house, dressed in body-hugging leather from stem to stern, and stood an easy six-four in the stiletto heels.

"Zed, darling," she said but never took her eyes from mine. "You're pretty friend was checking me out a moment ago. Would he like to dance with Mellina?"

Zed looked from the woman to me, and back again. "I'm sure the pretty man would love to dance with you, Mellina," she said. "But only if you promise not to bite."

Near the end of the evening the music slowed and I took the opportunity to talk to Zed about her past.

"I was born and raised on Blackbird Cay," she explained in answer to my first question. "It's a small island, ninety miles off the coast of Belize."

"Are your parents Mexican?"

Zed shook her head. "My father was Creole. And my mother could trace her roots all the way back to some English sailors who were shipwrecked there in 1638."

"They're both dead?"

Zed nodded. "It happened when I was five so I barely remember them."

"That must have been rough."

"Not really. The people of my village took care of me. I had a hundred mothers and fathers to love and scold me."

"But someone must have taken you in."

Zed smiled and at that moment I thought she was the most beautiful woman I had ever seen.

"I was adopted by the shaman of the village; a wonderful man named Zejuara who taught me his craft and the secret of life."

"Care to share it?" I asked. "I've always wanted to know the secret of life."

Zed flashed a crooked smile. "You won't like it at first."

"Try me."

"Okay. You ready?"

I nodded.

"For every outside there's an inside," Zed recited, then paused. "And for every inside there's an outside."

I shrugged and shook my head so Zed attempted to explain.

"Up," she said and pointed a finger at the ceiling, then reversing her hand. "Down. Pretty deep, huh?"

"Subterranean, Babe," I said thinking her secret of life echoed the Buddha's teachings and that of modern physics.

We looked at each other for a long moment before Zed continued.

"The discipline Zejuara taught me challenged both mind and body. But in time I came to love the strange man who talked to plants and animals like they were people."

"Did they ever answer him?"

"Of course."

"Can you talk to plants and animals?"

Zed raised an eyebrow at my question. "You have a cat, right?"

I nodded.

"Do you talk to him?"

"Sure."

"Does he answer you?"

I thought about the obvious communication that went on daily between Blue and me and nodded. "I see what you mean."

Zed smiled. "Zejuara trained me to be a medicine woman and by fifteen I was taking care of my entire village."

"Heavy responsibility for a teen."

Zed shrugged. "You grow up fast in that world."

"And how did you happen to find yourself in Michigan?" I asked, totally caught up in the story.

"As you can see," Zed answered while gesturing to the people around us. "I had connections here. And I came to meet my fate."

"Your fate?"

"Yes, Max. You know, destiny…karma…kismet.…You can wait for it to find you, or you can go out and confront it. I prefer the latter."

"And by that you mean your fate is somewhere in Michigan?" I asked amused by the concept of this exotic creature seeking her fate in middle America.

Zed nodded and drained the remaining ale in her glass. "I'm sure of it."

I didn't doubt her for a minute. If she said she was here to meet her fate, well, she was here to meet her fate. I only hoped I might be lucky enough to score a part in the play.

After looking around at the thinning crowd, Zed glanced down at her watch and back to me. "You about ready to go, Boss? I have to open the salon in seven hours."

The night was crisp and clear, the moon three-quarters full as we traveled down the I-75 Freeway with the Friday night bar crowd. So far no one had strayed from his or her lane, but it was probably best to assume at least a few people on the road were enjoying a buzz.

We had just zipped under the Nine Mile Road overpass when I spotted a familiar truck up ahead—a big, black bruiser of an SUV that made a quick lane change and pulled directly in front of me.

Zed noticed my change of mood and was instantly on the alert. "What's wrong?"

"The truck in front of us," I said. "I think it's the one that forced me off the road the other night. I need to check out the passenger side for damage." After slipping into the right lane I surveyed the crumpled metal. "Bingo, Babe."

As I spoke, the black bomber positioned itself to catch the upcoming I-696 interchange. I mimicked his move but hung back a bit. If the driver of the truck was the one who ran me off the road, there was a good possibility he might recognize my second vehicle. I allowed him to get several car-lengths ahead then regretted my decision when the black truck shot forward, weaved recklessly through a tight knot of traffic, and disappeared around the curvy entrance ramp leading west.

"Damn it," I said as my eyes scanned the road for a break in the traffic. "He's getting away."

"Easy," Zed advised. "Watch for your chance."

The woman's unruffled attitude helped me chill and when I spotted a safe opening between cars, I punched the gas and we roared up the highway.

After ten minutes I gave up the chase. The SUV had either gotten off on one of the two exits we passed or was too far ahead to catch.

"We'll see him again," Zed pronounced with confidence as I eased up on the gas.

I wanted to believe her but when the exit to the Rolling Pines mall came up, I pulled off the e-way and into the parking lot.

"Why the hell didn't I think to get the plate number?" I said shaking my head in disgust. "It was right in my headlights."

Zed didn't respond. Her eyes were busy scanning the dimly lit parking lot.

"There," she said pointing towards the far corner of the mall.

I looked in the direction she indicated just in time to see the black SUV moving quickly around the mall's ring road. "He's heading towards the theater entrance," I said excitedly.

I cut across the lot to head him off, but soon realized I had chosen the wrong path. We came within fifty feet of my quarry only to find ourselves blocked by the sunken driveway leading to the mall's underground delivery entrance. Forced to go around, we temporarily lost sight of the truck but when I swung into the theater parking lot, Zed spotted it again.

"Over there, Max. Parked near the entrance."

The midnight show must have just ended because as I skidded to a stop behind the truck, a small crowd of people exited the mall. I popped my door but Zed put a firm hand on my arm. "Be careful. Whoever it is might be armed."

Sound advice, but I was too pissed to listen so shaking her off, I jumped out, ran to the driver's door of the truck, and banged my fist against the tinted window.

There was no response from inside the vehicle, but several people passing eyed me with alarm. I was about to hit the window again when Zed slipped up beside me.

"Forget it, Max. It's empty."

With a keen sense of disappointment I cupped my hands and looked through the tinted window. Zed was right. We had lost the chase. Frustrated, I spun around and searched the faces of the people walking by. Any one of them could have been the driver.

Pulling out my phone I dialed Riff's work number. She ran an immediate trace on the SUV's plate, but it turned out to be another dead-end. The truck's owner had reported it stolen a week ago.

Chapter 7

Late the next morning as I dressed for my lunch date with Riff, I went over last night's failed chase for the umpteenth time. The driver of the black truck had indeed recognized my Lexus. And that suggested, at least to me, a connection between the assault on the road and the break-in at my house. A long shot but one that kept sticking its ugly nose in my face.

Before leaving the house, I checked out the clothes I was wearing in the full-length bathroom mirror. The heather-gray jeans looked good on me, as did the camel colored mohair sweater, but the new wrinkles, I mean laugh lines, that seemed to have formed overnight in the corner of each eye were a bit distressing.

"You little shits best behave yourselves in front of Riff," I said stretching the skin taunt and looking deeper into my reflection. "Or it's Botox-time."

After saying goodbye to Blue, I stepped into the garage and felt my heart sink. My truck was nowhere in sight. "Stinkin' good-for-nothing, piece of crap alarm system!" I shouted and slapped the heel of my hand on the wall above the security pad. "What's the sense of having your useless butt if you let every Tom, Dick and Harry waltz into the house whenever they damn well…"

I stopped in mid-rant, suddenly remembering I had parked in front of the house the previous night, and as I walked through the sunroom and out the front door I felt like a forgetful paranoid fool. Was I growing as a person or what?

Crossing the patio I was happy to see my Lexus waiting for me on the cobblestone drive that circled the house. It had rained early that morning and beads of moisture were glistening like diamonds on its British racing green body. That shade of green has always been a favorite of mine; a holdover no doubt from my teenaged fascination with sports cars like Triumph and MG, and I continued to favor the color if not the toy-like cars. In today's world, it's better to be up a little higher and have a bit more steel around you, what with monster-sized SUVs, drivers steaming with road-rage and practically everybody (including me), yakking away on their cell phone.

Rounding the front of my truck, I signaled the door locks, but instead of the usual answering chirp, the parking lights blinked twice in blatant incrimination. That meant I had forgotten to lock the doors last night, a bad habit I'd developed lately, and given what's been going down in my life, one that I could ill-afford.

Opening the driver's door, I settled into the leather seat and was instantly surrounded by the sound of…snoring. "Shit!" I said as I leapt out the door and backed away. There was somebody sleeping in my truck. A few seconds later, indignant curiosity prompted me to peek in the window, and when I recognized the sleeper stretched out across the back seat, a sense of relief was followed by some really righteous anger.

"Damn it, Kenny!" I said after jerking the door open. "What the hell are you doing in my truck?"

As if deep in a dream, Kenny's only reaction was to adjust his position and smack his thick lips. It was obviously going to take more than words to wake this sleeping beauty, so seeing that he was using the passenger side armrest as a pillow, I walked around and yanked the door open. The large head, with pink cap firmly in place, hung suspended in space, and when he still didn't wake up, I leaned down and shouted directly into his ear.

"Maxie," he said after yawning loudly and rubbing his brown eyes with a balled up fist. "What's up?"

"What's up?" I growled. "What do you mean, what's up? What the hell are you doing in my truck?"

"Thought we might do lunch," he said flashing an upside-down grin, "and discuss the case."

"Sorry," I said and backed off at the sight of the boxy white choppers and thick, pink tongue. "But I've got a date for lunch, and you're not invited."

"With who?"

"A police officer named Linda Riff," I snapped when the man made no move to get out. "And if I ever catch you sleeping in my truck again, I'm going to borrow her gun and shoot you."

Kenny ignored my bad mood, grabbed the headrest on the front seat, and pulled himself to a seated position. He took a dingy handkerchief from a pocket of his equally dingy jeans and blew his nose, honking as if he was an angry goose.

Finishing this gross display, he looked out at me and grinned like a Halloween pumpkin.

"Don't have a cow, man," he said rocking slowly back and forth. "I didn't sleep in your truck all night. Got here about an hour ago. The doors were open, so I figured what the hell? Along with being mentally challenged, I'm slightly narcoleptic."

"I don't care if you're freakin' Rip Van Winkle. From now on, consider my car, my truck, my house and my property off limits to your snoozing."

Kenny looked unfazed. "I know who Linda Riff is," he said and boosted himself through the door. "She's a police lieutenant in my city."

I slammed the door but before I could take a step Kenny piped up again. "So where we havin' lunch?"

I snorted and shook my head. "You are so not invited."

Kenny blinked his mournful eyes at me. "What are you talking about, man? I thought we were going to team up."

"I never agreed to that," I protested.

"So you're saying you're not interested in finding out who killed Andra and her mom?"

"Sure I am, but what's that got to do with your coming to lunch?"

"I might be able to help Lieutenant Riff in her investigation," Kenny answered eagerly. "We could share information. Maybe I could pick something up from her."

I ground my teeth together and snatched open the front passenger door. "Okay, fine," I said impatiently. "Get in the damn truck. But don't get the wrong idea. Taking you along doesn't mean I'm agreeing to any partnership. I just don't want to be late."

Riff and I had decided to meet at a small Coney Island in Southfield, and when I pulled into the lot with a chattering Kenny beside me, I was hoping he would stay centered in his semi-sane personality. Inside, I spotted the police lieutenant at a table near the back. She immediately noticed the odd little man dogging my heels and shot me a questioning look. At the table, I introduced him.

"I've read your name in the paper," Kenny said shaking Riff's hand a bit too vigorously. "You're a homicide investigator."

"That's right," Riff replied as she extricated herself from the handshake. "And I know something about you too. You claim to be psychic, and you've been in contact with my department to report your…what should we call them? Visions?"

Kenny swelled with pride at Riff's recognition, but his expression changed as she went on.

"Too bad you're rarely able to fill in the details."

Kenny gaped at her in defiance. "I explain everything I can."

Riff obviously had doubts about Kenny's mental powers. So did I. But she had not spent as much time with him as I had. Yeah, he was wacky, and it was like befriending a guy with two heads, but he'd been right-on about the Martin murders. And because of him, Jessica was alive.

A waitress in a blue jumpsuit approached and the three of us placed our orders. After she left, I steered the conversation toward more neutral ground.

"Has Kenny ever been able to tell your department where to look for trouble, Riff?"

"Once," Riff answered looking directly at Kenny. "But he's called the department five times in the past eighteen months. And even on the one he got right, his information was pretty sketchy."

"I don't get the whole picture at once," Kenny said. "It comes to me in pieces, like a puzzle."

"My department's loaded with puzzles, Mr. Dougland," Riff returned. "And frankly, we don't have time, or manpower to pursue them all."

Cop and busboy stared at each other for several seconds before Riff relaxed back in her chair.

"Sorry," she said in an abrupt about face. "I realize you're only trying to help."

I raised an eyebrow at Riff's sudden retreat, knowing it had to be difficult. My friend has a veteran cop's skeptical nature and using a psychic, particularly one as crazy as Kenny, to investigate a crime was a big stretch for her.

"If you have any insights about the Martin murders," Riff continued in a conciliatory tone, "my department and I would appreciate it if you shared them."

Caught off guard by Riff's change of direction, Kenny was uncertain how to respond. But when she smiled at him and nodded encouragingly, he mimicked her actions.

There was silence for several seconds, and as if a switch had been flipped in Kenny's brain, his face went flaccid and he began talking in a low, spooky monotone.

"Dark hands clutch the book, and marked passages point the way. Words on the page inflame his anger. Delight with promise. Inspire revenge."

Riff and I looked at each other then glanced around at the nearby tables.

"Can you see who's holding the book?" Riff asked.

"No."

"Is it a man or a woman?"

"I can't tell."

"Is it Mitchell Sanders?" Riff asked.

Kenny shook his head and seemed to come out of his trance as Riff pulled the familiar notebook from the pocket of her coat and jotted down a few lines. I could tell by the look on her face that she was unsure of what to do with the information.

"Well," she said as she tucked the pad away. "I'll keep what you told me in mind, Mr. Dougland. Thank you."

"What about Mitchell Sanders, Riff?" I said. "Any luck finding him?"

"Not much. Although he did make contact with his uncle trying to dig up information about Jessica's condition."

I looked at her in astonishment. "What uncle? There aren't any uncles."

"This would be Lila Martin's first husband's brother," Riff replied. "According to my information, Mitchell lived with him while his parents went through a nasty divorce. The two were close until Mitchell ripped him off for dope money a couple of years ago."

"Does the uncle know about the attempted murder?"

"Yeah," Riff answered. "He needed to know in case Mitchell made contact."

"Did you tell him what to say?"

Riff nodded. "We told him to stick to the suicide story, and act like Jessica was not expected to make it."

"Thought he might surface to claim his mother's estate?"

"That was the plan," she said. "But so far, no luck."

The waitress arrived with our order, and we turned our attention to the Coneys and fries. Kenny's psychic event didn't seem to affect his appetite. He ate with gusto, while Riff and I exchanged small talk, shoveling in the food like there was no tomorrow, and dripping chili and ketchup down the front of his shirt.

"Well, gentlemen," Riff said immediately after we had finished the meal. "It's been...interesting, but duty calls. You'll have to excuse me." She stood, and slung her purse over a shoulder. "I'll call soon," she said putting a hand on my shoulder. "And Mr. Dougland, thanks for your insights."

My eyes followed Riff as she left the restaurant, and I wished I were leaving with her. Instead I was stuck here with some loony who wanted me to join him in a murder investigation. And since I was actually considering it, I had to wonder who was crazier, the fool or the sucker who follows him?

Looking back at Kenny, I realized we had lost the semi-normal side of his split personality. His facial features, only a moment ago rational and interested, had morphed to goofy, and after slumping down in his seat, he began a mumbled conversation with himself.

Step right up, folks, I thought, picturing myself as ringmaster in a freak show. And see the rubber-faced man change personalities before your very eyes.

On Sunday I decided to visit Jessica in the hospital, but was unsure what her mental state might be. With Mitchell's attempt on her life, she had essentially lost all connection to family and I couldn't be sure how that might affect her.

At the hospital, I picked up a visitor pass from the front desk and when I arrived at Jessica's private room on the fourth floor, discovered a police officer standing guard at the door. He checked my pass and ID before giving me the nod to go in, and when I did I saw Jessica sitting up in bed, her face pale, the food on her breakfast tray untouched.

"Aw Jessie," I said moving to her side and leaning in for a hug. "I'm so sorry. I should have come over right after you called."

"Forget it, Max," she said swiping at her wet cheeks with a tissue. "I told you not to."

We were quiet for several moments; both of us thinking our own thoughts.

"So how are you feeling?" I asked.

"Disoriented. Doctor Gosh told me I was in a coma for three days but I can't recall any of it. My last memory is Mitchell pushing his way into the house and making me swallow those damn pills." Jessica paused and breathed in heavily. "I tried to fight, but he kept forcing them on me. When I started to puke, he cooked up some dope and shot it into my arm."

I hugged her tightly and felt tears well up in my eyes.

"Lieutenant Riff said it was you that found me and called for help."

"I can't take credit for that," I said straightening and giving her a lopsided grin. "It was Kenny Dougland who sensed you were in trouble. The man is freaking amazing."

Fresh tears slid down Jessica's cheeks but her face took on a look of defiance. "I accused Mitchell of killing Mom and Andra."

"Pretty brave, babe. What did he say?"

Before she could answer, there was a knock on the door and the cop who was guarding the room leaned in.

"Ms. Martin? There's a Kirk Robinson here to see you. Should I let him in?"

At the name, Jessica's haunted eyes brightened and she nodded her assent. When the door reopened a moment later, a slim, handsome-faced young man with shoulder length auburn hair stepped in clutching a bouquet of yellow roses.

"Hey, Jess," he said softly. "Am I interrupting something?"

"No," she said tucking her tousled hair behind her ears and sitting up straighter. "But how did you know I was here?"

A flush crept into the man's cheeks and he shifted his feet nervously. "My mom works down in Admitting. She told me you weren't accepting visitors, but I had to try."

Jessica's pleased smile lit up the room. "I'm really glad you did, Kirk. Come on in and meet a friend of mine. Max Snow, this is Kirk Robinson."

I stood and met Kirk's outstretched hand but his attention never wavered from Jessica. The look in the man's eyes told me he was head over heels in love, and when I glanced at Jessica, I saw her face wore the same expression.

"Hey," I said knowing it was time to leave. "I have to get going, Jess. When do you get sprung from here?"

"Doctor Gosh said maybe tomorrow."

"Need me to pick you up?"

Jessica locked eyes with Kirk and he shook his head.

"Thank for your offer, sir," he said. "But I'd like to drive the lady home if it's okay with her."

Chapter 8

▼

At home later that afternoon, I stood on the patio enjoying an iced cappuccino, and my view of Cradle Lake. My house is built on the side of a gentle rise, and the architect took advantage of the location by constructing a double tiered, terra cotta tiled patio that steps down toward the water.

The upper patio, actually a sunroom, stretches across the entire front of the house. It's laid-out in a half circle, thirty feet wide at the center and enclosed by a wall of light sensitive transition-glass, the same ingenious material used to regulate light in eyewear. I use the enclosed patio for dining with guests; it's the ultimate window table overlooking the water. As a workout room; there are free-weights, a treadmill and a Bowflex machine on the opposite side. And when the mood strikes, as it often does, a large sunken Jacuzzi is there to comfort body and soul.

The lower patio is open to the elements. It has a heated swimming pool, another Jacuzzi, a built in gas barbecue, big enough to roast a side of beef, and if weather permits, a wrought iron table capable of seating eight. Directly in front of that, a wide cobblestone drive circles the house, and beyond it, fifty feet of sandy beach fronts the mile long lake.

As I sipped my coffee, I thought about Mitchell Sanders. It baffles the hell out of me how people can be hardcore drug users. I mean, who wants to be that buzzed all the time? Not that my hands are clean, mind you. As a kid, I was an indiscriminate consumer of many street-drugs. But in my adult life, I hope I've learned to pick my poisons with more discretion.

Next up on my brain's hit parade was this Kirk Robinson guy. Who the hell was he? And where did he come from? The double-barreled question kept cycling back to me that whole morning. Through my relationship with Andra, I thought I had met most of her sister's close friends, yet here was a man in love with Jessica and I had never even heard his name. That kind of bugged me, but not in a resentful way. I felt protective of the grief-scarred woman.

There were times when seeing people in love made me wonder why I couldn't find anyone to share my life. You'd think being a millionaire, I wouldn't have such problems. But the truth is money only complicates the dating thing. There's always that underlying question. Is it me or my bank account they find sexy? I'd been in long-term relationships before. I was married once for over ten years. I've been single almost as long and am beginning to wonder if I've lost the capability to commit.

The late afternoon sun spread over the lake like syrup on pancakes. Fall in Michigan is a kaleidoscope of color, and when the days are warm, like they had been recently, it was my favorite season. Inspired by the Indian summer weather, I decided to clean the beach in front of my house. Living on the extreme eastern end of the lake has its advantages. Like privacy and spectacular views of the setting sun. The down side is the garbage that floats ashore with the current, especially during the summer season. I'm constantly picking up cans, water-toys, skis, tennis shoes, not to mention the occasional condom and woman's bathing suit top.

Moored on the beach directly in front of my house is a brand new 20' Hobicat with mainsail, jib and spinnaker. Secured firmly to a wood dock not far away, a sleek but comfortable pontoon boat bobbed gently on the waves. Both would soon have to be pulled out of the water and stored for the winter months, but I hoped to get in some sailing time before the inevitable Michigan winter set in.

Down on the beach, I scanned the shoreline for the Great Blue Heron that usually hangs out on my end of the wide bay. I hadn't seen the big guy around lately and suspected he had already booked south for the season.

Although my long-legged friend was nowhere in sight, something else had caught my attention. Forty yards ahead, exactly at the water's edge, a small mound of silver lay glistening in the afternoon sun. It had an odd shape, and from my perspective it looked like a wadded up beach towel or a child's stuffed animal.

Ambling down the beach to check it out, I raked any flotsam on the shore into piles for easy collection. When I got close enough to make out details on the mystery object, I flung the rake aside and broke into a run. It was my cat, Blue, and he was lying still as death on the sand; one side of his face crushed flat and matted with blood.

Dropping to my knees, I snatched up the tiny body and felt for a heartbeat. As I did, my ears caught the sound of a tinkling bell. And through a blur of horrific grief I noticed a slim black collar encircling the cat's neck. The anomaly jolted my senses like a speared fish and I knew instantly the animal in my arms was not Blue. The size and color were practically identical, but my cat had never worn a collar in his life.

"Shit," I hissed and breathed in jerkily. "Shit, shit, shit." But any feeling of relief I experienced was short lived when I realized who the murdered cat was. His name is Bulgaris and he was the prized pet of my nearest neighbors, Brad and Diva Black. Our two cats were the same breed, twins to their jade-green eyes, and it wasn't the first time I had mistaken the sleek feline for my own. In fact I had met Brad and Diva when I chased Bulgaris to their doorstep one evening thinking Blue had somehow escaped my house.

As I raced home to assure myself Blue was safe, my mind was filled with guilt and anger. Guilt because I suspected Bulgaris had been murdered in a case of mistaken identity. And angry because whoever killed the cat must have been someone known to me. Someone who'd been to my home and knew what my cat looked like.

My nerves were stretched tight as I stepped into the sunroom and called Blue's name. Of course he didn't answer; he's a cat not a dog, and unless I'm holding a treat, Blue deems worthy of his attention, he never comes on command. When a frantic search of the cat's lower-level haunts turned up empty, I sprinted up the stairs. My first stop was the master bedroom. His favorite place to nap was beneath the covers of my waterbed, and to my great relief, that's exactly where I found him, snoozing away, oblivious to my panic.

Sitting on the bed, I scooped the cat up and hugged him to me. After a few minutes, Blue squirmed to get down and I grabbed my cell phone off the night table. My first call was to Brad and Diva. They weren't home but I left a message for them to call as soon as they got in. Next I tried Riff at her precinct. She was out so I punched in her beeper number. Within moments, my friend was on the line listening patiently as I explained what had happened.

There was no immediate response and the uncomfortable pause lengthened into a full minute.

"Could be a coincidence," she finally said, her tone unconvincing.

"Sure, and all cops are saintly protectors of the people."

Riff ignored the sarcasm. "Did you get the gun permit?"

"Picked it up Friday morning."

"How about the CCW?"

"I passed the class and applied, but I haven't heard anything yet."

"All right," Riff said after sighing deeply. "This is what I want you to do. Take your permit over to Tactical Sports and buy a gun. The range is open until nine tonight, and I'm pretty sure Eden is working. She'll help you out."

"Wait a minute," I said before Riff could hang up. "What kind of gun do I want?"

"It doesn't matter what kind you want," Riff said. "Eden's going to sell you the .40 caliber Sig. She's obsessed with it. Thinks it's the best thing since sliced bread. And she's probably right. I'm considering buying one myself. Have her get you started in the range and practice until you're comfortable."

"Okay," I said. "I'm on my way. Any last advice?"

"Yeah. Be careful. With the gun, and with Eden. They're both—repeat both—extremely dangerous."

"Thanks for the warning. Nice to know you care. How do you feel about dropping by tonight? I could barbecue something."

"Sorry. I can't."

After Riff disconnected, I leaned back and chewed my bottom lip. Did I really want to own a gun? A month ago I would have answered an emphatic "no." But things had changed. Somewhere out there, a crazy-man was looking to hurt me and the things I love.

As Riff had predicted, Eden sold me her favorite .40 caliber Sig and I returned to the range every night that week to practice. I'm almost embarrassed to admit how quickly I became accustomed to the gun; embarrassed because I used to pride myself on being a non-violent peace loving sort. Owning the gun and applying for a permit to carry said I was willing to use it.

On Saturday of that week, the salon was crazy. By mid-afternoon I had done two cut and colors, touched up another stylist's highlights, gave the manager of Fantasy Footwear a quick trim, and did an up-do for a teenage client going to her first formal dance. After four more haircuts, my workday would be over and it couldn't come fast enough for me. I felt scattered. And depression, a rare emotion for me, was applying for permanent resident status in my brain. Thankfully my concerns about assuming salon management duties proved groundless. Fox had taken on Andra's job and with a big assist from Zed, things were running smoothly.

When Fox and I talked that morning, she told me Pete was still causing trouble. I hated that, mostly because there wasn't a damn thing I could do about it. I couldn't even offer my house as sanctuary, with thoughts of the murdered Bulgaris fresh in my head. In fact, I was beginning to think it would probably be best if I kept my distance from the salon as well.

Curious to see how her investigation was proceeding, I buzzed Riff. "Hey Lieutenant. How's it going?"

"Shitty, if you want to know the truth. The damn fire destroyed Lila Martin's entire bedroom and any clues that might have been useful. I've gone over everything a hundred times and still come up with zip. On top of that, I can't find that little prick, Mitchell Sanders anywhere."

"Maybe he skipped," I suggested.

"He's a junkie, Max," she said as if that explained everything. "And junkies never go far from their source."

I found that bit of cop-logic discomforting. I wanted Sanders in police custody or a thousand miles away.

"Look, Max," Riff said in a serious tone. "I suggest you watch your back. We don't know that Sanders wasn't scoping out the house when you showed up to save Jessica and spoiled his plans."

"A lovely thought," I said. "Thanks for sharing."

"Just doing my part to keep you alive," Riff replied, her pitch noticeably softer. "I might want to go to bed with you again sometime."

"May all your desires come true, Lieutenant. Especially that last one."

The remainder of the workday flew by and I was too busy to think about anything else. When I finished my last client, I grabbed a quick dinner at the mall's food court and by eight o'clock I was on the I-96 heading home.

As I sped down the dark, deserted expressway, a sense of unease overtook me. A quick check of my mirrors confirmed no one was following. Straight ahead, the headlights of my truck picked up nothing out of the ordinary. The night had turned cool and damp, and a thick fog had settled into low-lying sections of the rural highway. Each time I drove through one of the white patches, the knot in my gut tightened a little more. The tension built to a flashpoint when I zipped beneath the Webberville Road overpass and noticed a dark colored car on the entrance ramp pushing fast to match my speed.

At first I tried to rationalize my fear away. It was just another car using the expressway. But as if it had a mind of its own, my foot pressed down on the gas pedal.

I was doing eighty and all of my attention was focused on the rearview mirror when the road in front of me dipped sharply and I found myself driving down into a bowl of solid fog. Ripping my foot from the gas, I slammed on the brake. Probably not the best choice given the wet pavement but thankfully I slowed without going into a skid. Just as my heart restarted itself, a set of headlights flashed in the mirror.

Gradually I climbed out of the fog and increased my speed. The car behind matched me and narrowed the gap. That didn't have to mean anything sinister, of course. A lot of drivers can't stand traveling behind anybody. But after almost being killed on this very stretch of road, I couldn't help feeling jumpy.

Despite the dicey road conditions, I bumped up my speed, determined to shake my pursuer. When the headlights started to close in again, an idea suddenly pushed its way through my panic, and because my brain was churning out fight-or-flight chemicals by the truckload, the scheme actually seemed plausible. Just up the road was a long low valley that was sure to be filled with the night's pea soup. Once hidden in the mist, I could slip to the shoulder and let the Bozo on my tail pass me.

Holy lame-brained plans, Batman.

Within moments, the road ahead began a slow descent and the fog swallowed me up. After a count of five, I eased off the gas, angled to the right, and coasted to a stop when I felt the shoulder under my wheels.

I sat there, holding my breath, waiting for the trailing vehicle to pass. After several seconds ticked by with nothing in sight, I wondered if I could have missed him in the marshmallow fog.

Popping my seatbelt, I triggered the power window. As the tinted glass slid down, gossamer wisps of fog rushed inside like tiny ghosts. Two quick steps sounded on the gravel behind me, but before I could react, my door was wrenched open.

"Police officer!" shouted a blunt voice. "Keep both hands on the steering wheel."

My slamming heartbeat pounded in my ears. Did that guy say "police"? Yes. It was a cop. I could see his uniform, his badge, and the barrel of his gun pointing directly at me that looked wide enough to drive a truck through.

"Keep your hands in plain sight."

"Yes sir," I said and gripped the leather wheel cover to make sure my fingers stayed put.

The policeman produced a long-handled flashlight from behind his back and snapped it on. After a quick search of the interior, he shined the beam directly into my face then snapped it off again.

"Mr. Snow?"

"Yes?"

"I'm Officer Mike Kenel. I drove you home the night you were run off the road."

I blinked several times, straining to see through the tiny blue circles seared into my vision by the powerful flashlight. "Yes, of course," I answered still feeling disoriented. "Officer Kenel. This must look so bad. I thought you were following me. I'm sorry."

The policeman nodded sagely before he spoke.

"Can't say I blame you, sir. At your suggestion, I talked to Lieutenant Riff the night of your accident. She briefed me on your situation. Sorry for the scare but you were driving too fast, and when you tried to lose me I had no choice but to investigate. You sure you're all right?"

I sank back into my seat and ran a trembling hand over my forehead.

"I'm fine," I said. "Thanks."

The remainder of the ride home was uneventful and when I finally made the turn into my drive, I was never happier to get there. But my relief was cut short by the sight of several large chunks of concrete lying helter-skelter across the driveway. It took all of a moment to figure out what they were. Someone had toppled the Buddha sculpture, causing it to break up into pieces.

"Son-of-a-bitch," I said and felt the pit of my stomach go hollow. I had worked on that piece for five months.

Stepping out to clear a path, I heard the scream of my home security alarm and realized there was more fun yet to come. Without thinking, I ran up the drive towards the house. Halfway there it came to me that whoever triggered the alarm might still be around so I stepped into the surrounding woods. The underbrush was wet with the recent rain, and after a few steps, my jeans and shoes were soaked.

The closer I got to the house, the more I thought about how stupid this was. I was alone and unarmed. What the hell would I do if I met anyone? Make a citizen's arrest?

My senses were geeked to hyper-drive when I felt something touch the back of my leg. I yelped, sprang forward, tripped over a tree stump and sprawled headfirst into the wet brush. A second later, I was on my feet again ready to fight for my life, but when I turned to confront my assailant, there was nobody in sight. A quick movement caught the corner of my eye and as I peered into blackness a familiar howl sounded alongside the security alarm.

"Blue? Is that you? Come here, bud."

The thoroughly soaked cat streaked into my outstretched arms and nuzzled me forcefully under my chin. "Sorry about this, Babe." I said, stroking his wet fur. "But you're okay now. I've got you." The cat's body trembled with cold and stress, and when I unzipped my jacket he tucked himself inside. Cradling his weight with my left arm, I continued cautiously toward the house.

When I stepped up onto the patio, the clouds broke, and as if on cue, a single shaft of moonlight sliced across the sunroom windows. There embedded neck-up in the half missing glass of the patio door was the head of my Buddha sculpture, the ever-present smile still playing out across his wide lips.

The moment was pure Hitchcock. The only thing it lacked was a suspenseful soundtrack to scrape across my raw nerves. Crouching low at the edge of the patio, I swept my eyes from left to right, sprinted to the security panel beside the door, and silenced the alarm.

Inside, the soft green glow of the hot tub illuminated the room enough to tell me it was empty. Gathering what courage I had left, I slid my key home and watched the door swing back on its own weight. The moment I stepped inside, Blue squirmed from my jacket and disappeared into the house.

My only thought at that point was to get to my gun. It was tucked in the drawer of a table at the foot of the stairs, and I hoped to God it was still there. If not, whoever had it was probably pointing it at my head, ready to add me to the statistics of people killed with their own weapon.

Keeping low, I crossed the sunroom, entered the dark house and reached for the light-switch on the wall above me. "That's right," shouted the little voice in my head, "light the place up. Make yourself an easier target."

My hand froze in midair, and for a moment I wondered if retreat wasn't my best course, but at that point the thought of what might be waiting outside seemed scarier than what might be inside, so stayed where I was. Forcing my feet to move, I duck-walked to the table at the foot of the stairs, opened the single drawer quietly as possible and reached inside. When my fingers touched cool steel, I snatched up the gun, popped the magazine, and checked the load in the diffused moonlight. Finding it full, I jacked a ready-round into the chamber and moved to the phone beside the couch.

An hour later, the local cops had come and gone. They found no one lurking in the house and a quick check outside revealed nothing out of the ordinary.

Vandalism was their glib explanation for the damage done to my sculpture and patio door. Their advice? I shouldn't worry about it. Probably only kids looking for cheap thrills.
   Right.

Chapter 9

▼

I didn't sleep at all that night. Who could sleep with a loaded semiautomatic under their pillow? At 6 a.m. I was in the kitchen drinking coffee and trying to dodge the first rays of the sun.

Vulnerability is good in small amounts; it keeps you open to new experiences, but too much of anything can kill you and I was fading fast. Of course, staying awake all night hadn't helped. Now I was sleepy, spooked, sad, mad and depressed. Add dopey, which wasn't much of a stretch, and bashful, something I'd been most of my life, and I could be the seven dwarves.

My friend, Blue, was keeping his distance that morning as though he sensed I was dangerous to be around. He might chance the same room, but always looked ready to bolt at the slightest provocation. His standoffish behavior could be interpreted as a warning to me of impending disaster, but it was a better bet he was more concerned about his own furry little butt.

Closing my eyes, I dozed off in the kitchen chair. When I awoke a few seconds later, the face of a man I had known all my life was flashing on my mental screen. It was an innocent face, kind of like an altar boy in a Norman Rockwell painting, with grass-green eyes, red bow lips and a head full of wavy-orange hair that covered his scalp like bumpy moss.

Bobby Deegan had been my best friend all through childhood and adolescence. We grew up next door to each other in a no-collar neighborhood on the northeast side of Detroit. From the get-go of our youth, he was always Mr. Tough Guy; ready to take on anything or anybody. I on the other hand, was usually Mr. Chicken, who'd rather run than fight eight black guys chasing us through a Detroit park because Bobby screamed out the 'N' word. Call me a wimp.

At nineteen, Bobby joined Gomer Pyle's branch of the service, spent two years killing for Uncle Sam in the jungles of Southeast Asia, and came home a very intense patriot. Three months out, he joined the Detroit Police Force, scoring the nickname "Ole Slip n' Fall" after several of his busts fell down the concrete stairs leading to the precinct holding cells. But there was more to that story as a *Detroit Free Press* exposé on "dirty cops" revealed. In less than five years on the force, Bobby had pulled the trigger on seven men; all of them black. And although Internal Affairs had judged every one of the shootings justifiable, he flunked the mandatory psychological exam and was forced to resign.

After that he went into some kind of undercover work, but for whom I couldn't say. At the time I assumed it was the government but his "business associates" drove expensive cars, dressed in designer clothes, and appeared more greedy than righteous, a sure sign I might be wrong. Whatever they were, I didn't like them, and for quite a while, Bobby and I drifted apart. I still cut his hair and we got together occasionally, but he had changed from amusing cynic to hard-core mercenary and it was a challenge to remain friends. One day he just disappeared, and for weeks, my phone calls to his house went unanswered. When I finally managed to track down his mother, she claimed to not have a clue to his whereabouts.

Eight years went by with no word from Bobby. Then one night he showed up at my home in Royal Oak and I almost didn't recognize him. His face had aged twenty years, he was hairless as a statue, and his normally muscular body was reed thin and stooped slightly at the shoulders.

For three hours, Bobby sat in my living room drinking beer and rambling on about our childhood adventures together. Never once did he offer an explanation about his absence or his bizarre appearance, and although curious as hell, I didn't ask.

Deciding my dream about Bobby was an omen; I picked up the phone and punched in his home number. He lived twenty miles north of me in a high priced subdivision built around a world class golf course. After three rings, an answering machine clicked on.

"If you don't know I'm on the golf course at this time of day," said the familiar voice, "I don't want to talk to you. If it's important, dial my cell number. If you don't know it, I don't want to talk to you."

I smiled at my old friend's irascible sense of humor. The funny thing is he wasn't kidding. Years of being a marine, a cop, and who knows what else, had honed his edge of intolerance for people.

I looked up Bobby's cell phone number in my phone book and after seven rings; an abrupt voice came on the line.

"What the fuck do you want, Maxie?"

"Hey now," I teased, knowing how my friend hated to be disturbed on the golf course. "Is that any way to answer the phone? Suppose this was your mother calling?"

"My old lady doesn't have this number," Bobby kidded back. "And I don't want to hear about you giving it to her either."

"Not under penalty of death, man. Unless of course, you refuse to help me."

"Now how could a poor chump like me help a rich bastard like you?"

I gave him a brief accounting of the original break in, the assault on the road, and the recent damage to my house.

"And you're thinking the three are related?"

"I don't know what to think."

"What are the cops saying?"

"Not much. The local boys called the damage to my house 'vandalism'. I haven't heard zip from the Sheriff's Department or the State Police."

"So why call me?"

"Because I thought I'd start investigating this thing for myself and I have no idea where to start."

Bobby barked out a sarcastic laugh. "Get a grip, Maxie. You've been reading too many detective novels."

I could feel my face grow hot with irritation. "Look, I obviously can't depend on the cops to protect me, so you're it. Are you going to help or not?"

"You want advice?" Bobby said still sounding amused. "Here it is. Rent a grass shack on the beach in Tahiti and pay some big-breasted island babe to screw your brains out for a month."

"That's not the kind of help I'm looking for."

"Well I am," Bobby said. "How 'bout sending me?"

"I'd like to send you somewhere, but it ain't Tahiti."

"Maxie, listen to me, man. You don't want to go up against a whacko stalker…if there really is one."

"There is, dammit."

"Then my advice stands," Bobby said. "Leave town."

"Leaving town," I hissed through clenched teeth, "isn't going to solve shit, and you know it."

Bobby's laughter rang through the phone, and I felt my blood pressure spike even higher.

"Look, Deegan," I said trying to keep my voice calm but failing. "I think somebody's trying to kill me here."

"Big deal," he said. "I've had people trying to kill me for years."

"I'm sure they all have a good reason too," I said. "And if you don't serious up, I might join their club."

"Hey," Bobby mused. "A hairdresser hit man? Why didn't I think of that? Just a slip of the shears and…"

A huge sigh escaped me. "I didn't call to suggest cover possibilities for your hits, man."

"No, but I appreciate the idea. And to pay you back, I'm going to help out with your problem."

"Finally."

"First you want to decide where your troubles began."

I nodded, taking mental notes.

"Then stretch that peroxide-soaked brain of yours back a little farther. What was the most significant event in your life before that? Start there. Write down everything you can think of. People, places, everything. When you're done, send it to me. You on the Net?"

"Yeah, but…"

"Cool. Here's my email address."

I scribbled it down.

"Get it to me soon, old friend. Your life expectancy doesn't sound too promising."

I decided to take Bobby's advice, but I needed a little fresh caffeine to kick-start my brain. When the coffee finished brewing, I poured it into a thermal carafe, grabbed a mug and sprinted up the stairs. My PC is in a corner of the art studio, and once seated I booted up the powerful little Dell and opened a new file.

After a few false starts, I chose Andra's death as my "most significant event" and racked my brain for the details that followed. It wasn't easy. I don't have the best memory, and it took more than two hours to get it all down. When I finished, a second and third read stimulated no further insights, so after a run through the spell check I punched in Bobby's email address and shot the document off into cyberspace.

Bobby emailed me back that night with instructions to meet him on the golf course the following morning, and by 9 a.m. he had already finished eight holes. Little had been said about my problem so far, but I wasn't surprised. Bobby was a serious golfer, and I knew the real conversation would take place in the clubhouse.

He scored the ninth green with two spectacular drives, birdied with a fifteen-foot putt that would impress the hell out of Tiger Woods, and ten minutes later, we were seated on stools at the clubhouse bar. After ordering us a pair of Irish coffees, Bobby lit a cigarette, and took a long, greedy drag.

"Christ, Maxie," he said after blowing the smoke toward the ceiling like a steam engine. "You look better than ever. Are you taking youth pills, or what?"

"I don't feel better than ever. In fact I feel like shit lately."

The deep-set lines around Bobby's eyes crinkled with amusement. "Yeah," he said sliding a palm over his slick dome. "Good looks don't mean squat when you've got a psycho-killer on your tail."

I raised my eyebrows questioningly and watched his mouth spread wide in a shit-eating grin.

"That's right, man," he exclaimed almost gleefully. "Whoever took out the Martin women has decided you're next on the list."

"What?"

Bobby lit another cigarette from the stub in his hand and squinted at me through the smoke. "It wasn't hard to figure, man. Most of the story was in your email, and I hacked the rest out of the Southfield Police computer."

I sat there shaking my head as Bobby continued.

"Somebody has detailed information about your life, Maxie. Ever think about where they're getting it?"

I mentally reviewed the email I had sent to Bobby and after adding in his wild theory, deduced the answer he was looking for. "Andra's journal."

Bobby smiled at his old friend's quick pickup. "Did Andra know about the shrine room and Lott's four million, you lucky fuck?"

"Yeah."

"How about the code to your security system?"

I nodded.

"Would she write about your cat, the kind of vehicles you drive, your Buddha statue?"

"Yes to all that," I said, disgusted I hadn't made the connection for myself.

From the corner of my eye I saw the bartender approach.

"Another round, gentlemen?"

I nodded as Bobby drained what was left in his cup. Within moments two more were placed before us and after throwing down two fives, I watched the bartender walk to the register.

Bobby leaned into me and spoke in a low voice. "Keep your eye on that guy."

I did as instructed; following the bartender's every move as he deposited the bills. Next he pulled out a handful of change from his pocket, selected two coins and added them to a short stack beside the register.

"Did you catch that?" Bobby asked.

"The coin thing?"

He nodded. "The coins in the stack represent the number of drinks the little crook didn't ring up today. When he cashes out his till, he can pocket that much without anybody being the wiser."

I shook my head in wonder and watched the bartender serve another customer.

"Don't be too impressed," Bobby said sipping his coffee. "I used the same scam when I tended bar."

"You going to tell anyone?"

"None of my business," he said dropping a fiver on the bar as he slid off his stool. "Besides, this guy's easy prey. He'll get greedy and hang himself."

Bobby clamped an arm around my shoulders and planted a wet kiss on my cheek. "If I were you, Maxie, I'd start packing that new gun of yours. Better to get busted for carrying illegal than stuck somewhere with no way to defend yourself."

I looked at him quizzically. "You really think I'm going to need it?"

"You're being stalked by a crazy who's already offed two of your friends. What do you think?"

"I think I'll move into your place and let you protect me."

"Move in if you want," he said. "But I'm going to be out of town for the next few days; got business in San Francisco. Then I fly down to Augusta."

"What?! You said you'd help me?"

"And I will, but I'm not going to hold your fucking hand. Get in touch through email if you need me before I get back."

Chapter 10

I had mixed feelings as I drove out through the gates of the private golf course and turned east on the e-way service drive. Bobby's theory about Andra's killer being my stalker sounded tight but it wasn't exactly what I wanted to hear. The truth, they say, will set you free. It can also scare the bejesus out of you.

Bobby's offer of help was encouraging but the problem, as far as I could see, was still all mine. And the number one priority was to unload this damm depression. If I couldn't, my plan to stalk my stalker was fucked.

For the umpteenth time I reconsidered my decision to take the offensive. I had no experience, no skills in criminal investigation, and no way to acquire them on short notice. What I did have was the certainty that running away would do no good. And scary as searching for my psycho stalker might be, it somehow felt better than letting him hunt for me.

At the entrance ramp for the expressway, I merged into the traffic, settled into the middle lane, and checked out the occupants in the cars around me. Bobby's advice was to pay attention to everything, but that was easier said than done. I hadn't been able to focus on shit since Andra died, and my short-term memory, much in dispute even before this nightmare began, was beginning to fray around the edges.

As I considered my options a black Corvette pulled up on my right and paced me. The dark haired driver reminded me of Zed and I immediately had the idea of enlisting the mysterious beauty's help. Zed was, by her own description, a healer of mind and body. And if she could she help me get back on track I might have a fighting chance.

Picking up the cell phone from the seat beside me, I punched the preset number for the salon. Zed answered on the second ring, her rich accent soft and melodious.

"Hello, Max."

The personal greeting threw me for a second then I remembered the salon had caller I.D.

"Hey, Zed. Just thought I'd check in and see what's going on."

"Everything here is fine," she said then paused as if awaiting the real reason for my call.

Before I could chicken out, I took a deep breath and jumped in with both feet. "How would you like to come to my house for dinner?"

"Maybe. What's on the menu?"

"I don't know yet," I said playing along. "But if you're willing to gamble, I promise not to disappoint you."

I could feel her smile on the other end of the line.

"Guess I could take a chance."

"Is tonight too soon?" I asked crossing my fingers.

"Tonight would be good," Zed replied. "I'm out of here at six."

After giving her directions, I snapped the phone closed, and released the anxious breath I'd been holding. It was the same breath I'd held as a teenager when calling a girl for a date. Guess some things never change.

Before going home, I stopped at Inn Season, the new gourmet market in downtown Cradle Lake. The place was pure yuppie with a snooty staff and inflated prices but their merchandise was always top notch, and their wine selection unbeatable in the area. After considering several possibilities, I decided on the fresh Yellow-fin tuna, a nice mix of assorted greens and sprouts, two golden sweet potatoes, a pound of dark Michigan cherries and a 1997 Mondavi Fume Blanc.

On the drive home, I was in a much better mood. I was even whistling Led Zeppelin's "Stairway to Heaven" but then what man wouldn't whistle if he knew Zed was coming to dinner?

At 6:45 I heard a car pull up behind the house and a few seconds later there was a single knock on the back door. I opened it to find Zed standing on the granite stoop looking like Emma Peel in Amazon mode. Despite the cool temperature, she wore no coat. What she was wearing (be still my beating heart), was the proverbial little black dress and matching thigh-high suede boots. I knew it was rude, and my mother had taught me better, but I was unable to stop myself from gaping at her magnificent form.

When I finally managed to drag my eyes back to her face, her smile told me she was neither embarrassed nor offended by my carnal reaction.

"May I come in?" she asked.

Entranced by her seductive aura, it took me a moment to process the simple question. "Yes. Please," I finally said and opened the door wide.

When Zed swept past me, I was enveloped in her intoxicating scent. It smelled like spicy green tea, and the effect was strong enough to make me consider giving up my lifelong love of the coffee bean.

"I love it," Zed said taking in the first level. "Can I get a tour?"

"I think that can be arranged," I said offering my arm. "Why don't we start with a look at the lake."

A few minutes later, as we reentered the house from the patio, a timer in the kitchen demanded my attention.

"Why don't you check out the upper level on your own," I said, "while I finish making dinner."

Zed's black eyes twinkled at the suggestion. "You trust me in your bedroom? I might sneak a peek at your underwear."

"You'd have a hard time finding it," I said. "I gave it up years ago."

"Me too," she said gazing deep into my eyes before starting up the stairs. "What a coincidence."

My brain released a bunch of rowdy hormones as I watched Zed climb the stairs. I kind of wished she hadn't told me about the underwear thing. I'd been looking forward to enjoying my dinner. With the vision of Zed, sans underwear, bouncing around in my head, I probably wouldn't taste a single bite.

I decided we would dine in the sunroom, where candles and the glow of the hot tub would set the ambiance. When everything was ready, I called up the stairs to Zed but got no response. The second time I called; she appeared at the top of the stairs and made her way slowly down.

"Sorry," she said. "I was caught up in that abstract painting in your studio."

"What painting is that?" I asked, as if I didn't know.

Zed only stared at me. "Why didn't you sign it?"

"Because I'm not sure it's finished?" I said lying to the mind-reader.

"I can't always read you," she said. "So don't get paranoid about it."

"Right," I said turning up the wattage on my smile. "Nix the paranoia."

Escorting Zed to the patio, I pulled out her chair before taking my own seat.

"Somebody's been watching the Cooking Channel," she said gazing down at her artfully arranged dinner. "The salad looks wonderful."

"It's a mix of mesclun and adzuki sprouts, with my homemade citrus vinaigrette."

Zed tasted the salad and paused with her fork in the air. "You made this dressing?"

I nodded.

"Mind if I try to guess what's in it?"

"Guess away."

Zed took another taste. "Mmmm," she murmured running a pink tongue across her full, dark lips. "Okay, I'm ready. Orange juice, lemon juice and lime juice, olive oil, rice wine vinegar, Dijon mustard, of course, and a dash of…cinnamon."

The ingredients Zed named were absolutely correct.

"Did you read that in my mind?" I asked impressed with the woman's discerning palate. "Or can you actually taste all of those flavors?"

"A little bit of both," she confessed. "You're easy to pick up when you feel passionate about something."

"Like cooking?"

She nodded.

"I'm not sure if I like that," I said trying to control my widening grin. "Seems like an unfair advantage somehow."

"That depends on your perspective," she said. "Some men might consider it a blessing."

"Everything about you is a blessing," I said. "And I might as well admit it because you're just going to read my mind anyway, right?"

Zed leaned into my shoulder, treating me to a glimpse of the shadowed valley between her breasts. "About this wonderful food you prepared," she whispered her lips only inches from my own.

"Yes?"

"Let's eat it. I'm starving."

When we finished dinner I cleared the table and poured us both a second glass of wine. Zed raised hers, and peered at me through the amber liquid.

"Men who can cook well," she said, "usually make good lovers. Something about the way they attend to preparation and presentation."

"If that's a compliment on my dinner, it was a nice one."

"Who taught you?"

"My ex-wife, Susan. She encouraged me to share the kitchen duties when we first lived together, and I found myself enjoying the hell out of it."

"What happened between you two?"

"I lost her to Zen Buddhism, believe it or not. We took classes at a temple in Ann Arbor and she was hooked. Decided we should move to Japan and find a Zendo that would accept Americans."

"I take it you didn't want to."

I shook my head. "At the time I wasn't ready for that kind of change."

"Is she happy?"

"I don't know. We've lost contact."

"How about you, Max? Are you happy?"

"I am right now," I said joining my palms and bowing Japanese style. "And according to Zen, now, is all there is."

The twin candle flames danced in Zed's coal black eyes as she put a hand on my arm. "The hot tub looks very inviting. Can we go in?"

"Sure. But I don't think I have a bathing suit that would fit you."

The corners of her mouth tipped up. "Do I need one? I mean, is it a house rule or something?"

I shook my head, not sure I could actually speak.

Zed stood and headed for the hot tub, her hip-sway subtle, but enough to pull the bottom of her dress in alternate directions. There was the soft purr of zipper as the boots were stripped off. A shrug of her shoulders released the dress, and I watched it float down like a whisper to form a silk puddle at her feet.

Mere words could not describe Zed's voluptuous but powerful form, and I'm pretty sure I was drooling as she stepped down into the bubbling water and settled in. It had not been my intention to try and seduce Zed that night, although my hormones were definitely urging me in that direction. And just because my lifelong fantasy woman was naked and waiting for me to join her in the hot tub didn't mean I had to try. Did it?

As I stripped off my own clothes I could feel Zed's eyes on my body. Thank God I'd been hitting the gym on a fairly regular basis. Not that I was full of bulging muscles, but my body was slim and tight. I'd be embarrassed to show anything less to this superbly sculpted woman.

My physical reaction to Zed's stunning figure was obvious as I stepped into the water and settled across from her.

"Very nice," she said, meeting my eyes. "Whatever you're doing. Keep it up."

My carnal desire surged to new heights at the promising double entendre but before it could smother the last dregs of rational thought, I decided to confess my duplicitous intensions. "You've probably already guessed, that dinner wasn't the only reason I invited you here tonight."

Zed boosted herself up so that only the softly rounded bottoms of her exquisite breasts were below the waterline. "It wasn't much of a stretch," she said. "But other than the obvious, I haven't a clue what's on your mind."

My eyes followed a stream of water sliding like a skier down the curve of one breast, and I tried hard to ignore the tightening between my legs. "You know how you told me you're a medicine woman?"

"She nodded.

"Well I need something healed."

Zed raised an eyebrow, and her smile was indulgent "Everything about you looks to be in excellent shape. Where do you hurt?"

"Here," I said tapping my head with a forefinger. "I've been fighting a losing battle with depression ever since Andra died, and I really need to dump it."

"Why?"

I explained my decision to stalk my stalker, and how the effects of depression might compromise the effort.

"What you call depression," she said after listening patiently to my story, "is part of the healing process everyone goes through when they lose a loved one. I have no skill to take it from you, and wouldn't even if I could."

I shook my head. "Well then I'm screwed, because whoever's after me isn't fooling around."

Zed stared at me for a long minute, and then seemed to come to a decision. "Western culture teaches that death is an ending, but nothing in the universe can be completely destroyed. Matter changes form and consciousness evolves, but if you look without opinion, you'll discover what we call *death* is only an illusion."

"Well it's a damn good one," I said. "And illusion or not, it hurts."

"Without a doubt," Zed agreed. "But that hurt helps lock the memory of people in our hearts forever."

I stayed quiet as she continued.

"If you'll trust me, I may be able to help ease your feeling of loss. It won't take away the hurt, but it will allow you to do what you need to."

"That would be great," I said brightening at her offer. "What does it involve?"

"A ritual cleansing in a fresh body of water," she said. "It's fortunate we have a lake right outside your door."

"The lake?" I asked feeling chilled at the thought. "You want us to go in the lake? The water is freezing."

Zed gave a short nod as if to acknowledge my observation. "I'm sure you'll survive. Are you ready?"

Reluctantly I followed her from the hot tub, snagged two fleece robes from a nearby coat-tree, and offered her one.

"Sorry," she said, taking both robes from me and dropping them on the floor. "The ceremony has to be performed au naturel."

Outside, a full moon and cloudless sky capped the lake, and as Zed stepped knee deep into the dark water I checked out the beach for any late night strollers. Seeing no one, I moved to join her, but she held her arm straight out to me in a *stop* motion.

"Wait for my signal," she said, and after wading in up to her waist, raised her arms as if to embrace the bold shaft of moonlight shining down on her like a spotlight.

Maybe it was that second glass of wine or the cold air numbing my brain cells, but as I watched her sway in perfect synchronization with the rolling waves, her solid form seemed to take on a water-like transparency.

It was a bizarre scene and more than just a little scary. For a moment I considered running back to the house, tossing her clothes outside and locking the door. Instead I massaged my eyes. When I opened them again, a solid Zed beckoned me forward.

I hesitated for only a moment before I stepped into the water. It was, as I feared it would be, icy-cold and as I moved to stand face to face with the mysterious sorceress, everything below my waist went numb as a rock. Zed's smile was encouraging as she offered me her hands. The moment I grasped them, the cold disappeared, as did any doubts I harbored about participating in the cleansing ritual.

Silently guiding us into deeper water, Zed stopped when our shoulders were completely submerged. She took a deep breath, and after nodding at me to do the same, we slid beneath the lake's inky surface. What I experienced in the lake, under the spell of the awesome woman would be hard to explain. But when I somehow found myself standing on the shore several minutes (or was it hours) later, enfolded in her powerful embrace, the sharp pain of Andra's loss had been reduced to a dull ache.

Inside the house, we stepped into the hot tub, and as the welcome warmth surrounded me, I tried to make sense out of what had just happened. The details were already fuzzy around the edges, and the harder I attempted to recall them, the faster they seemed to slip away. Five minutes later my mind abandoned the effort, turning instead to something a bit more tangible, namely Zed's incredible curves sitting inches away from my fingers. I wanted this woman more than anything I had ever wanted in my entire life. Wanted to hold her, stroke her, make mad passionate love to her and never stop, but the timing seemed wrong. Given what we had just experienced, sex seemed like the last thing I should have on my mind.

Jumping out of the tub before I made a move I might regret, I snatched one of the robes off the floor and slipped it cape-like around my shoulders.

"I'm going to grab a quick shower," I said without looking at her. "If you want, you can use the guest bathroom. You'll find everything you need there."

Standing beneath the twin showerheads I wondered how I ever got to be so weird. Not half an hour ago Zed had offered me a glimpse of enlightenment. Now all I could think about was making love to her. A link had been forged between us in the lake that night, something that went much deeper than sex, but at the moment none of that mattered.

My back was to the shower door when I heard it click open and spinning around, I found Zed standing there.

"Hope you don't mind," she said slipping inside the spacious marble stall. "I didn't see any reason to run two showers. And it's quite obvious," she said reaching out a hand to encircle my erection, "that you've been thinking about me."

Chapter 11

▼

When I woke early the next morning, Zed was asleep beside me. On top of that good fortune (like it could get any better), my head felt clear for the first time in weeks. The thought of Andra's death still made me sad, but with Zed's help I had let go of the depression.

Slipping quietly from beneath the covers, I noticed Blue at the side of the bed. He was sitting high on his haunches, kangaroo-style, his graceful neck stretched to its full length, his pea-green eyes peering curiously at the sleeping Zed. The cat was interested in everything that happened in the house, including the women who shared my bed. And as I ran my cupped palm up and down the silky smooth fur on his neck, Blue responded with a raspy purr.

At the sound of a yawn, I looked behind me to see Zed had pushed back the covers and was in the throws of a full-body stretch. The sight was invigorating for a morning man like me, and a whole lot more energizing than a bowl full of Wheaties.

Propping herself up on an elbow, she raked a hand through her tousled hair and smiled seductively. "Morning encore, Maestro?" she asked as the point of her focus sprang to immediate attention. "How wonderful."

In the kitchen, over toast and coffee, I questioned Zed about what had happened in the lake. She seemed reluctant to speak about it, finally settling the matter by advising me to never question a gift from the universe. Twenty minutes later she was on her way home to shower and change clothes before going to work. And despite my best efforts to convince her to stay, including offering to write a letter to her boss excusing her for the day, she declined, saying Fox needed her.

Sporting a grin from ear to ear, I made myself a cappuccino and sat in the sunroom planning my next move, or attempting to anyway. For weeks I hadn't been able to think straight because I was sad and depressed. Now I was having trouble because I was as happy as a clam.

About nine thirty, I called the salon and Fox picked up.

"Hey, you," she said. "How was dinner last night?"

"Excellent. My culinary skills passed inspection. And Zed and I got to know each other a little better."

"I bet," Fox teased. "That little black dress she was almost wearing when she left here didn't leave much secret."

"Was she wearing a dress? I can't remember."

"Big surprise," Fox said. "I'd be willing to bet a week's pay you don't remember what you had for dinner."

"I could if I wanted to," I said. "But why fill my brain with unnecessary details."

Fox laughed.

"So, Ms. Queen-of-the-Office, how are things there?"

"Busy, as in your books are filled for the next month. Want to add another day?"

"Funny you should ask that, Fox, darling, sweetie, because I need you to do something for me."

"Uh oh," she said. "I don't think I'm going to like this."

"I know you're not. But I need you to take care of it anyway."

"Take care of what?"

"Clearing my appointments for the next couple of weeks," I said, and pushed ahead before she could pose any objections. "Offer to book people with whoever is available. And try to reschedule the rest."

I held my breath and waited for her unhappy response.

"Some of these people are going to be so pissed, Max. Are you sure?"

"Sorry, Fox. I know it'll be a hassle but I need the time off."

"Is something wrong?"

"No," I lied. "Everything's fine. I've got some personal business to take care of and I need to give it my full attention."

"What kind of business? Can I help?"

"The personal kind, Ms. Fox," I answered gently. "And no you can't, but thanks." Before she could raise another question I asked about her ex. "So what's up with Pete? Is he still causing problems?"

"If you'd call slashing all four of my tires a problem, he is."

I shook my head in disgust. "You're not staying alone at your apartment I hope."

"No, I'm bunking with a friend in Eastpointe. It's a long haul to work but I feel safer."

"What's the number there?" I asked, and scribbled it down as she recited it. "I want you to call mall security and remind them about your trouble with Pete. Give them a picture if you have one, and ask them to scope out the salon a little more often."

Fox grunted dismissively but I knew she would do it.

"So when is Daddy Warbucks starting this unscheduled vacation?"

"Today."

"And when can we expect you back?"

"It's hard to say."

"Is that what you'd like me to tell your unhappy clients when they ask to reschedule?"

I grimaced at the thought. "Just tell them I'll be back soon, and that I'll give them a break on the price for their inconvenience."

"How much?"

"I don't know. Make up a number."

"Don't tempt me, buster. And you best call every day."

"I will. I promise."

"I love you, Max."

"I love you too, Foxy."

By ten, I had finished my morning shower and shave, stretched my fuzzy muscles with a few yoga positions, and after slipping on jeans and a heavy black sweatshirt, jogged out to the roadside mailbox. I hadn't collected the mail for three days, and as I leafed through the thick stack, an envelope with the state seal caught my attention. Settling the stack back in the box, I tore the legal size envelope open and after reading the accompanying letter, wasn't sure if I should whoop for joy, or sit down and cry. I had been approved by the Michigan Gun Board to carry concealed. All I needed to do was report to the appropriate office, sign the papers and it would be legal for me to walk around with a deadly weapon. Damn scary, if you ask me.

Retrieving my gun from its place in the drawer, I popped the magazine and slipped the weapon into a small leather gym bag. After saying goodbye to Blue, I headed for Tactical Sports. Bobby advice was to carry my gun, and I was going to do exactly that. But I needed more practice, and something to carry it in. No way was I going to stick it in the front of my pants like tough guys on TV. Shit happens, you know?

After securing range time from one of the now familiar men in black, I inquired about Eden.

"Day off," was his friendly reply as he rang up two boxes of shells and a target. "But she's on the schedule tomorrow. Any message?"

I thought about that for a moment and decided it was best not to encourage the volatile woman. Riff was right on target about Eden. She could be as aggressive as a Black Widow in heat. My last encounter with her in the dark gun range was hair-raising to say the least.

"No," I finally said scooping the shells and rolled up target off the counter. "I'll catch her another time."

After practicing for almost an hour, I felt totally comfortable handling the weapon. Gone was the queasy stomach and fear of shooting myself. Taking its place was a growing confidence in my ability, plus a keen sense of pride at the accomplishment. The last thing surprised the hell out of me because I had always been an opponent of handguns. Thought they should be strictly regulated and carried only by cops and the military. But in light of my own experience, I was forced to rethink that position.

Before leaving the store, I purchased two lightweight, black nylon holsters for my gun. One fit snugly under my left arm; the other, was designed to be worn on a belt. At the clerk's suggestion, I also picked up a vial of pepper spray called Lil' Brut, made to be hooked to a key chain. The sign on the display said it could stop a two-hundred-and-fifty-pound man dead in his tracks.

"Potent stuff," I said handling the tiny can by two fingers. "Any chance of it going off in my pocket?"

"That would be a bitch," the salesman said, his voice chock full of amusement. "But the safety cage on top is supposed to prevent accidental firings. Just make sure that when you do press the trigger, it's pointed in the right direction."

I had forty-five minutes before the glass repair people were scheduled to meet me at home so I took my time on the interstate. Of course, taking your time on the I-96 means doing at least eighty, and that's in the right lane. You want excitement in your life? Forget about extreme sports. Just jump on that puppy during rush hour.

When the repairmen had done their work and departed I checked and rechecked the job. Blue watched me from inside the house, and for a brief second I thought about shipping him out of harm's way. I finally decided against it, knowing the cat would be too stressed away from home. Not to mention the fact that my cunning feline friend had already eyeballed the original intruder, and that he had hiding places throughout the house even I couldn't find.

The rest of that day was uneventful. I spent the evening watching a Gilligan's Island marathon on cable while I cleaned my gun and reloaded the clip. I had always been curious about how Marianne and Ginger made all those coconut-cream pies. What did they use for crust? How did they bake them? Useful information if I'm ever shipwrecked during a three-hour tour. After the sixth episode, Gilligan and the gang still hadn't been rescued so I went to bed secure in the knowledge of tomorrow's reruns.

About 4 a.m. I was rudely pulled from a dream by the sound of the telephone. Damn, I thought as I struggled to open my eyes. Nobody calls this early in the morning with good news. The answering machine was programmed to pick up after four rings. At the sound of the fifth, I realized I had forgotten to reset it. After the tenth ring I couldn't stand the suspense, so I dragged myself out of bed and hustled down the stairs making a mental note to have a phone jack installed in my bedroom ASAP.

When I reached the phone I snatched it up, irritated at the caller's persistence. "What?"

"Max? It's Riff."

"Aw shit," I moaned. "You're not going to tell me something creepy, are you?"

The line was ominously silent.

"Please tell me nobody I know is dead."

"No one's dead, but it isn't good news. Pete Deville kidnapped Fox last night. He beat her up, and sexually assaulted her."

My reaction to yet more bad news was raw and angry. "What the fuck is going on here? Has the whole goddamn world gone crazy?"

Riff didn't respond.

"Where the hell is she?" I demanded. "I want to see her."

"She's at Providence," Riff replied. "I spoke with her father a few minutes ago."

"I'm on my way," I said still furious. "You meet me there."

"Wait, Max. Her dad told me they'd be leaving for home soon. He said the doctor gave Fox a strong sedative, so don't call until tomorrow."

I wanted to scream out as rage bubbled up inside me. "Did you catch that fucker?"

"No," Riff replied quietly. "But we will."

"Yeah, right," I said giving way to sarcasm. "You haven't nailed him yet, Riff. What the hell makes you think you're going to get him now?"

"We're doing everything we can, Max."

I picked up a pillow off the couch and sent it sailing across the room like a Frisbee. "Shit!" I spat into the phone-line. "This whole thing is like some kind of freaky fucking nightmare."

Riff waited while I got a handle on my anger. When I finally did, I apologized for ragging at her but held on to my edge. I figured I'd need it for the next part of the conversation.

"As long as I've got you on the line, Riff, we need to discuss something."

I explained how Bobby Deegan, using police records and my account of what had happened; put together the theory about Andra's murderer being my stalker and how the personal information about me was probably coming from her journal.

There was a pause as Riff ran the information through her logic filters. "Could be a fit," she replied in a noncommittal manner. "You say this Bobby Deegan guy hacked into our computers? You'll have to tell me about him some time."

"One more thing," I said, positive she wasn't going to like what came next. "I've decided to go on the offensive. And I want you to know about it in case anything happens to me."

"The hell you are," Riff ordered. "If your friend is right, we're dealing with a bad ass killer here. Leave it to us."

"I *have* left it to the police," I said risking her anger. "So far they haven't done diddly. I figure I've got nothing to lose."

"Only your life, Bucko."

"That's already on the line," I shot back.

I could feel Riff's frustration, but I wasn't going to back down.

When she spoke again, it was in a barely controlled tone. "And just what the hell are you planning to do? Join up with your psychic buddy?"

"Maybe."

"Oh yeah. I can see it now. The blind leading the blind."

"That's not fair, Riff. I'll admit Kenny's a little out there but he's been right twice about the case. No, three times. He called the murder before you guys had a clue. He helped save Jessica's life. And his vision about someone looking through a book was probably the murderer reading Andra's journal."

Riff was quiet for a moment. "I don't care if he's the great fucking Carnac, Max. He's crazy. Do me a favor and stay out of it. You'll get yourself killed."

"That's what I'm trying to avoid, Riff."

I heard a phone ring in the background and Riff's name being called out.

"I gotta go," she said with finality. "Take my advice and use some of your goddamn money and go on a long vacation."

"It's not going to help, Riff," I said, but I was talking to dead air. She had already hung up.

Chapter 12

▼

I awoke again at six that morning, amazed I could have fallen back to sleep after the heated conversation with Riff. My best bet, if I wanted to avoid a lot of grief, was to stay out of her way for a while. I was getting enough of that from the little voice inside my head.

At six-thirty I considered calling Fox but opted to wait. The family would probably still be asleep and although anxious for news, I didn't want to disturb them. After my shower, I emptied the dishwasher, fed Blue and decided to go for a run. For the last two weeks I'd been trading my workout time for the gun range and I was feeling more than a little out of shape. Want another true confession? I really don't like to exercise. But when I remembered Zed's stark evaluation of my body the other night I decided to go for it.

My optimistic ego told me we were destined for a rematch and I didn't want to disappoint her. Not only that, but my mind kept flashing back to the men at Zed's club. Next to those buffed giants I looked like a ballpark weenie.

For my run I dressed in roomy jean cutoffs, a Halloween orange sweatshirt imprinted with a dancing skeleton, white socks and white high-top runners. I grabbed the pedometer I had recently purchased at Runners' World in the mall and clipped it to my belt. Sliding on my Oaklees, I did a few warm-up stretches, and with Queen's "Innuendo" playing on my Discman, I started off down the driveway.

An hour and a half later I staggered back through the door, my thighs screaming for mercy, the bottoms of my feet hot and steamy. The breath I had lost a mile down the road was caught somewhere in the back of my throat. And despite the chilly temperatures, sweat was running liberally down my back and between my butt cheeks. I grabbed a half-gallon of OJ from the refrigerator and drank half of it straight from the carton. The ice-cold juice helped revive me, and I pressed the cool container to my forehead inviting my muscles to relax. After some follow up stretches, I began to breathe easier. It had been a tough workout but now that I was pretty sure I wasn't going to die of a heart attack, I felt damn good about it.

Snapping the pedometer off my belt I glanced at the read-out expecting to see a double-digit reward for my Herculean effort. "What?" I screamed startling Blue who had crept silently into the room. The numbers stared back tauntingly. I had run a measly 4.3 miles. 4.3! It felt like at least ten.

On the way to my second shower, I sprinted up the stairs two at a time. Things went well, most of the way up, but I was tired, and when I misjudged the step near the top, I went down hard and cracked my right knee on the last riser.

"Shiiiit," I yelled sitting down hard on the landing and exploring the shocked joint for signs of damage. There wasn't much, unless you wanted to count the big ugly bruise that had already spread across the entire kneecap. That's why I love exercise, you know. It's so fucking *good* for you.

After my shower, I reexamined the knee. It hurt, but there was barely any swelling, and I could walk on it without limping. Sort of. Remembering an old Ace bandage that had been bouncing around my sock drawer for years, I wrapped the knee and made my way carefully down the stairs.

It was ten-fifteen when I phoned Fox at her parents' house. Her mom answered but without her usual cheeriness.

"Carly's still asleep, Max. But she'll be up soon. Why don't you come over for breakfast?"

Thirty minutes later I parked in front of the Fox house, a well kept sixties-style tri-level that looked pretty much like every other house on the wide boulevard. I always thought the architectural redundancy in that area of Southfield smacked of a "Stepford Wives" cult, and I fully expected to see women, dressed like June Cleaver, out gardening or sweeping the front porch.

John and Rita Fox met me at the door. Both looked stressed and slightly punch-drunk from worry.

"Come in, Max," said Rita after giving me a quick hug. "I told Carly you were on your way over."

"Is it all right?" I asked suddenly nervous about the visit. "I mean, maybe she needs more time."

"Yes, it's all right," Rita said and pulled me gently inside. "She wants to see you."

I shook hands with John Fox and he inclined his head toward the kitchen. "It's not pretty, Max," he whispered as tears filled his tired eyes. "That bastard hurt my daughter. If I find him, I'll kill him."

I nodded my understanding.

"Go on in," he said tightly. "She's waiting for you."

Fox sat alone at the kitchen table, wrapped in a voluminous black robe that made her slender form appear childlike and vulnerable. When she put a hand up to hide her face I lowered it gently and knelt on one knee beside her. I stared past the stormy bruises that circled her eyes, past the swollen, split lips and the angry red welts covering her neck, and smiled. Smiled because my friend was safe, and because I could still smile at her. But mostly because she returned the smile and despite her horrific experience, I knew she would be okay.

Kissing both of her cheeks, the taste of salty tears evoked both sympathy and anger in me. "Can't leave you alone for a minute, girl," I said and bit my bottom lip hard. "What the hell am I going to do with you?"

The four of us had breakfast in the dining room and after helping Rita with the dishes I felt a bit more relaxed. A stack of pancakes and six pieces of bacon proved to be a great stress reliever. Fat-wise though, it canceled out my run that morning.

When her parents left the room, I slipped an arm around Fox's shoulder and pulled her against me. "If you want to talk about it, babe, I'm ready to listen."

Fox nodded and stood up slowly. "I need to say it to someone other than the police. But let's go out on the porch. I don't want to put my parents through it again."

I followed her out to the sun porch where floor-to-ceiling windows offered a perfect view of the home's well-kept backyard garden. There was a rainbow of pansies still in bloom as well as several varieties of roses, all back-dropped by tufts of ornamental grasses that glowed golden in the late-morning sun.

Fox and I sat side by side on a padded wicker loveseat but before she began her story, fresh tears filled her eyes.

"Pete attacked me in the parking lot at Kroger," she said feigning bravery. "I had just opened my car door when he came out of nowhere and punched me hard in the face. I hit the ground with the groceries and went out like a light. When I woke, I was lying on a bed in a dingy motel room."

Fox paused in her story and stared out the window before continuing. "My hands were tied in front of me with a leather belt, and when I was awake enough to feel the pain I almost passed out again. I ached everywhere, especially my face, and there was blood all over the bed." Fox's expression turned panicky as she continued. "Pete was in the bathroom so I decided to get the hell out of there. My hands were on the door knob when he grabbed the back of my hair."

Fox went on to describe what happened. Believe me; you don't want to know the details. I didn't want to know the details. But I listened because she needed to talk.

"He was drunk on Tequila." Fox sounded angry now. "And he kept screaming that Andra got what she deserved. When he fired up a crack-pipe I knew I was going to die too. Liquor makes Pete mean, but crack makes him evil." Fox paused to swipe at her free-flowing tears. "After he raped me, he passed out. And even though I was afraid to get caught trying to escape again, I knew it was my only chance. Somehow I managed to untie myself, find my car keys and make it to the parking lot. I'm not exactly sure how."

At home later that day I stood on the beach and stared blindly out over the water. I could confess to murderous thoughts about Pete, but why ruin my nice guy image? Still I knew if I spotted him on the street, I might not be able to stop myself from running his ass over once or twice.

Hate is not a comfortable emotion for me. Whenever it shows up I usually drop it like a hot potato, but I was going to use that fire in my belly to sharpen my guard. Pete was going to help me pay attention.

For some reason my thoughts kept returning to Andra's missing journal and our last conversation together. She had been at my house the Saturday before her murder, and during dinner we managed to polish off two full bottles of Cabernet. Both of us were buzzed and when Andra started dissing Pete, I cheered her on. We slammed everything about our mutual enemy, and pumped up by the power of the grape, what we didn't know, we made up. As the evening ended, the two of us swore a drunken pact. We would convince Fox to dump Pete, no matter what it took.

Because we'd been drinking, Andra spent the night in my guest room. Climbing the stairs a bit unsteadily, she held tight to the wood handrail and in her free hand she clutched the ever-present journal. My young friend had a peculiar penchant for writing when she was high, and probably spent some time detailing her impressions of our last evening together before going to sleep.

As I thought about our conversation that night, I was struck by a troubling question. What if Pete had somehow gotten hold of Andra's missing journal, and blamed her for Fox dumping him? How far might the ass-wipe go to extract revenge? We knew for a fact he was capable of kidnapping, assault and rape.

Could murder be far behind? I went over the idea several times, piecing it together like a puzzle. The picture that emerged presented a plausible motive for murder, and perhaps the stalking of yours truly. If Pete had killed Andra, and I decided to work with the assumption that he did, wouldn't I be his next logical target?

I considered calling Riff and suggesting my idea, but her reaction was predictable. She'd dismiss the implication based on lack of evidence and invite me to keep my nose out of it. Unfortunately that wasn't an option any longer. Not if Pete actually was Andra's murderer.

Somehow, I was going to have to find Pete before he found me, but Sherlock Holmes I'm not. Instead of the famous detective's larger than normal brain, logical sense of deduction, and network of "Irregulars" I had half-baked suspicions, a prejudicial attitude against my lone suspect, and only one person who might be able to confirm my theory. You guessed it; wild-man Kenny Dougland. And after considering the pros and cons of his proposed partnership, I decided there was nothing to lose by joining forces with him.

Checking out my pocket watch I saw it was 3:54. If Kenny was working, he'd still be at the mall. Running down the phone number of "Litsa's" from Information I called and was connected with the restaurant's assistant manager.

"Kenny's not here today," she said in a friendly tone. "Any message?"

"No," I said. "Thanks anyway."

The phone number for the Dougland residence on Cradle Lake was unlisted, so I jumped in my truck and drove over there. It was a gamble, but I was in the mood. And even if Kenny wasn't visiting, someone might know where to find him.

I'd never been to the home on the far west side of the lake, but there was no mistaking the property when I saw it. A wooden sign carved in the shape of a casket hanging at the end of the drive announced it as the "Dougland Digs." Guess that's what you'd call, undertaker humor, and I'm sure you need all you can get in that type of work. I mean, who thinks of working with the dead as a career choice?

I turned right and proceeded slowly towards the house. The tunnel of trees above me was bare of leaves, and the sunlight streaming through twisted branches created a patchwork of mottled shadows on the black topped drive. I spotted a bed of flowers behind the two-story gray cedar manse and when a familiar pink cap popped up from behind a cloud of colorful pink roses, I parked my truck and walked over to greet the man beneath it.

Kenny wore the same outfit he usually sported at the mall, plus a quilted vest and a pair of well worn leather gloves. He stood there watching me approach, squat body bent back and belly jutting out like he was pregnant with twins.

"Maxie," he called out. "How do you like my garden?"

He doffed his gloves, and we shook hands as I took in the mass of blooms surrounding us. I wasn't a rose expert but I knew they could be high maintenance. My mom grew several varieties when I was a kid. And Marie Snow is a lady who knows how to care for a rose. Looked like Kenny did too.

"What can I say, man? It's awesome."

Kenny smiled at the compliment. "Thanks. You into roses?"

"Sure. Love them but I'm minus the green thumb it takes to keep them alive. What are these?" I asked pointing to some of the reddest roses I had ever seen.

"A French shrub rose called Sevillana. Cool, huh? She explodes with blooms like that from spring to winter. I've even seen her flower in the snow. Over there's another form," he said pointing to a huge bush enveloped in creamy white petals. "They call that one 'Pearl'."

I trailed behind as he gave me the fifty-cent tour. When we finally sat down on a bench beneath an overgrown arbor of tiny yellow roses, Kenny pushed back the cap on his head.

"You come here to ask me about Pete?"

I shook my head in amazement. "Kenny, you are such a bizarre dude."

He nodded in agreement.

"How did you know?"

Kenny shrugged his shoulders. "Been thinking about him myself so it was easy to pick up."

I decided to cut right to the meat. "Do you think Pete killed Andra?"

Kenny closed his eyes and rocked back and forth several times. "Not totally sure but, yes."

"Do you think he's the one stalking me?"

"Do you?"

"Yes," I finally said after adding Kenny's psychic hunch to my own amateur hypothesis. "But there's no proof. Maybe I should just suggest it to the cops."

Kenny shook his head. "They won't believe you."

He was right, of course. I was going to have to come up with some kind of concrete evidence. But as to how and where I was going to find it, I was clueless.

"Don't you mean how are *we* going to find it?" Kenny said fixing me with his signature goofy grin. "We're partners, remember?"

Chapter 13

▼

Insanity must be catchy. You know, kind of like a cold or the Herpes virus. The evidence of that theory, at least in my case, was two-fold. First, despite some misgivings, I was beginning to trust Kenny's psychic insights. And second, I had decided to throw caution to the wind and hunt for Pete.

Both choices were a stretch, and a more rational person might question my sanity. Especially since Kenny informed me that his psychic ability works best in what I call his wackier mode. Despite that little wrinkle, Kenny's dual personalities had joined my investigative team, and as if to be funny, my warped imagination conjured up a logo for our future business cards.

Crazy, Crazier and Craziest
Private Investigators

Back at home, I nuked myself a cup of the morning's coffee and took it up to the art studio. I had a few ideas about how we might find Pete, although none of them filled me with any great amount of confidence. Searching for inspiration, I powered up the Dell and scrolled through two weeks of unanswered email until I noticed that Bobby had sent me his phone number in California.

I dialed and waited through six rings; Bobby answered on the seventh. He was golfing of course, and when he had finished the hole, I briefly explained my theory about Pete being Andra's murderer.

"Bravo, Maxie. Glad to see your brain hasn't been entirely dissolved by hairspray. What's your next move?"

"To find Pete, but the cops are already looking in all the obvious places. Any suggestions?"

Bobby didn't miss a beat. "Ask the girlfriend where his buddies hang and stake the place out. You might get lucky."

"Good idea."

"And what is Mr. Cosmetologist going to do if and when he finds his man? Threaten to give him a bad haircut?"

When I admitted I didn't have the slightest idea, Bobby snorted. "You and Stephanie Plum would make a great team," he joked, referring to author Janet Evanovich's incompetent skip tracer. "Neither one of you knows what you're doing but it's a hoot watching you fumble along."

After disconnecting, I phoned Fox at her parents' home. "Hey, girl. How you feeling today?"

"Good enough to go back to work, but these black eyes might freak the clients."

"Don't be in so much of a hurry. Just rest and let your mom take care of you."

"I've got an idea," Fox grumbled. "How about if you rest and let *your* mom take care of you?"

My mind quickly ran down the chilling scenario. "Okay. Okay. I get the point. Go back whenever you want."

"Thanks, boss. And for you, I'll wear sunglasses and look mysterious instead of scary."

"Mysterious is good," I said. "And speaking of mystery, do you happen to know where Pete hangs out with his buddies?"

"Why do you want to know?"

"I don't," I lied. "Riff told me to ask you."

Fox was no fool, but the request wasn't out of line with what was going on. "There is a place in Detroit," she said. "A bar near the corner of Seven Mile and Livernois."

"What's it called?"

"I don't remember. I was only there once. But it's right near that ritzy Palmer Park neighborhood."

"There might be more than one bar in that area," I said prompting her. "Care to elaborate?"

"I remember a pink neon sign flashing the words 'Draft Beer' in the window. Would that help?"

"Probably. I'll give the information to Riff."

I thanked her, and after dodging a couple of questions about what I'd been doing, we hung up and I called Bobby back.

"Be nice if you had a stooge to work with," Bobby said after listening to my report. "Someone you could wire up and send in the bar to eavesdrop."

"I know the perfect man for the job," I said, thinking about Kenny. "But where am I going to get a wire?"

"A friend of mine can hook you up," Bobby said. "Name's Jack."

"Is he any good?"

Dead silence followed my question, like I had asked if water is wet. And after giving me a phone number, Bobby disconnected without another word.

Following a bathroom break, I dialed the number Bobby had given me. The call was picked up but all I heard was heavy mechanical breathing, ala Darth Vader.

"Hello?" I said, wondering if Bobby forgot to give me the secret password. "Can I speak to Jack?"

There was a long pause and then a voice clinked in my ear like copper-filled quarters. "Who's calling?"

"My name is Max," I said deciding Jack must have been using some sort of scrambler to disguise his voice. "Bobby D. gave me your number."

Silence filled my ear, followed by more clipped metallic syllables. "What can I do for you, Max?"

I gave him an idea of what I was looking for.

"Not a problem. Where should we meet?"

"How about the Rolling Pines Mall in about an hour?"

"Look for an unmarked gray step-van in the last row of the Sears parking lot."

Before leaving the house, I tapped Johnny Lott's stash for three grand. Jack's estimate was less, but you never know. Something from the 007 or Maxwell Smart collection could catch my eye.

Thirty minutes later, I parked my Lexus beside Jack's step-van. The passenger side door slid open as I approached, and a shadowy figure waved me in. Climbing the two metal stairs, I glanced around. The inside of the truck looked like Radio Shack on wheels.

The roving electronics' salesman was as nondescript as his truck. Jack was medium height, medium build, with medium brown hair. He wore khaki pants, a pair of scruffy, brown wingtips, and a sand-colored windbreaker zipped to the neck. Large, mirrored sunglasses hid a good part of his face.

Although not the snappiest dresser, Jack did seem to know his business, and after a few questions about my specific needs, he put together a neat package; two wireless microphones designed to look like St. Christopher medals, and two receiving units worn in the ear like a hearing aid. The fifth piece, a slick, ultra-sensitive listening-bug, was tucked inside a sealed pack of Kools. My impulse buy was an infrared night-scope.

After some brief instructions and a quick test of the equipment I was out the door with no receipt, no service contract, and Jack was on his way to meet his next cash customer.

I drove home, called Kenny, and made arrangements to pick him up about seven. By eight we had located the bar, a squat single-story structure that looked as though it had been stepped on in one corner. There was no name in evidence but there was a pink neon sign flashing in the window.

I parked half-a-block down the street, killed the engine, and looked around at what had once been a classy shopping district. Remnants of faded glory were evident even in the dim light although the neighborhood had fallen prey to poverty and crime.

Traffic in the area was light and because of the cool temperatures, street people were down to a minimum. Good thing too because my new Lexus SUV stuck out in that part of Detroit like the proverbial sore thumb.

"Now," I said as I fit Kenny with the earpiece and snapped the St. Christopher medal around his neck, "if anybody inside gives you a hard time, just act a little crazy. But don't overdo it. Keep the Kool pack in your shirt pocket and when you see people talking, casually turn in their direction. If you get in trouble, I'll come in."

Kenny nodded like he understood and his conversation seemed rational, but it was impossible to be a hundred percent sure which of his personalities I was talking with. Staring into the funny looking man's trusting face, I searched my soul, wondering if I actually had the guts to save him if he got into trouble. And what if he got hurt? Could I handle the guilt? Frankly I didn't know, but there was no way I could go into the bar myself. If the men inside really were friends of Pete, one of them might recognize me.

"And last but not least," I said emphasizing the words. "Try not to piss anybody off."

Kenny exited the truck and as he ambled down the street I could hear him mumbling. No…correction…rapping. The man was improvising a rap as he headed toward the bar.

> "Okay, Kenny's gunna follow Maxie's plan.
> Needs me to front a little crazy, yes I'm the man.
> Listen for some talk about Pete, he say
> And when you pick it up

Point the Kools that way.
Try not to be noticed and not to be heard.
Don't ya dis nobody, or say the wrong bleeping word.
And big time important if ya wanna get out alive
Don't piss nobody off, don't start no jive."

I laughed out loud as he repeated the verse, and felt the tightness in my chest subside to a more manageable level. Picking up the little night-scope, I watched Kenny pause in front of the bar, look my way, and raise his arm in a wave.

"Kenny," I hissed. "Don't do that."

"Oh yeah," he said lowering his arm and glancing around. "Sorry, Max. Going in."

"Riiight."

When Kenny walked inside, my ear-jack picked up a mixture of voices, laughter, and the click of pool balls.

"Man, is it dark in here," Kenny whispered and a moment later a loud crash made me grip the steering wheel. Obviously my mole was no longer underground.

Suddenly another voice spoke; its tone low and confrontational. "You got a problem there, Slick?"

"Nope. No problem. I just tripped over a chair."

Great, I thought. The man has the stealth of a cow, and while picturing every set of eyes in the place giving him the once-over, the low-pitched voice spoke again.

"Yeah, well follow the yellow brick road over to the bar here before you hurt yourself."

I heard Kenny huffing and puffing as he lifted himself from the floor and settled at the bar.

"Whaddaya gonna have?"

"Ummm," Kenny said obviously thinking it over. "A large Diet Pepsi."

There was an uncomfortable pause.

"This is a bar, monkey boy. Not MacDonald's. We serve beer, wine or liquor."

"Okay," Kenny said. "I'll have a beer."

I could picture him sitting there, elbows on the bar, goofy grin, half-hooded eyes. Perfect. People usually underestimate the mentally challenged. I hoped that held true in this crowd.

Kenny sat at the bar for a good half-hour. I could hear him drinking the beer and munching on something crunchy. Our target wasn't there or he would have said so by now, and although the Kool pack mike picked up various conversations, I caught nothing about Pete. Next came the sound of footsteps, water hitting water, then a toilet flushing. Obviously my spy was in the bathroom taking a leak.

"Max? Hey, Max. This is Kenny speaking."

"No shit," I said. "This isn't a freaking party line, you know. Can anybody see or hear you?"

"Nope. I'm alone in the john. I had to pee really bad. That guy at the bar made me drink two beers already. I don't think I can take another one. I feel funny. Kinda floaty. I never drank beer before."

I rolled my eyes up as far as they could go and leaned back against the seat.

"But don't worry," Kenny said with alcohol-laced bravado. "I won't quit. In fact I was thinking of getting this party rolling a little."

"Negative, Kenny," I said as a pang of anxiety tweaked my gut. "Stick with the original plan."

"But Max..."

A loud bang assaulted my ear like a door slamming against the bathroom wall, and a moment later two new characters joined the audio drama.

"Yo, Casper," said a smart-ass voice. "Check out the mug on this ugly motherfucker."

"Not without my shades on," a second man said. His tone was deep and clotted. "Face like that turn folks to stone you look at it directly."

"Very funny," Kenny said and a stab of laughter met his comment.

"Who you talkin' to, dawg?" asked smart-ass. "Nobody in here 'cept you and the roaches."

"I wasn't talking to anybody," Kenny answered without a trace of alarm. "And what's it to you, anyway?"

"Kenny," I hissed into the mike. "Don't mess with these guys." But it was already too late.

"You brave for such an ugly-fuck," the first man said and laughed again. "Ain't he brave, Casper?"

"Brave or stupid," answered Casper. "But he got good taste in smokes. How about you lay a couple of Kools on us, ugly man?"

The moment of silence stopped the breath in my throat. And when Kenny finally did answer it was absolutely the last thing I wanted him to say.

"I don't smoke."

"Say what?"

"I said I don't smoke."

"Then why you got a pack of coffin nails in your pocket?"

There was another short pause and I pictured Kenny staring at the man with a clueless expression.

"Coffin nails?"

"Yeah, you know, fags, smokes, Cancer sticks. The things in your shirt pocket."

"Oh," Kenny said before I could prompt a response for him, "you mean cigarettes. I couldn't give you any of these. I'm holding them for a friend."

"You're going to be holding your fuckin' teeth if you don't, man, and I'm sure your friend wouldn't want that to happen."

From the sounds coming through my earphone, I assumed Kenny was lifting the cigarette pack from his pocket. My next thought as I heard him snap the seal was, "Please, God, let Jack be as good as Bobby thinks he is". Next came the tearing of the inner foil. If there were no cigarettes inside, my wacky friend was in deep shit.

"Here," Kenny said prompting me to breathe again. "Take three apiece. I don't want no trouble."

I was about to tell Kenny to get his buns the hell out of there when he spoke to the men again.

"Hey, do you guys know Pete Deville?"

"Kenny! No!" I screamed as my hand shot to the ignition key, but before I could start the truck, the passenger door clicked open.

"You okay in here, honey?" a high-pitched voice asked, and a moment later a petite woman with a set of boobs that would make Dolly Parton look flat, swung the door wide.

I stared in disbelief. The woman was Betty Boop come to life; complete with arched, pencil-thin eyebrows, a pair of bright red, kewpie-doll lips, and a head so full of untamed black curls, Medusa would be jealous as hell. A fuzzy purple sweater stretched heroically around her enormous chest, and a black latex micro-mini, tight enough to outline every detail it was supposed to hide, hugged her curvaceous hips.

"Hey there, handsome," said the woman as she popped the lock on the rear passenger door and climbed in, casual as you please. "If you're lookin' for love, I'm lookin' for you."

It took a moment to register her offer but when I did, I shook my head. "No thanks."

In response the hooker gripped the hem of her sweater and peeled it upward until one perfectly sculpted breast was completely exposed. "You sure about that?" she said slowly uncovering its twin. "I'm having a two-for-one sale tonight."

In my ear I heard the men in the bathroom confront Kenny again, and despite the distraction behind me, turned to stare at the bar.

"You lie, motherfucker. Pete don't hang with whacked-out shits like you."

Maybe Kenny's response was the result of the two beers he downed. Whatever the reason, he seemed to be keeping it together.

"Is that so," he said loudly. "Then how'd I know he played pool here?"

There was silence for a beat and I imagined the two men staring the question at each other. "If you know my home-boy, Pete," smart ass said, "then you must know Stumpy."

"Stumpy?" Kenny said his voice a tad less confident. "Oh yeah. Pete and me party with him sometimes. Great guy."

"Then this is your lucky day," the voice growled in mock delight. "Because Stumpy's shootin' pool right outside the door here. I'm sure he'd be glad to see an old friend."

My sense of doom doubled as I turned to look at the hooker behind me. In anticipation of turning the trick, she had stripped to her birthday suit and was lounging against the back seat, legs tucked neatly beneath her.

"If you don't stop staring at me like that, sir," she said palming her wide nipples in feigned modesty. "I'll be forced to call a policeman."

"Here," I said offering her my cell phone. "Call and go. I'm kinda busy right now."

The hooker rocked forward between the seats and positioned one of her breasts barely an inch from my face. Her eyes took in my gun lying on the passenger seat, and the St. Christopher medal I was holding near my mouth.

"I can see that," she said. "Like, are you a private dick or do you always talk to your jewelry?"

I hushed her when a new voice sounded in my ear.

"Yo, Casper," it said; the inflection measured and filled with menace. "Showing off your new lover? He's way too pretty for you, man."

There was an explosion of laughter from the men inside the bar.

"Claims he's a friend of Pete," Casper replied. "Say's he knows you too."

That was it. I was going to have to bail Kenny out. I only wished God or the devil would clue me in as to how. Cranking the engine, I looked back at the naked woman. She wasn't going anywhere in her present state of undress, so I would have to take her with me. By the time I screeched to a halt in front of the bar, my desperate mind had formed the beginning of a plan.

"Look, uh…"

"The name's Bette with an 'e'," she said in her squeaky cartoon voice. "Exactly like the Divine Miss M."

"Okay, Bette with an 'e,' how would you like to score an easy hundred?"

"Sure," she said and ran a blood-red fingernail down the inside of her left breast. "Who do I have to kill?"

"All you have to do is walk inside this bar, like that," I said waving my hand at her naked body.

Bette leaned over to glance at the bar through the window. "No sweat," she said smiling. "I've been naked in there plenty of times."

Bette opened the door, stepped out, and bent forward to adjust the ankle straps on her towering pumps. At that precise moment, an ancient church van driving by rocked visibly sideways as an entire Boy Scout troop rushed to catch a glimpse of Bette's up-turned fanny. She straightened at the boys' calls, waved back, and to their extreme delight, shook her incredible chest in a memorable farewell.

Stepping out, I spoke into the mike, hoping Kenny was unhurt and could still hear me. "I'm coming in, man," I said with more confidence than I felt. "Break for the door when you see your chance."

Gun in hand, Bette and I approached the entrance, and despite the terror clutching my insides, I pushed open the door, and signaled her to enter.

Straightening her shoulders like she was about to go on stage in the Miss America pageant, Bette strutted inside. She was bare ass naked, totally defenseless and obviously enjoying the hell out of the whole experience. I was fully clothed, armed with a .40 caliber semiautomatic, and hoping big time that I wouldn't leave skid marks in my pants. Scooting in behind her, I let the door swing closed and tucked myself into the shadows. Bette moved forward a few feet and stepped into a pool of light from an overhead spot. With legs spread wide and spiked heels firmly planted, the petite hooker placed fists on hips and threw out her chest.

"Hey boys," she squealed. "How they hangin' tonight?"

All sound ceased as the small crowd took in Bette's stellar performance. There was a chorus of wolf whistles and several men called out her name. That exchange was followed by shouts of anger as Kenny suddenly broke free of the men surrounding him and ran towards us. When two guys brandishing pool cues took off in pursuit, I gulped, stepped out of the shadows, and pointed the barrel of my gun directly at them. Thankfully the angry duo skidded to a stop several feet away.

Thank you. Thank you. Thank you.

One of the men, a huge dude about the size of a refrigerator, raised his cue. I aimed the gun directly at big boy's forehead and quickly thumbed back the hammer. In the silent bar, the ratcheting steel made a sound that could freeze the abominable snowman's gonads.

Would I shoot if those bad-boys tried to rush me? Bet on it. Maybe not to kill but what they didn't know couldn't hurt me.

"Good man," I said keeping up the macho act. And stepping forward I pulled Bette back toward the door. From the corner of my eye, I saw the bartender pick up a phone. "No need to call anybody," I said keeping my gun trained on the bully-boys. "We're leaving. Kenny, Bette, go out to the truck."

I backed out behind them and jumped into the driver's seat. As I fired up the engine, the bar door opened and two faces looked out. I didn't want anybody catching my plate number so I popped the Lexus in reverse and squealed down the block to the nearest cross-street. Breaking hard, I whipped the wheel to the right and blasted out of there.

I drove blindly for several minutes, speeding down side streets, until I felt we were safe. Pulling to the curb, I breathed in jerkily, and pressed the side of my face against the cool window glass.

The sound of someone humming breached my sense of safety and I shot a glance at Kenny in the passenger seat. He was stiff-backed, bug-eyed, and staring straight out the windshield.

"Kenny?" I said wondering if the night's adventure had wigged him out entirely. "You all right, man?"

Kenny didn't move a muscle, but when the humming turned into Bette's rendition of the Britney Spears hit "Oops I Did It Again" I realized what the trouble was. My weird friend was shook because there was a naked woman in the truck, but I guess I couldn't blame him. There wasn't one in there when he left to go into the bar.

It took some convincing and another hundred-dollar bill to get Bette to put her clothes back on. Kenny never turned around, but from the strained look in his eyes I'm sure he wanted to.

I offered to drive Bette home and she directed me to a narrow, three-story apartment building about a mile away. The neighborhood looked somewhat safer than that surrounding the bar on Seven Mile, but immediately after she exited through the driver side door, I hit the automatic locks.

"Sure you don't want to come in?" she asked pressing her breasts against the half-open window. "I could do both of you."

I grimaced internally, as my brain conjured up an image of the too bizarre menage-a-trois.

"Thanks," I said slipping the truck into drive. "Maybe some other time."

Chapter 14

When we pulled away from the curb, Kenny broke his silence and then some.

"Wow! Wow! Wow!" he said craning his neck to get a last look at Bette. "Who was that? Oh, my God. Do you know her, Max? She was naked."

Incredible, I thought. And proof positive, that for the male at least, sex is stronger than violence. A little while ago, the man was a breath away from getting his butt beat or worse. Now all he could think about was the naked woman.

When I stopped for a red light and looked over at him, he was still staring out the back window.

"Man, oh man, oh man." he whooped and bent forward in his seat.

For a moment I thought he might throw up, and then he started laughing hysterically. To break the spell I gave him a firm poke on the shoulder. I didn't want him getting too excited in my truck and doing something weird, if you know what I mean.

The light changed. I turned west on Seven Mile and caught the entrance for the I-75 about a quarter mile up the road. Traffic was light and Kenny was quiet as I slipped into the left lane and bumped up my speed.

"Hey man," I said glancing over and offering him my hand. "First, I want to thank you for helping me out tonight. You were very brave going into that bar."

Kenny shook my hand.

"Second," I said turning to look him square in the eyes. "What the hell is the matter with you? You got us into some serious shit. We were supposed to be working undercover. Remember? Nobody told you to mention Pete's name."

Kenny shrugged his shoulders and flashed a big, dopey grin. "Sorry. I guess I forgot. But it did get things moving."

"You're right about that," I agreed nodding my head. "Things were moving so fast I almost had a heart attack."

"What do you mean, Maxie? You were great. Just like Joe Friday on Dragnet."

I did a silent scream and gripped the wheel. If the night's adventure was an example of our working relationship, my guardian angel better beef up security. On the plus side, the experience wasn't a total loss. We had met the boys most likely to help Pete evade the law, especially the walking refrigerator. And having met the big man once, I never wanted to get within arm's length of him again.

After dropping Kenny at his parents' house, I made my way slowly around the lake toward home. The experience in the bar had unearthed several uncomfortable emotions I had buried long ago, and I wasn't too sure about digging them up. The thing is I don't fit the role of tough guy. My one and only fight had been in the sixth grade. I started it thinking the kid was an easy mark but I was wrong. The fight was over before I had a chance to throw a single punch. Since then, violence and I had been virtual strangers. And when I saved Kenny in that bar, it was the bravest thing I had ever done.

My body felt electrified by the fusion of adrenaline and testosterone in my bloodstream. If I was going to sleep, I had to find some way to release my pent-up energy. Turning into my driveway, I contemplated a night run and a soak in the hot tub. But when I noticed the motion detector lights shining behind my house I had to scrap that plan.

I should have stopped and called the police, but being fully charged with A and T, a potent brain cocktail that can push almost any man into asinine behavior, I didn't think of it. Punching the gas, I shot up the drive and skidded to a stop beside a black Jeep Cherokee. When I spotted Zed leaning casually against the front fender (is the woman cool, or what?), I heaved a sigh and my body relaxed. Sort of.

I remember waking up about eight the next morning, just in time to watch Zed snug a pair of black leather pants around her shapely butt. The sight was poetry in motion. And when she noticed that my eyes were open, she placed a hand on each hip, turned and modeled the day's outfit.

Attempting to hold her breasts in check was a corset-style bustier I'd gladly change places with, and over that, a form fitting bolero jacket, cinched tightly at the waist. With a knowing smile, Zed took in my lusty expression and the tent erecting itself beneath the sheet. Turning, she reached for a pair of sleek leather gloves atop the nightstand, and when she faced me again, her eyes were hooded.

One finger after another was guided into the satiny leather and as she moved in my direction, I felt that ole black magic put me in its spell.

When I awoke for the second time that morning, Zed had gone and the clock beside me read nine thirty. Jumping out of bed, I did my regular morning routine, slipping in twenty minutes of meditation to juice up the soul. It proved impossible to quiet my mind so instead I focused on that night's plan of action. I'd revisit the bar on Seven Mile, follow "refrigerator" man home, and watch for any sign that Pete might be hiding out. Before I could do that, I'd have to score a surveillance vehicle the boys in the bar wouldn't recognize. But, did I want something badass? The kind of thing people would think twice about messing with? Or sad ass—so pitiful looking it wouldn't be worth the effort.

Once again I made a withdrawal from Lott's stash, counting out one hundred of the bills, and stuffing the fat wad into my pocket. I drove to a used car lot in Detroit, near the corner of Six Mile and Evergreen. Not the kind of neighborhood I would normally do my car shopping but I figured they'd be more likely to have what I needed. With doors locked and my gun holstered beneath my left arm, I circled the dealership twice. On my third pass, I spotted the perfect thing.

Less than an hour later I was the owner of a ten-year-old black Ford Econoline. It had dark tinted windows, gang symbols painted on the driver's side and a spray of eleven bullet holes across the passenger door. The truck obviously had history. And despite appearances, kind of halfway between badass and sad ass, everything seemed to be in working order.

"The price out the door," said smiling Al of Smiling Al's Used Cars and Trucks. "Ten-thousand-five-hundred."

I smiled. Smiling Al smiled, and when he saw the roll of hundred dollar bills appear from my pocket, his smile grew broader.

"Do I hear ninety-five hundred?" I ventured fanning out the cash. I knew anything over ten thousand had to be reported to the Feds. "Half now, half on delivery."

With a vigorous nod of his shiny brown head, Al agreed to deal. He even threw in the cost of plate and title changes, assuring me the final paperwork would be ready by five.

Before heading home, I zipped to Tactical Sports to purchase a larger can of pepper spray. The Lil' Brute on the key chain was convenient, but having it dangle between my legs while I drove made me nervous.

Inside the store, I bought the baddest looking can of pepper spray they had; an eight-inch long, two-inch wide, rock-hard can of burnished stainless steel. Waving off the offer of a bag, I slipped the can into a front pocket of my jeans, and turning to leave, collided with Eden.

"Is that a can of pepper spray in your pocket, darling," she said eyeing the bulge in my jeans before giving me an amorous hug. "Or are you just happy to see me?"

Back at home I spent the rest of that afternoon in pursuit of hedonistic pleasures. I brewed myself a double shot of hazelnut espresso, soaked in the hot tub until my brain began to melt, and then chilled in the pool.

After showering, I did a half-hour of yoga. My version of the ancient positions anyway, the slight modifications being forced upon me by a touch of arthritis in my wrists and knees. And as I held the "downward dog" position (grrr, ruff, ruff) I visualized my plan for that night going off without a hitch. I only hoped real life matched my fantasies.

A taxi delivered me to Smiling Al's a little before five. Twenty minutes later, I was headed for the bar. It was early but since I had no idea when or even if the big guy would show, it was the only thing I could think to do. Never having planned a stakeout before, I brought along my take on essentials: the gun (God, I hope I wouldn't need that), my new can of pepper spray (ditto), the night scope, a king-sized Three Musketeers, a package of miniature Reese's Peanut Butter Cups, and a Snickers. To keep me awake and hydrated, there was coffee and iced cran-raspberry juice.

It was a little after six when I pulled into the same spot I had parked the previous night; kitty-corner from the bar and a perfect location for watching the door. There was still enough daylight left to check out the neighborhood. What I saw was pretty skanky. Most of the stores on the street were boarded up. The few still in business were gated and had signs announcing police-link security systems.

By eight, I was bored but jumpy from the caffeine and chocolate. On top of that, I had to pee. By nine I was desperate to pee and wondering if I was brave enough to take a leak between the buildings when the passenger door of my van jerked open. In a quick movement, I snatched the gun from the seat beside me and pointed it at the intruder.

"Oh excuse me," said a squeaky voice. "I thought this was my van."

Care to a guess who? I'll give you a hint, It's a woman. Well, if you count her chest measurements, a woman and-a-half. That night she was dressed in a leopard print leotard, matching four-inch pumps, and a sheepskin coat that barely skimmed the tops of her fishnet encased thighs. Give up? How about one more clue? She ends her first name with an "e".

Bette squinted into the van's dark interior and squealed with delight. "Max? Oh my God. This is so cool."

Ignoring the gun pointed at her, she climbed into the passenger seat and closed the door.

"Damn," the lady said popping off her shoes and massaging first one foot and then the other. "If I ever quit being a hooker it'll be because it's so freakin' hard on the feet."

I set the gun in my lap and looked at her questioningly. "Bette, how the hell do you do that?"

"Do what?" she asked cocking her head my way.

"Open locked doors."

"Oh that," she said dismissively. "My step-dad was a master locksmith and ran a home security business out of our basement. I was always hanging down there so he taught me all about locks and security systems. Want me to teach you?"

"No thanks."

Bette pointed at the night-scope in my hand. "Am I interrupting again?"

I rolled my eyes. "Would it matter?"

Propping her feet on the dash, she looked at me with an amused expression. "You can dump the tough guy bullshit, Max 'cause I'm not buying it. Unlike those butt-heads in the bar, I saw how shook you were last night."

I returned the spunky little woman's smile and relaxed against my seat.

"See?" she said opening her shoulder bag and rummaging around inside. "I knew you liked me. But then, how could you resist?"

"You make it hard," I agreed. "No doubt about it."

Bette stopped her search of the voluminous purse and shot me a mischievous glance. "Why, honey," she said kissing an index finger and pressing it against the front of my pants, "making it hard is part of my job description."

I gulped and looked down to see if my pants were on fire.

"Go ahead and do whatever you were doing," she said smiling in satisfaction. "I'm going to take a break. Is that coffee I smell?"

"Drank it. But I still have cran-raspberry juice."

Bette grimaced as if I'd offered her pond scum. "You don't really drink that shit?"

"I happen to like it," I said defensively.

"Yeah, right," she chuckled and dug deeper in her bag.

I was about to enumerate the health benefits of my favorite juice combo when I noticed three men standing in front of the bar. As I watched them through the night-scope, I heard the click of a lighter beside me and a few seconds later, thick, sweet smoke wafted my way. Reflexively I checked my mirrors for cops. That wasn't Virginia Slims she was smoking, and the powers that be take a very dim view of mixing guns and pot. Turning in my seat I stared at her, eyebrows raised. She grinned impudently and blew a stream of blue smoke towards the roof of the van.

"Hope this is cool," she said, offering me the joint. "I was dying for a couple of hits."

I shook my head. "No thanks. I kind of have to stay focused."

Still looking at me, she took a long drag and held the smoke tight in her lungs. "So, what are we doing tonight?"

Those six simple words made my ass tighten. I needed another kooky partner like a hole in the head. Still, I was desperate to pee and maybe she'd be willing to watch for the big guy while I slipped off to relieve my bladder.

Reluctantly I explained my reason for being there. "I'm trying to get a line on one of the boys from the bar."

"Yeah?" she said and took another hit off the joint. "Which one?"

"Big guy. No neck. Could double as a refrigerator."

"What do you want him for?" she asked taking a long last drag before tamping out the roach in the ashtray.

"I don't want him. I'm searching for a friend of his. Guy named Pete Deville. Ever heard the name?"

Bette shook her head from side to side as she released the smoke. It must have been really good dope because I was definitely beginning to catch a secondhand buzz.

"The big guy," Bette explained as I rolled my window down, "is known around the neighborhood as Stumpy. He scored the nickname after a hooker friend of mine sliced off his swizzle stick during one of those 'tie-me-up-and-treat-me-bad' domination things. People said you could hear him screaming for blocks. Cops found him with his dick duct-taped to his forehead."

I held up a hand feeling my own intact equipment shrink between my legs. That's not the kind of story men like to hear. It makes us realize how vulnerable the so-called stronger sex really is. Swallowing hard, I promised myself never to let anyone tie me up again.

"So," I said, steering her away from the gory subject, "do you happen to know where this Stumpy guy lives?"

"Sure, at the Ambassador Arms. I was over there a few times before he lost his wanger. You wanna check it out?"

I considered her offer, remembering the size of the man in question and the malicious glint in his cold dark eyes. But Bette was offering me exactly what I had been hoping to find; the next logical step in my search for Pete.

Breathing out a sigh I nodded my head. "But I want to be sure Stumpy's in the bar while were doing it."

"No problemo," Bette answered as she slid into her shoes, and before I could stop her she was out the door and making her way briskly across the street towards the bar.

"Bette!" I yelled through the windshield, "get your ass back here," but the exasperating little shit never even turned around.

After five minutes of indecisive hell, the bar door opened again and Bette stepped out into the night. Strutting her stuff, she gave me a little finger wave as she swivel-hipped her way back to the truck.

I kept an eye on the bar door and as Bette neared the van, popped the passenger door lock. When she settled into the seat, I glared at her. "Why the hell did you do that? Don't you think somebody in the bar might be pissed off about you helping me last night?"

Bette looked confused for a heartbeat. Then her eyes widened in delight. "Aw, Maxie," she said leaning over to plant a wet kiss on my cheek. "That is so sweet. You were worried about me."

"I was worried I'd have to come in and save your butt," I said attempting to keep up the irate father act.

Bette dismissed the threat to her safety with a wave of her hand. "I used the dumb bimbo ploy. Works almost every time. When it doesn't, I rely on my little MK40." She reached into her purse and extracted a palm-sized semiautomatic. "A girl can never be too careful."

I let out a relieved sigh and slouched back against my seat.

"Stumpy's in there all right," she said. "Drunk as a skunk and whippin' everybody's ass at pool. If we're going to his place, now's the time."

I stopped at a nearby MacDonald's to pee and was feeling a little less tense when we parked in front of Stumpy's apartment building, a four-story wood and stucco edifice that looked older than dirt. Arched windows and wrought iron rimmed balconies hinted at its past heyday. But the best thing it could be called now was seedy.

In a flash, Bette was out of the truck and on the covered porch, smiling broadly like she was there to visit her Aunt Fanny. When she gestured for me to come up, I shook my head and waved her back. I had only wanted to scope things out. No way was I ready to act, even if Pete happened to be there.

Bette cocked her head and feigned confusion.

"Yeah right, you little…I recognize the dumb bimbo ploy when I see it."

With arms folded across my chest, I steeled my resolve not to be dragged into anything prematurely. Bette's response was to sit down on the concrete stoop and light up a cigarette.

"Get your ass up on that porch," ordered the pushy little voice in my head. "You look like a fucking wimp sitting here."

"Better a wimp than dead."

"Not by much, sissy-boy, and besides Bette already told you Stumpy ain't here."

"What about Pete?"

"What about him?"

"He might be there. And he might blow your comfortable little home in my head to smithereens with a shotgun."

"I'm not afraid."

"Well I am!"

"But you got to go, man," the voice argued. "Think how we're going to look in front of Bette."

"Fine," I mumbled as I slid the pepper spray into a jacket pocket and holstered my gun. "You want to follow this hooker nutcase, fine with me. I only hope we'll both be happy with your advice in the end. And I mean alive happy, damn it. Not dead happy."

Before leaving the van I noticed Bette's purse on the floor. Snatching it up, I searched for the little gun and was relieved to find it tucked inside. The woman was totally unpredictable and somehow I felt safer knowing she was unarmed. At least I hoped she was. There was no telling what she might be hiding inside that bottomless cleavage of hers.

When I finally joined Bette on the porch she grinned at me and flicked her half-smoked cigarette out on the shabby lawn.

"Took you long enough," she said. "Why the hold up?"

"I was trying to decide whether to crap my pants now, or wait until you get me killed," I answered while glancing around to make sure we were alone. "Want to tell me what we're doing up here?"

"You said you wanted to check out Stumpy's apartment."

"I said I wanted to know where it was," I protested, "not go inside."

"You ain't going to learn jack-shit out here," Bette said. "His apartment's on the third floor and unless you can sprout wings, there's only one way to check it out."

I would have argued if I thought it would do any good. But one look at Bette's determined face told me to save my breath. "So what are you going to do?" I asked jerking hard on the tightly secured glass and steel-mesh door. "Pick the lock?"

"Can't," Bette answered. "The damn thing's on the inside. We're going to have to get someone to buzz us in."

"How do the people that live here get in?"

"Buzz a neighbor?"

"That would be a big hassle," I said.

"Yeah. But it would also be an unbeatable security system."

I nodded and checked out the six mailboxes flanking the front door. Each had a bell for the apartment it served and intercom button. Below that the tenant's last name was printed neatly in black marker.

"What's his apartment number?"

"3-B."

The tag for 3-B read "Dumpert". I raised my brows. "Stumpy Dumpert? Now there's a mouthful."

"Used to be," Bette giggled. "But not anymore."

I stared at her and tried not to react but her cutting comment (no pun intended) cracked me up and I doubled over laughing. Maybe I had caught a buzz from the pot she'd been smoking. I don't know. But every time I tried to control myself she'd let loose with another set of giggles and I'd start laughing all over again. The distinct possibility that Stumpy might come strolling up the walk finally sobered me up; that plus the fact that another couple was climbing the stairs and eyeballing us like we might be escapees from the loony bin.

As they stepped up on to the porch, I composed myself as best I could and flashed what I hoped was a disarming smile. "Good evening, folks."

The couple nodded coolly as the guy pushed the bell to a second-floor apartment. A woman's voice on the intercom asked who it was, and when the man said his name, the buzzer sounded, the door clicked open, and they walked quickly inside. Before it could close, Bette used her toe as a doorstop.

"We'll have to hoof it up three flights," she said, as a devilish spark lit her eyes. "There's no elevator in this dump."

By the time I reached the top of the sixth riser, my sore knee was giving me hell, and as I stepped on to the landing Bette was standing in front of Apartment

3-B, hand poised to knock on the door. I opened my mouth to protest but it was too late.

Knock, knock, knock.

My body froze in mid-stride while my brain played twenty questions. What if somebody actually came to the door? What if it was Pete and he rushed out with a gun in his hand? Would I be willing to use mine? And finally, why the hell was I following the lead of this crazy woman?

I turned and started back down the stairs, but stopped when Bette called to me. Glancing over my shoulder I felt a shiver of apprehension streak like lightning up my spine. The ballsy little babe had one hand on the handle of Stumpy's open apartment door and the other was waving at me like she was on a float in the Thanksgiving Day parade.

"Come on, Maxie," she whined reaching inside to flick on the lights. "Nobody's home."

Chapter 15

By the time I got to the door, Bette was already inside. "Damn the little vixen," I thought. How could she be so nonchalant about breaking into someone's apartment? It was taking everything I had just to resist the marching orders my feet were giving me. Unfortunately, running away at that point was not an option. I would have to abandon the spandex tornado, and the guilt I'd suffer for leaving her in danger wouldn't be worth it.

Through the open door I could see a spacious living room with stucco walls that looked like they hadn't felt the touch of a paintbrush in twenty years. Judging from the stale smell, the sickly yellow color had more to do with cigarette smoke, dust, and neglect than the ancient paint's original tint. Area rugs scattered about were old and threadbare, and the hardwood floors looked like somebody had been ice-skating on them. To the right sat several mismatched pieces of furniture; a DVD player balanced on a chrome and vinyl bar stool, and the biggest, big screen TV I'd ever seen. Straight ahead, was a dimly lit hall with two doors on either side. My guess was that they led to the kitchen, bedrooms, and bath.

Curious to see more, I peeked around the door at what must have once been a formal dining area, but like the adjoining living space, that too had fallen on hard times. The white marble floor was dull and cracked, and an ornate chandelier that had once added class to the room had lost most of its dangling glamour. A wood table directly beneath it wasn't set with Stumpy's best china that night. Instead, the entire surface was stacked high with stereos, DVDs, CD players, car radios, cell phones, beepers, and other assorted electrical equipment. Looked like our man Stumpy was running a five-finger discount house out of Apartment 3-B.

I craned my neck to look farther in and saw TVs of all sizes lined up three and four deep against a far wall. Stacked on top, were at least a dozen, still in the box Sony DVD players. I was contemplating how the hell Stumpy could have gotten that amount of inventory up the three flights of stairs when I heard my name being shouted from the kitchen.

"Hey, Maxie. You want a beer? The Stump's got Miller or Sam Adams. Can you hear me, Max?"

If the little hussy's intent was to terrify the shit out of me, she was on the right track. And I'd bet every cent I had she was in there congratulating herself on a job well done. As I listened to her bellow my name through the apartment, it dawned on me that everything this woman did was calculated to get the most dramatic response. She played the moment like an improv-actor, and my nervous quiet in the empty apartment was just too irresistible.

After a last glance around the living room to make sure no one was lying in wait, I quick-stepped to the kitchen door but caught my breath when I entered. "Shit," I hissed trying not to breathe the putrid air assailing my nostrils. "What the hell is that smell?"

Bette looked at me over the top of the open refrigerator door and shrugged like she was oblivious to the rancid odor. "Which one you want?" she asked, holding out our absentee host's two beer selections. "He's got cans or bottles."

"Nothing for me, thanks," I answered sarcastically, and marveled at the woman's chutzpah. "Do you always raid the refrigerator when you break into someone's house?"

"Not always," she said matter-of-factly. "But that joint gave me cotton-mouth and nothing soothes like a cool brewski." She popped a can of Miller, chugged the contents and tossed the empty into the sink where it rattled noisily around the chipped porcelain before rolling to a stop near the drain. When our eyes locked, she mimicked my stern expression, and I heard the sound of a second beer being opened as she ducked her head back inside the fridge.

"Eywww," Bette whined dramatically. "There's something creepy growing in here. Wanna see it, Max? No wait," she said and waved me back. "Stay away. I think it's alive and moving toward the light." She giggled at her own joke and continued to rummage around.

Great, I thought. The world's only combination hooker-cat burglar-comedienne and I'm lucky enough to be doing my virgin B&E with her.

"Bette," I growled, "What the hell are you looking for?"

"Stumpy stores his pot in here," Bette reported. "I figured as long as we're visiting I'd relieve him of a couple of bags. He'll never miss…" She paused mid-sentence and when she spoke again her squeaky voice held real surprise. "Well, looky here."

"What?" I asked anxiously. "What did you find?"

Clenched in her tiny fist was an assortment of shimmering crystal jewelry, and something about the style looked very familiar. My heart skipped several beats as I moved to her side. "Let me see those. Are there any more?"

"Oh yeah," Bette nodded and let the refrigerator door swing wide.

My eyes followed her hand as she reached into the crisper and dragged out another fistful of the sparkling jewels. Filling the drawer was what looked to be the entire contents of Lila Martin's missing jewelry box. I almost exploded with excitement. Here was the proof I needed to connect Stumpy to Pete.

I hugged the tiny woman, overjoyed at her discovery. "This is it, babe. This is the proof Pete's the one."

"The one what?" she asked popping open a third beer.

But before I could answer there was a loud crack as the front door to the apartment flew back on its hinges and crashed against the wall.

I looked at Bette, my eyes widening with alarm. She aped my expression and whispered the words I least wanted to hear. "Stumpy's home."

Reflexively, my fingers wrapped around the gun inside my coat.

"Sorry, Charlie," said the little voice in my head. "The gun is out. You and the happy hooker aren't exactly invited guests, you know."

"And whose fault is that?" I wanted to shout as I pulled out the pepper spray and shook it to activate the chemicals. "I remember that 'don't be a wimp' crack, you little bastard."

Bette chugged the beer in her hand and set it noiselessly down on the counter. Putting a finger to her lips, she signaled me to follow and led us across the kitchen to a walk-in butler's pantry. Grasping the curved wood handle, she swung the door open triggering the single light bulb inside. But before we could enter, a wave of fetid air emanating from within told me we had found the source of the malodorous odor. My heart sank as I scanned the kitchen and realized there was no place else to hide. It was the stinking pit from hell or prepare to face the big guy.

The pantry was wide and deep with floor-to-ceiling shelves on each side. Half a dozen large boxes were stacked shoulder high near the rear, and as we scooted behind them, the door swung closed, and the light clicked off. Hiding in the dark room an idea wormed its way through my panic, and stepping from behind the boxes I searched the low ceiling for the single light bulb. When I found it, I twisted it free and tucked it into the pocket of my jacket. Returning to my place beside Bette, I heard the sound of a rolling burp being stifled.

"Excuse me," she whispered suppressing a giggle. "It's the beer bubbles."

I hushed her when we heard footsteps enter the kitchen, followed by the sound of a really bad James Brown impersonation.

"I feel good. Do da loo da loo da loo. I knew that I would now."

Stumpy's voice was slurred. He sounded very drunk.

"I feel nice. Sugar and spice."

I flinched at the sound of a metallic crash that could only be pots and pans hitting the floor. Stumpy must have lost his balance but his song never lost a beat.

"So good. Uh uh, So good. I've got you. Uh, uh, uh, uh. Wow."

Once again I felt a strong urge to draw my gun. But shooting Stumpy in his own apartment would probably earn me time in the big house and I didn't relish the thought of spending years with my butt pressed against the wall. Not to mention I didn't want to take out the only man who could implicate Pete in the Martin murders.

Bette grabbed my elbow and I almost jumped out of my shoes.

"Max," she whispered her lips close to my ear. "I have to pee."

"Well hold it," I hissed back through clenched teeth.

"I can't," she whined. "Beer goes right through me."

I should have realized she was about to do something crazy but before I could protest, Bette thrust her coat into my arms and slipped around me. A moment later, there was the whisper of spandex being slipped off skin, and the next thing I heard was a stream of pee splashing against the tile floor.

"Shit!" I moaned and pressed my forehead against the box in front of me. "Somebody please tell me this is not happening."

Finally after what seemed like an eternity, Bette's steady flow slowed to a trickle and a moment later the little minx was at my side working hard to tuck her huge boobs back into the skimpy leotard.

"Sorry," she said, after slipping her coat back on. "Weak bladder."

I put a hand over her mouth and listened intently. Stumpy's singing had stopped and the sudden silence was deafening.

"Uh oh," I said, and shook the pepper spray again.

"What?" she whispered.

But before I could answer, the door to the pantry was literally ripped off its hinges. Stumpy stood like a mountain in the pantry entrance, only this particular mountain was very unsteady on his feet. Leaning forward, he attempted to see into the room but his massive bulk blocked the light.

"Who the fuck's in here?" he roared but after taking one step inside, his unsteady gait met Bette's puddle of pee and he crashed to the floor.

Seeing our chance, I grabbed Bette's arm in a tight grip and putting my shoulder against the stack of boxes, dumped them onto the prostrate man. In the ensuing confusion the 'toon and I sprinted towards the door, leaping in unison over Stumpy's enormous body. Even in her four-inch heels, Bette made it easily. I almost made it but at the last second a beefy hand shot out and gripped my ankle like a vise.

Somehow I managed to stay on my feet, make that foot, but I was going nowhere fast. And in horror, I watched Stumpy sit up, using my ankle for support.

"Well, well, well" he said, grinning like only a drunken maniac could. "Look who we got here. Mister Tough Guy. Hey, Tough Guy. Glad you could drop in. Saves me the trouble of looking your ass up."

Bracing my hands against the frame of the pantry door, I jerked my leg back with every ounce of strength I had. The human mountain swayed forward giving me hope, but a quick flex of his muscular arm brought me down to the floor beside him. As I struggled to escape, my eyes locked onto an object that had spilled from one of the toppled boxes. The thing lay on the white tile floor, inches from my face, softly illuminated by the kitchen lights beyond. It was a man's arm.

My first thought was that Stumpy was storing manikin parts in the pantry. But it was so lifelike, right down to the short dark hairs covering the top of the arm and dirt under the fingernails. Dirt under the fingernails, Gracie?

Understanding finally broke through shocked confusion, and I felt bile rise in my throat. Bette and I had been hiding behind a dead guy. A cut up, boxed up, very smelly dead guy. And the odious thought triggered a wave of intense nausea that almost took me out of the game. Thankfully the sobering fear that I might share the same fate if I didn't get the hell out of there pushed me to act, and I shot Stumpy square in the face with the pepper spray.

The bellow that followed us out the door and down the stairs rang in my ears. Surely it must have rivaled the infamous Stumpy-looses-his-wanger scream that once reverberated through the hall of that very same building.

When we hit the street, Bette and I jumped into the van and rocketed down the block. My first impulse was to call Riff for help, but how would I explain what I'd been up to? I passed on that and decided to call the Detroit P.D. instead, hoping they'd get their butts in gear before the effects of the pepper spray wore off.

Spotting a gas station on the next corner, I parked beside a pay phone and dialed 911. Using my cell phone was out because the call could be tracked.

"Emergency operator."

Frantically I searched my freaked-out brain for the right words.

"Uh...one of my neighbors is screaming in his apartment. I think he might have been shot."

I gave her Stumpy's apartment number and the location of the building. She immediately asked for my name but I pushed on, leaving no room for her to comment.

"The guy deals drugs and hot goods out of his apartment. Make sure the police check the refrigerator. There's also a suspicious smell in the kitchen pantry like somebody died in there."

I paused for a breath and the operator repeated her request for my name.

"Look lady, I don't want to give my name. You know how it is in a neighborhood like this. I have to protect myself. Just tell the cops to get over there in a hurry."

For added insurance, I phoned the Southfield Police Department and left the same anonymous tip, stressing that if they moved fast, they could find Lila Martin's missing jewels in Stumpy's vegetable crisper.

As Bette and I drove away, I explained what I had seen in the pantry.

"Gross," she said crinkling up her face in disgust before plucking the Snickers bar off the top of the dash. "Were you going to eat this or what?"

We circled back to Stumpy's apartment and parked a block away. Five minutes later, two of Detroit's finest parked in front of the building. An EMS truck pulled in behind them and through the night-scope I watched curious neighbors gather on the sidewalk.

After what seemed like an eternity, the cops brought Stumpy out in handcuffs and loaded him into the back of a cruiser. I knew from listening to Riff talk shop that the apartment would be secured until they obtained a search warrant. After that the law would discover everything they needed to indict Stumpy on several charges and hopefully net Pete as well.

When the last cop car pulled away, I drove Bette back to her apartment. Reaching in my pocket I pulled out the five one-hundred-dollar bills left over from the van deal and paired them with my business card.

"Thanks a lot, Bette," I said pressing the cash into her hand. "Take this for your trouble. And if you ever need me, don't hesitate to call."

Bette counted the cash and stashed the lucky bundle between her breasts. "That's seven hundred dollars you've given me so far, Maxie, and I still haven't seen you with your pants off. You're not gay are you?"

"Not that I know of."

"Then why don't you come up," she said and inched a hand up my thigh. "I want to show you how good I am at earning my money."

Her offer was tempting but as I paused to consider it, Zed's face flashed through my mind. I wasn't sure why, but I didn't want to mess things up with the Amazon princess.

"Thinking about your girlfriend?"

"How did you know?"

Bette shrugged. "Most of my customers are men from the burbs. They wear the same look when they're afraid the wife will find out about me. I usually help them overcome the fear by sticking my hand down their pants."

"You going to do that to me?"

Bette's hand snaked closer to my crotch but stopped just shy. "You want me to," she said confidently eyeballing the sudden swell behind my zipper. "But I don't think I will."

"Why not?"

"Because you'll remember me more if I don't," she said raking me with her baby blue eyes. "And I want you to remember me."

"Like I could ever forget?" I said while wrapping a fist around the fur collar of her coat and pulling her to me. Our lips met in a wet, provocative kiss. When we parted, her face was set in a satisfied expression.

"Told you," Bette teased and pecked me on the cheek.

She looked much more desirable through my haze of horny hormones. "Told me what?" I asked as she popped her door open and stepped down to the sidewalk.

"That it would be more exciting if we didn't do it tonight."

I opened my mouth to protest but she checked me with a finger to her lips. "Chill, babycakes. Think about how cool it'll be when we finally do it someday."

At home the next afternoon, I had just finished combing out Blue's coat when the phone rang startling both of us. Crossing the room, with the cat hot on my heels, I checked the caller ID. The name and number of the Southfield P. D. glowed green in the window. Four rings later the answering machine clicked on.

"Max. It's Riff," said the no-nonsense voice. "Pick up the phone."

I paused with my hand over the receiver. Something told me this wasn't a social call.

"I mean it, Max," she continued. "You pick up or I'll come out there and find you."

It was an idle threat. Riff was way too busy to come looking for me, thank goodness. And I preferred to wait until she calmed down a bit.

The determined woman changed tactics, softened her tone and trolled for a response. "I've got information about Mitchell Sanders."

I snatched up the phone. "What information?"

"He's dead."

"What?!"

"Detroit discovered his body last night. Seems they got an anonymous call about a man screaming inside his apartment. When they arrived on the scene, they found the guy had been gassed with pepper spray. He kept insisting a man and a woman had been hiding in the kitchen pantry. The cops checked it out and found a very dead Mitchell Sanders. Parts of him anyway."

I gulped and pictured the severed arm lying on the floor.

"Seems Sanders went all to pieces and somebody packed him up for trash. The head was missing but Forensics was able to ID the body from prints. Detroit also discovered Lila Martin's stolen jewelry in the refrigerator crisper drawer."

She paused and waited for my reaction.

"No kidding," I said. "What a break for you."

"Yeah. Isn't it?"

There was a strained silence before she asked the question I knew was inevitable. "You wouldn't happen to know anything about that, would you?"

"Me? No."

"Where were you last night?" she shot back.

"I was with a friend at home."

"Who?"

"Zed. My new receptionist."

"That's interesting, because I stopped by the salon last night a little after nine and met a woman by the name of Zed locking up."

I swallowed hard but stayed silent.

"You know what else?" Riff said tightly. "I listened to the 911 call to Detroit, and the message that came in here about the same time. Both voices sound surprisingly like you."

"Like me? How bizarre is that?"

"The caller tipped off the police to look for Lila Martin's jewelry in the guy's refrigerator. Now how could Mister Anonymous have identified the owner of the jewelry unless he'd seen it before?"

"That's a mystery all right," I answered wondering how the hell I could get out of this conversation without hanging myself. There was no way to talk around the woman. She was too sharp.

"Anyway," Riff continued, "turns out the guy who rents the apartment, a Mr. Clarence Dumpert, is a good friend of Pete Deville's. Dumpert is downtown right now, spilling his guts. Claims Pete was the one who snuffed Sanders."

"No shit?"

"No shit," Riff repeated. "I just got a fax of his statement. Seems Sanders had been buying dope from Pete and came to a bar on Seven Mile two days ago to connect. Dumpert brings Sanders back to the apartment, and when they walk in, Pete's there, going through Lila Martin's jewelry box. Sanders recognizes his stepmother's collection and decides to get pushy, demands cash and stash for his silence. Deville pretends to go along, and when he tempts Sanders with a free hit, the junkie can't resist. Sanders was dead before the needle came out. They threw him in the bathtub; Pete did the carving, and packed away the pieces in the pantry. The plan was to take him out with the trash little by little. Guess they didn't figure on the smell."

Memory of the sickening odor sent a wave of queasiness through me.

"They're lifting prints from Dumpert's apartment," Riff said. "Especially from the pantry. Please tell me they're not going to find a match for yours."

"My prints aren't on file in Detroit," I answered and then wished I could take the words back.

"Damn it, Max. If I find out you were there, I'll arrest you and throw your ass in jail until all this is over."

"On what charge?"

"I'll think of something," Riff said heatedly. "Criminal stupidity comes to mind."

I ignored the remark, realizing it was spoken out of frustration. "Seems to me," I said, "that the mystery caller did you a big favor. You found Mitchell Sanders and the missing jewelry, plus you now have a bridge connecting Pete through Stumpy to the Martin murders. I'd think you'd be happy."

In the lengthy silence that followed I realized how I had slipped up.

"Yeah, well," Riff said solemnly. "Even a lucky boy like you comes up short occasionally. Do yourself a favor and back off."

Chapter 16

I thought long and hard about taking Riff's advice and truly wished I could. There's nothing I enjoy more than kicking back and relaxing at the end of the day, but the way things were going that wasn't an option. In America boring is a bad word, but when you haven't had it for a while, boring is actually very nice. The world should celebrate boring with an international holiday because human beings need it so much to remain sane. It's also the backdrop for exciting. In fact, when you think about it, boring makes exciting happen.

At the moment however, I'm sorry to say my life was anything but boring. Well not totally sorry because Zed was one of the not boring parts and I wouldn't trade meeting her for anything. I thought I might be falling in love with the mysterious medicine woman. It certainly wouldn't be hard. She's everything I've ever wanted and more. Unfortunately it was the more part that gave me pause. Zed was so extraordinary, she was a little intimidating.

Another cool part of my not so boring life was uncovering the evidence linking Pete to Andra's murder. And although Riff was reluctant to concede me any kudos, I knew my discovery would be a big assist to her investigation. She could now focus her attention on a single suspect and begin a more aggressive search. Regrettably that didn't alter my role in this little performance. Pete, the murderer/stalker, was still out there. If he had slowed his harassment in the last few days, it was only temporary. Once the crazy bastard found out he was wanted for the murder of Mitchell Sanders he'd have nothing to lose by taking crazy chances.

I needed an edge, which meant I had to find Pete but my only lead to his whereabouts was a dead end. No way would go near the bar on Seven Mile, and I could forget the surrounding neighborhood as well. The cops would be watching the whole area.

The question of where to look for Pete ran through my mind several times before my logic filters kicked in and gave me the obvious answer. If Pete made another attempt on my life, and I was sure he would, it would happen right here in my home, the only place he could score Johnny Lott's bankroll and me at the same time. The hunch had to be right. I could feel it in my bones. And if facing him down was the only way to settle things permanently, fine, let him come. At least I'd have the home-court advantage.

Now if that sounded like I was being macho, don't you believe it. Fear and uncertainty were motivating my every decision. The one thing I did know for sure was that I wasn't ready to die. Not that I feared death, at least I didn't think I did. But I was sure sick of being afraid.

After pouring a cup of coffee I wandered into the sunroom and pondered the big question. If Pete did play his hand in my home how could I defend myself and capture him for the police? Asking Riff for help was out. As a cop, she had to follow the rules or risk losing the conviction. No way would she condone what I was planning. Leaning against the sunroom's curved glass wall, I stared out at a murky sky and the seamless black lake. It was strange how the lake had begun to mirror my moods the last couple of weeks.

"So, Mister Moto," I asked my reflection in the window. "What is next step on path?"

"Must keep plan simple," my reflection answered. "Better to cover honorable ass in case you screw up."

The simplest plan I could think of was to hide somewhere and get the drop on Pete, but I had better choose carefully. The guy was no dummy, and unlike me, he seemed to have this cat-and-mouse thing nailed down tight. Walking back in the house I surveyed the lower level critically. The entire first floor was one big room, with only a minimal amount of furniture. True, there were several concealed closets, but none seemed to be a good position for an ambush.

Climbing the stairs, I checked out the art studio. There was a long, rectangular worktable in the center of the room, a double-sink against the inner wall and my computer in the northwest corner. None of these offered much in the way of protection so I stepped across the hall into my bedroom. The moment I entered, it hit me that here was the one place Pete was sure to visit, hoping I was too stupid to have removed the cash after he tried for it the first time. That nixed the concealed space as a place to hide, but did offer a slight advantage. If Pete's attention stayed focused on the Buddha shrine and the money he thought was inside, it just might allow me to get the jump on him.

A quick glance around didn't offer much hope. There was my waterbed sitting dead center to the bank of windows facing the lake, an oval rattan nightstand to the left, and a carved winged-back chair on the right. Running the length of the south wall was a walk-in closet. Directly across from the foot of my bed, the entrance to the Buddha shrine.

Wandering into the guest bedroom, my eyes fell on an antique hope chest that had definite possibilities. It measured approximately four-and-a-half feet long, two feet wide and three feet deep, easily big enough for me to fit inside. An added bonus was that the lock, a brass hook and eye clasp setup, had always been defective; a fact that used to bug the hell out of me, but now was just what the doctor ordered. To the eye, the clasp appeared fastened, but the slightest upward tug would usually allow it to open.

To test my idea I unloaded the spare guest linen from the chest, stepped in and squatted to my hands and knees. The fit was tighter than I thought it would be, but not terrible, and after lowering the top, I heard the brass hook slide home. It was pitch black inside, and not the smartest thing to do for my sore knee. But if all went well, I wouldn't be there for very long. Out of nowhere, a panicky feeling of imprisonment tightened my throat, but when I arched my back, the lid popped up easily.

Always fascinated by my inexplicable human ways, Blue watched through narrowed eyes as I pushed the heavy trunk down the hall. The cat considered it his duty to check out all changes in our home décor and he never missed an opportunity to express an opinion.

When I angled the chest into my bedroom, Blue jumped on top and rode the beast to its final destination beside the nightstand. I took that as a positive sign, because if the perceptive cat hadn't agreed with my decision to place it there he wouldn't have come in the bedroom for a month.

My next task was how to handle the security system. Shutting it down might make Pete suspicious, so I reset the code to the one he had obtained from Andra's journal.

To make it look like I wasn't home, the Lexus would have to go, so after grabbing my keys, I drove it over to Brad and Diva's and parked around the far side of their house. They were vacationing in Arizona, and I was sure they wouldn't mind.

Walking home I debated whether or not to return the four million to the shrine room. Anything could go wrong, especially since Pete hadn't been privy to my hastily drawn up script. And if the worst happened, I certainly didn't want the shit to score the money. In the end I baited the trap with two dummy suitcases loaded down with phonebooks and newspapers. If luck was with me, Pete would come out carrying both at the same time.

My strategy was basic. Wait for Pete to enter the shrine room, quick-step to the entrance, and zap him with pepper spray when he came back through the door. The slimy bastard should only hope it happened that way too. This disgusting excuse for a human being had brutally murdered Andra and her mother, and he'd be damn lucky if I didn't put a bullet through his head. Well, okay. Maybe I wouldn't shoot him. Not if I didn't have to. That would let the son-of-a-bitch off way too easy. In my revenge fantasy he would go to prison for life and become the girlfriend of the biggest, baddest, most well hung dude in the joint. And when the big guy got bored, I hoped he would pass Pete along to his pervert friends.

That sounds spiteful, I know, and if there's any truth to karma I'm going to be in big trouble in my next life. But Pete didn't deserve mercy. I was going to do everything in my power to see that he spent the rest of his life behind bars.

The final detail to work out was what to do with my gun. I considered bringing it with me inside the chest, but I needed to have the pepper spray in hand. Not to mention the damn thing could go off and who knows what body part I might lose? In the end I decided to tuck the gun between the mattress and frame at the foot of my bed. That put it only steps away if I needed it.

About seven o'clock that night I was startled out of an anxious trance when the phone rang. It was Zed. I had been so busy preparing for the big showdown with Pete I forgot I was supposed to call her an hour ago.

"Sorry I didn't connect with you, babe." I said. "It totally slipped my mind."

Zed's voice was husky and sensuous, and I could feel her indulgent smile. "Not a problem. I only want to tell you I've decided to visit my friend, Ajen in Toronto for the weekend. We're going to catch a show, and shop the sexy leather boutiques. Of course I'll keep you in mind when making my selections."

My brain flashed back to the outfit she had worn the day before, and the lascivious thrill of her butter-soft leather gloves. "Please do."

"And what will you be up to while I'm gone?"

I hadn't told Zed what I was planning and now I was relieved there wouldn't be a need to. She'd only worry or try to get involved and I didn't want her in harm's way.

"I'm still working to get a line on Pete," I said trying to make it sound innocent. "I'll probably play at that for a while."

There was silence for several heartbeats and I could almost feel Zed probing my brain across miles of phone lines. When she spoke, it was slow and deliberate.

"You don't have to bullshit me, Max."

"What do you mean?"

Zed laughed softly. "Just be careful. You and I have unfinished business together."

Pete didn't show that night or the next and I was beginning to think he wouldn't after all, but about five the following morning he finally made his move.

I had been pacing the bedroom in an attempt to stay awake when the exterior lights at the rear of my house snapped on. The sudden brightness caused me to jump in place, and after re-swallowing my heart several times, I crossed the room and stood beside the open hope chest. Peering down into its rectangular interior, my plan to hide while a mad killer roamed the house struck me as very lame. The thing was an overgrown shoebox box for crissake. Better to have my gun in hand, and shoot the bastard when he came through the bedroom door.

I stood stock-still unsure of the right course of action. When the motion detector lights snapped off two minutes later, I closed my eyes in relief but my heart still beat its warning. Time inched along. My determination to face Pete outright wavered. But at the soft tread of footsteps on the stairs, I knelt in the chest and let the lid close over me. The inside seemed to have shrunk, and I was uncomfortable almost immediately, especially the sore knee which throbbed in concert with my drumming heart.

Minutes later a muffled crash from across the hall met my ears. When the sounds of breaking glass followed, I realized Pete must have been trashing the artwork in my studio.

"They're only things," shouted the little voice in an attempt to dissuade me from doing anything stupid. "You just stay put."

Footsteps entered my bedroom. I heard the familiar squeak of the bathroom door, and a moment later the triple report of a large caliber weapon shattered the glass shower doors. The sudden blast snapped my head up against the lid. Brilliant white stars zipped in every direction across my field of vision. But blindness was the least of my worries. I had voluntarily packed myself in an oversized towel hamper, and the only thing I had for protection was a spicy condiment in a spray-can. If it was Pete that had shot out the shower doors, and I felt in my gut that it had to be, I had overestimated the guy's sanity. The man was totally nuts. And I was about to be plugged like a beer can on a fence post.

As I listened intently, footsteps crossed the room and stopped in front of the hope chest. Pete was either checking the window for trouble, or contemplating the contents of the hope chest at his feet. At a time like this Luke Skywalker would call upon the "Force" to bamboozle the mind of his enemy. So I figured what the hell, I might as well give it a shot. Concentrating, I sent out my strongest mental command, "Nobody in here but us chickens."

As added insurance I racked my brain for a protective prayer, but the only thing I could come up with was Grace. "Bless us, O Lord for these thy gifts which we are about to receive..." I stopped, startled by a toe tapping lightly against my precarious sanctuary. If I hadn't been packed in so tight, the adrenaline careening through my veins would have made me jump a mile high. Another kick to the side of the chest sent my soaring stress levels into the stratosphere and for a moment I imagined I was pounding on the sides of the wooden chest with my fists. Thankfully, before I did anything stupid, I realized that the booming sounds resounding off the fillings in my teeth was blood beating against my eardrums like tom-toms. At the peak of panic, the footsteps moved away, and I exhaled the breath I'd been holding. "Shit," I thought then slapped a hand over my mouth afraid I had said the word out loud. That was too fuckin' close.

Rallying my senses I attempted to calm my wildly racing heart. When I did finally manage to regain some control, I nudged the lid up an inch and peeked out. The soft light of the waning moon was enough to illuminate Pete's lanky profile, and I watched in fascination as he ran his hands across the wrong end of the wall mural. Even in my wigged out state, that struck me as odd. He had found the hidden entrance on his first visit with very little problem.

Pete worked his way to the other side and stopped when he noticed one of the bullet holes. Bending to inspect it, he slid his finger inside, pushed with a fist, and the door clicked open.

Corralling my fears, I watched Pete take a single step inside the shrine room, pause, and turn back to scan the surrounding darkness. Did he sense I was there? Did a sicko like this actually have normal human senses? Or do they morph to super normal, like an animal that knows it's being hunted? I certainly hoped not, but just in case I ducked down and allowed the lid to close.

I counted to ten, three times before working up the nerve to look out again. When I finally did push up against the top of the hope chest, the damn thing would not budge. Yeah right! I whispered to myself, thinking my imagination was playing games. Very funny. After my second try, I realized with horror that the lid was stuck fast.

My brain railed against the cruel joke. Why would something like this happen to me? I'm a good person. I love my family and friends, at least most of the time. I give unselfishly to charities. Adopt several needy families at Christmas. Hell, one time I even gave five bucks to a street-person who washed my windshield with a greasy rag and left it all smeary. I didn't deserve this kind of shabby treatment.

Feeling panicky I arched my back against the top but the damn thing still wouldn't budge. I'd become a prisoner of my own asinine plan. That's okay, I thought, trying to buck up my courage. So you can't get out. So what? Pete doesn't know you're locked in the chest.

The now familiar footsteps exited the shrine room and instinctively I shrunk down as far as I could. With eyes closed I strained to pick up any sound and caught a muffled double thud of two suitcases being tossed onto the bed beside me. I heard the locks pop on one case, and pictured Pete swinging open the top. A menacing silence confirmed his discovery of my ruse. After opening the second case, he screamed out like a wounded animal.

"You motherfucker, Max! Your ass will pay for this. I'll tear this fucking dump apart then burn it to the…"

Pete stopped his rampage abruptly, and in the silence that followed, I caught a faint voice calling my name.

"Maxie? Maxie, it's Mom. You left your back door unlocked."

I did a silent scream and felt my throat tighten. What the hell was she doing here at this hour of the morning?

Pete's footsteps quickened as he headed for the door and I knew calling to Marie would be useless. My only hope was to break out when he left the room, and grab my gun.

I heard nothing for a moment. But when the sound of Marie's scream cut through the chest, any reserve cool I had abandoned me. Roaring in anger I pushed against the top with all my strength.

"Open-up-you-son-of-a-bitch!"

It should have been one of those intense moments where I would gain super strength and be able to lift cars off babies. Unfortunately it didn't happen like that.

"God dammit!" I screamed and thrashed hopelessly around inside the chest. "Somebody let me out of here!"

I stopped suddenly and felt a stab of guilt pierce my heart. By playing my little game of hide and seek, I had exposed my mother to a murderous crazy man who might hurt her, or worse. At that last thought, my shoulder muscles tensed and I rolled right, then left, determined to break out. Right. Left. Right. Left. The hope chest began a steady rocking and finally toppled onto its backside. The shift in position freed the traitorous lock and when the top swung open I rolled out and hit the ground running.

"Mom!" I screamed as I grabbed my gun and ran down the stairs oblivious to any danger that might be waiting. "Mom. I'm coming."

But by the time my feet hit the first floor the house was empty and silent as a grave.

Chapter 17

Webster's describes the term hysterical as a nervous affection, characterized by laughing, crying, convulsive struggling, a sense of suffocation, etc. That pretty much described me during those next few minutes as I rushed around and frantically called out for my mom. I opened closets, looked behind furniture and scoped out the garage. In wild desperation I even checked the doublewide refrigerator-freezer. I did not want to accept the fact that Pete had kidnapped Marie. I kept telling myself she was hiding; if not in the house, then outside in the surrounding woods. After all, Marie Snow was no ordinary lady. She could outrun, out swim, and out yoga most women half her age. She was just too cool and competent to be taken prisoner.

My heart was doing a hip-hop beat as I burst out the back door and skidded to a stop on a carpet of fallen leaves. On cue the motion detector lights snapped on above me, and I stared wildly around trying to catch any sound or movement in the woods. When nothing happened I ran toward the road, screaming my mom's name, fully expecting her to step out from hiding the moment she heard me.

I was halfway down the drive when a black Jeep Cherokee turned in and sped toward me. A moment later it skidded to a stop and a wide-eyed Zed jumped out. She approached cautiously, taking in the gun and my panicked expression.

"What's happened?" she demanded.

I stared at her, speechless.

"Max?"

"He took her," I managed to whisper and felt tears pool around my eyes. "Pete kidnapped Marie."

Thankfully one of us was good in a crisis; unfortunately it wasn't me. I was totally freaked and desperate for direction.

Zed leaned into the Jeep and switched off the engine. "Let's go inside."

"But maybe we could catch them," I said staring desperately down the empty road. "Did anybody pass you on the way in?"

Zed shook her head, slipped an arm around my shoulder and guided me back to the house. Somehow I managed to sit at the kitchen table to give her a recounting of the night's tragic comedy of errors.

"It's my fault," I said cradling my forehead in the palm of my hand. "God, I am such an ass. What if he hurts her?"

"He won't," Zed answered confidently. "Not yet anyway. He'll use Marie to lure you to him."

I leapt to my feet and began to pace the floor, ranting, and flailing my arms like a madman. When my anger boiled over, I snatched an empty crystal vase off a counter, hurled it against the wall and watched it explode into a million pieces.

Throughout my tirade Zed never said a word. She understood my need to vent. When I finally sat down beside her again, I was quieter but not much calmer.

"Should we call the police?"

Her eyes narrowed as she thought it over. "No, let's wait. Pete will call."

Not thirty seconds later, the phone on the kitchen wall rang and I snatched it up.

"Hey, Maxie," chirped a ghoulishly cheery voice. "Guess who?"

"If you hurt her, Pete," I threatened through clenched teeth. "I will hunt your ass down and kill you. I swear it."

His response to my threat was a cutting laugh. "Ooh I'm so scared. Save me from the big bad hairdresser."

I squeezed the receiver tight and did my best to control my anger. "I mean it, Pete. Hurt her and I'll spend every nickel I have to get you."

"You don't have the balls for revenge, Maxie. If you did you would have crawled out of your rat-hole tonight to save your old lady. Where were you hiding by the way? Wait. Don't tell me." He paused for a moment. "That big chest in the bedroom."

When I didn't answer he knew he was right.

"Damn! You are a lucky shit. I almost pumped a cap into the top of that sucker just for fun."

"What do you want, you sick fuck?"

"Lott's four million of course. You owe it to me for taking Fox away."

"You can have the goddamn money," I said. "Just don't hurt my mom."

"I ain't going to hurt her," Pete said. "Not unless you do something stupid."

"I won't. I promise. I'll give you what you want."

"I know you will, man. I know you will. But I'm digging this trip way too much to let it end just yet. No, I gotta have time to think of something cool. Something to make you sweat."

"Whatever!" I said, unable to hide my annoyance.

"Don't be mean, Maxie," Pete admonished. "And don't expect to hear from me again until tomorrow night."

I sat in stunned silence as Zed took the handset from my fingers.

"Well?"

"He wants money," I answered flatly.

"The cash from the shrine room?"

In spite of my troubles I couldn't help but be amazed by Zed's psychic abilities. I had never told her about the four million or the Buddha shrine.

"Pete found out about the money from Andra's journal," I explained. "He tried for it once and I figured he'd come back."

"Guess you were right."

I shook my head in disgust. "Yeah, I'm a regular Mr. Know-it-all."

"You did what you thought was best, Max. You had no way of knowing Marie would show up."

The sound of her name reignited my panic. "Are you sure we shouldn't call the police?"

Zed shook her head. "They would only complicate things at this point. If Pete feels pushed, he'll strike back."

She was right. Involving the police could only stoke an already explosive situation. It was obvious Pete wasn't playing with a full deck and there was no telling what might set him off. My only hope was that the man's greed would keep him from hurting Marie.

Too antsy to sit still, I grabbed the broom from a nearby closet and swept up the broken vase. "Don't want Blue to step on this," I said glancing at Zed.

She nodded but remained quiet.

I felt guilty about endangering my mother and incredibly stupid for thinking I could capture Pete when the police could not. If I didn't come up with something useful to do, I might lose control.

Plucking the phone off the wall I punched in Bobby Deegan's home number. Maybe he could give me advice or even some help if he had returned from California. After three rings the answering machine picked up. I left a detailed message then tried his cell phone. That also drew a blank; ditto the number in California.

Climbing the stairs, I checked out the studio and felt my heart sink to my toes. Pete had been a busy boy. Sculptures had been toppled, ceramic bowls smashed to bits and every painting slashed from top to bottom. Years of my work destroyed in minutes.

By the time I rejoined Zed in the kitchen I was beyond anger. "Do you know what that bastard did?" I demanded.

Zed nodded.

"And I let him do it!" I screamed in frustration. "I just hid in that trunk like a fucking wuss and let him trash my entire life."

Zed grabbed my arms as I neared her chair and stared deeply into my eyes. "I know you're feeling defeated, Max and I understand why, but if you're going to help Marie you've got to let it go."

I knew she was right. But I wasn't sure I could muster the self-control necessary to overcome my conflicting emotions.

"Of course you can," Zed answered addressing my unspoken doubts. "You're stronger than you think. And despite what went wrong tonight, your plan was a good one."

"A fat lot of good it did," I muttered, reluctant to trade my self-recrimination for her encouraging words. "I screwed-up everything."

"No," Zed returned. "You made choices and so did Marie. She chose to visit the house at that particular moment. Random chance is life, Max, and although it's hard to accept, your mom is entitled to her share."

I had only a vague idea what she was talking about, but the sincerity in her timeless black eyes softened my resistance. "Shit," I hissed as my rage was replaced by uncertainty. "What the hell am I going to do?"

"You're going to work with me to prepare yourself," Zed answered confidently. "So when Pete calls back, you'll be ready."

A few minutes later, following Zed's instructions, I booted up the gas fireplace, we both stripped, and I laid face down on the knotted silk rug before the roaring blaze. Kneeling beside me Zed began massaging a series of acupressure points across my back. When she combined that with a rhythmic humming I gradually began to relax. Her steady manipulations induced a trance-like state and when her hands finally came to rest at the small of my back, a comfortable sensation of heat flooded the length of my spine. After that, I dozed off, or maybe lost consciousness. With Zed directing traffic, it was hard to say.

When I opened my eyes a moment later, everything within my vision seemed to glow with an intense light. The couch, the stone floor, the rug beneath me, even the tiniest dust bunny in the corner pulsed with an energy aura that sparkled like the sun. The visual effect was enthralling, to say the least. And I would have happily spent the rest of my life pondering the subtle nuances in color if Zed hadn't restored my normal perceptions by lifting her hands and directing me to sit up.

"Breathe deeply," her voice whispered behind my ear, "and concentrate your attention on each exhalation."

I did what Zed advised, taking in long, slow breaths and paying particular attention to their release. The narrowed focus allowed me to center myself, and as Zed stroked my temples with the tips of her fingers, my body surrendered its last bit of tension. I was still angry, but my desire to go off half-cocked and risk everybody's life had been abandoned.

"How do you feel?" Zed asked, slipping behind me to massage the base of my neck.

"At the moment," I answered tingling to the touch of her hard nipples against my back, "a little horny. So I guess I'm okay."

Zed stayed with me the whole next day, urging me to meditate and do laps in the pool to disperse my nervous energies. Keeping busy helped but as each hour passed I grew more anxious and uptight. At seven-thirty that evening, the call we'd been waiting for came. It had been the longest fifteen hours of my entire life.

Pete's voice on the line sounded thin, as if it was being carried away by a rushing wind. "Are you ready to play delivery boy, Maxie?"

"Is my mom all right?"

"For the moment. And she'll stay that way if you do what you're told."

"And what's that?"

"Put Lott's cash in a backpack and head for the zoo."

"The zoo?"

"Yeah. Mommy and I are waiting up on the water tower. Come alone and unarmed. If I see one cop or anything funny, I swear I'll dump her ass over the side."

"You're not up on the water tower," I said shaking my head in disbelief. "How the hell would you get up there?"

"We climbed. Just like you're going to do, unless you're ready to become an orphan."

I didn't respond.

"So what do you say?" Pete asked tauntingly. "Is your momma worth four million?"

"Yes."

"Okay then, let's get this freak show on the road."

Pete's instructions were pretty complicated and showed exactly how sick he was. The zoo he was talking about was the Detroit Zoo. The water tower: a massive hundred-and-seventy-five-foot behemoth that had awed me since I was a kid. The metallic monster always reminded me of a giant spider, straight out of classic science fiction.

"Let me talk to my mom," I said swallowing down my dread at the thought of climbing the tower. "I still don't believe you're up there."

"Fuck you!"

"No, fuck you!" I shot back trying hard to sound in control. "You want the four million; you put her on the phone. If you don't, I'm going to assume you already killed her and call the cops. They'll be waiting when you come down."

Several seconds passed before my mom's voice came on the line. She sounded too calm, and far away.

"Maxie, we are on the water tower, but don't come up here. He wants to kill you."

There was a sound like she had dropped the phone and then Pete came back on the line. "Don't pay any attention to Mamma. I just poked her with some primo H."

"Don't hurt her, Pete."

Pete chuckled in amusement. "She ain't hurt. Climbed up here like a fucking monkey. Now she's enjoying a well-earned buzz. Ain't you, Mamma?"

Static broke up Pete's next few words, but after that he came in loud and clear. "Do what I told you, Maxie and your old lady goes free. If I see anything suspicious, she goes over the side."

He disconnected and I related the conversation to Zed.

"He's lying," she said. "He won't let her go."

I nodded. We were dealing with a madman who could only be trusted to do the wrong thing.

Thirty minutes later, I placed a large backpack bulging with one-hundred-dollar bills on the kitchen table. The nylon pack had originally held a two-man tent. It was designed with a single, central pocket, fastened at the top and sides with Velcro strips. Pull anywhere on the main flap and the pack would split wide open.

Only about one million dollars would actually fit inside, but I wasn't concerned. How many people know what four million looks like? I had to have faith in Pete's greed and trust that the sight of the fat prize would be enough to entice him. I was about to shoulder the heavy bundle when I remembered something that might come in handy, and after climbing the stairs, found what I was looking for on a shelf in my closet. A few minutes later I was back in the kitchen, and swinging the heavy pack over one shoulder, faced Zed who was leaning against the door.

"Are you ready for this?" she said her dark eyes full of concern.

I shook my head. "No. You want to try and talk me out of it?"

We looked at each other for a long moment without speaking.

"I'll be okay," I said and took her in my arms.

"I know you will," she replied.

"Is that an I-know-you-will because somehow you can see into the future and divine everything will be okay?" I asked hopefully.

"No."

We kissed and her lips caressed mine.

"No, what?" I asked when the kiss broke.

"No, I can't predict the future," Zed answered looking me square in the eye. "But I told you once I was here to meet my fate and I'm not ready to let you go that easily."

The determination in her words frightened me. "I couldn't handle it if you were hurt," I whispered against her cheek. "Promise me you won't try anything."

Zed gave an almost imperceptible nod.

"I love you," I said and hugged her tighter.

Another nod, but no reply.

Chapter 18

▼

As I drove to the zoo, I tried hard not to think about the danger awaiting me. Of course trying not to think about something is thinking about it, so I gave up and indulged in my fears. Worst-case scenario, I was driving to my death. But, what the hell. Who wants to live forever anyway? Not me. Maybe another forty, fifty years tops.

Don't ask me why, but the Detroit Zoo is located in the city of Royal Oak. Right on the corner of Woodward Avenue, world famous for its Dream Cruise, a two day orgy of classic cars and a million people so high on exhaust fumes they think they're having a good time, and the I-696, a curvy, hard-for-cops-to-hide expressway that inspires people to drive like they were in the Indy-500.

As I approached the Woodward exit, I caught a glimpse of the zoo water tower in the distance. The massive tank glowed blue-violet against the night sky but the catwalk circling its base was not visible. I thought about what my mom must have gone through climbing that monster. From here it seemed impossible.

Was Marie still alive? The shadowy question haunted me. Maybe Pete had killed her the minute he knew I was on my way. If that was the case (and I hoped to God it wasn't), the smartest thing for him to do was shoot me when I climbed up on the catwalk. But I didn't think he would. The whole elaborate scenario was about vengeance. I knew he'd want to play and watch me squirm. In fact, that was the only thing I could really count on.

I eased my truck up the exit ramp and stayed to the left, all the time keeping the tower in sight. When I stopped for a red light on the service drive, I gave it my full attention. Originally built in the 1920s, the water tower had been given its latest facelift approximately two years ago. Huge graphics on the side of the tank depicted a procession of animals, including humans, in silhouette against a lavender-blue sky. Spotlights illuminating the scene were affixed to the ends of long spokes extending out from the base of the tank. They highlighted the colorful graphics but left the catwalk in almost total darkness.

Following Pete's instructions, I turned north on Woodward, and pulled into the old Big Boy parking lot directly opposite the zoo's main gate. The lot was empty; the restaurant had been closed for more than a year. Weaving around the potholes and broken glass, I parked facing the water tower and flashed my brights three times to signal Pete. That done, I sat there and attempted to raise my faltering courage from the depths; not exactly an easy task.

I struggled with what seemed like overwhelming inertia for several minutes before stepping out of the truck. The surrounding night air was clear and cool; the new moon a jester's smirk as I fit the million-dollar pack across my shoulders. Reaching back in the truck I retrieved my gun from the glove compartment. Pete had warned me to come unarmed, but screw that. The sick little game had no rules, none that he would follow anyway.

In the shadows of the abandoned parking lot, I tucked the gun into a holster at the small of my back and dropped my heavy sweatshirt over it. Did I really want to shoot Pete? You bet your ass I did. But I would only do it to save Marie or myself. Like I said before, I wanted Pete imprisoned for the rest of his unnatural life. But if dropping a cap in him was the only way, then que sera sera.

I took a deep breath and started walking toward the zoo. Halfway across Woodward, I sensed Pete watching me from above and my ego urged me to give him the finger. Thankfully my ego was only in control ninety percent of the time. My more rational ten percent didn't want to detonate the ticking time bomb too soon.

The view of the tower even from that far away was intimidating as hell. I guesstimated the catwalk, where Pete and Marie were waiting, to be at least a hundred and twenty feet off the ground. A bubble of fear caught in the back of my throat and I began to feel lightheaded; probably the only known case of vertigo while standing on terra firma.

Shaking off the dizziness, I reached the west side of Woodward and stepped onto the curb. To my left, the zoo's parking structure extended over the busy highway's southbound lanes creating a tunnel. To my right, approximately thirty yards ahead, stood the park's main fence. I waited for a break in traffic to be sure I wasn't observed, sprinted across the well-kept lawn and dove into the shadows behind a ten-foot tuft of Miscanthus grass growing against the fence.

I knelt in the thick cover for several minutes, my heart thumping out the 1812 Overture, my ragged breath attempting to fill my lungs in short, painful jerks. "How the hell did I get myself into this mess?" I whispered as I peeked through the giant blades of grass at a suddenly busy Woodward Avenue. And what made me think I was capable of going up against a crazy man who had already murdered three people?

Suddenly the air was saturated with the high-pitched whine of police sirens. I was on my feet, ready to run, certain someone had seen me lurking near the fence and called the cops. It was during those next few heart-straining seconds that I realized how committed I was to saving Marie. Why else would I be so paranoid about being discovered? Seconds later two marked police cruisers flashed into view and after slowing for the intersection, screamed past my position heading east. Thank God I wasn't the only lawbreaker at large that night.

With my renewed sense of commitment, I shrugged off the backpack and tossed it over the fence. Now it was my turn, and by the looks of things it wasn't going to be easy. The imposing wrought iron fence was a good ten feet tall with the top two feet arcing in a soft curve over my head. Pleasing design to look at; a bitch to climb over. Somehow I managed without giving myself a second vasectomy, but I wouldn't want to watch the action on instant replay.

When I retrieved the backpack, I saw one of the Velcro closures had split open and before I could refasten it, a score of loose hundreds whipped away in the brisk wind. Ah well, I thought as I watched the Franklins skip helter-skelter across the lawn, Pete would never miss a few.

Keeping low, I made a beeline to the security fence surrounding the water tower and looked it over critically. It was steel chain link, twelve feet high with barreled razor wire scrolling across every inch of the top. Good thing I didn't have to go that way.

The base of the tower was shrouded in darkness and it took me a while before I located a ground level split where the two ends of the fencing came together. How Pete could have possibly known about that little detail was a complete mystery.

Forcing myself to keep moving, I got down on my knees, pushed the weighty bundle through the narrow gap and followed a moment later. Once inside the fence I refit the pack across my shoulders and looking up at the imposing structure, felt a wave of dread wash through me. Nobody could climb that sucker in the dark. And how the hell could I be sure Pete and Marie were really up there? He could be hiding nearby waiting for me to get halfway up the tower before plugging me in the back with a deer-rifle. It was just the kind of thing the sick bastard would do.

Without warning, a set of headlights cut across the scene and at the sound of a racing motor, I hit the ground with a thump. Holding my breath I prayed I hadn't been spotted. Several seconds passed and when no one ordered me to come out with my hands up I lifted my head and watched as a white pickup truck slowly circled the lot bordering the tower. The driver stopped a dozen yards away. A hood-mounted spotlight snapped on. And almost as if they knew I was there, it swept slowly across the entire area. I flattened myself against the earth, and begged Kuan Yin, the most compassionate of all Buddhist saints, to make me invisible. The grand lady must have been feeling generous that evening because the spot closed down only inches before illuminating my body. Seconds later the truck disappeared around the curved entrance leading out of the parking lot. I lay still as a statue for several minutes, my heart slamming against the earth, not entirely trusting that the security vehicle wouldn't return with reinforcements.

Rising shakily to my knees, I gazed up at the tower and spotted the ladder leading to the catwalk. The bottom rung was a good twenty-five feet above my head. To reach it, I would have to make my way up two sets of crisscrossed steel cables that bound the tower's steel support structure.

Once again I questioned whether Pete had been telling me the truth. How the hell could my mom have managed that climb? That she was in great shape for her age, I won't deny but I had a hard time believing she had the strength to scale the tower. If she was up there, I was going to be impressed as hell. And in the event that we both survived, I was going to adopt her exercise regimen immediately.

Approaching the tower, I balanced my weight on the lowest of the three-inch support cables and made my way slowly up the steep incline like a tightrope walker. The climb proved less hazardous than it looked but only because I was able to use the crisscrossing cables above my head for support. After ten minutes of intense concentration, I stood on the bottom rung of the ladder and wrapped my arms around the smooth guardrails flanking me. Every nerve I possessed pulsed with tension; and raw adrenaline, my new best friend, felt like hot needles surfing through my veins.

I counted to ten, taking long slow breaths and encouraging my muscles to relax. When I was finally convinced that gravity wasn't going to rip me from my perch, I began the arduous ascent to the catwalk. Halfway up I had to stop and readjust the bulky backpack; a million bucks is some heavy bread, if you'll excuse the pun, and my long-suffering knee was already aching under the extra weight. It took another ten minutes, but I finally managed to crawl onto a small steel platform twenty feet below the catwalk. I was panting like a dog and humbly grateful to have reached any kind of stopping point, even this three-by-three foot spit of cold metal was better than doing a balancing act on that friggin' ladder.

The blustery winds charged me from every direction and looking out from my perch I checked out the seemingly endless line of vehicles snaking down the I-696. Hundreds of people were traveling on that freeway, all of them completely oblivious to the life-and-death drama unfolding above their heads. If the story made the news, some might remember driving past the zoo that night but no one would report seeing anyone climbing the water tower. I was an ant on the side of the Empire State Building.

Straight ahead I could just see the lights of the Rolling Pines Mall some thirty miles west. And to my left, the downtown Detroit skyline flickered through the scant cloud cover. It was a spectacular view but I didn't have time to appreciate it; my brain was too busy scrambling for a way to approach the disaster that waited twenty feet above. I would love to have the gun in my hand when I stepped up on the catwalk, but that probably wasn't the best idea. If Pete spotted it, there was a good chance he would kill Marie.

When I could finally get my feet moving again, I climbed the ladder and boosted myself on to the catwalk. At that height the wind had more speed and power. I had to hold tight to the waist-high guardrail to steady myself. Ten yards away, Pete stood over my mother who was seated on the steel-mesh walkway. Her eyes were half-closed, and her arms hugged her chest against the cold. She wore no coat, only jeans and a flannel shirt. And I could see from where I stood that she was shivering. Catching sight of me, she tried to rise but Pete held her down and pressed the tip of his revolver to her temple.

"Set down the backpack," he screamed over the rushing wind, "and turn your pockets inside out."

I did as he ordered.

"Now lift your shirt and turn around."

I hesitated.

"Do it!" he screamed cocking back the hammer of his revolver.

I had no choice but I lifted the shirt only high enough to expose the gun.

"That was very stupid, Max. Take the gun out nice and slow and throw it over the side."

I did.

"Now pick up the backpack and bring it over here."

With one hand, I reached down and grasped the front of the weighty bag, hefted it and laid it on top of the catwalk's flat security rail. A quick rip of the main flap exposed the loosely stacked cash and the strong wind whisked dozens of bills out into space.

"Stop!" Pete screamed. "Or I'll kill her."

I held the flap down lightly. "You're not going to kill her," I shouted back trying to sound more confident than I felt. "Not if you want this money."

He raised his gun and pointed it at me.

"Shoot," I said. "And over it goes."

Pete returned the tip of the barrel to Mom's temple and I talked fast hoping he wouldn't fire. "Here's the deal," I said wiping cold sweat from my eyes. "When my mom goes down the ladder, you get the money and me."

I could almost see the sick little wheels churning out mayhem inside Pete's brain. After a moment he seemed to come to a decision. Reaching down he grabbed my mom by the shirt and hauled her to her feet. A push to her back sent her staggering forward. When she reached me, her eyes were filled with tears.

"Maxie, I'm sorry. I tried to fight but he shot something into my arm." She swooned against me, unsteady in the high winds.

"It's okay, Mom," I said removing my belt and handing it to her. "Strap this around you and one of the safety-rails next to the ladder. Make sure it's good and tight. Then start down."

The drug was slowing Marie's reactions but she was doing her best to fight it. Smiling gratefully she touched my face.

"Go," I said firmly, not sure how long Pete would be willing to play. "I'll see you down on the ground."

She did as I asked and when her head disappeared below the catwalk, I turned to face Pete who was moving slowly forward, the revolver pointed directly at the center of my chest. Five feet away he stopped and extended his free arm toward the pack.

"Okay, Max. Mommy's safe now. Hand me the cash."

My options were limited so I chose the only one that might save my mom's life. "Sorry," I said shaking my head. "You get nothing for being a fucking asshole."

With a flip of my wrist, I ripped open the backpack's central pocket, exposing the million inside. Before Pete could react, a gust of wind scattered several hundred thousand dollars across the night sky. I heard him curse and the pop of an exploding shell, then hot lead smashed into my chest with force enough to lift me off my feet. My hand still clutched the backpack and as I crashed to the catwalk, it rolled out into space. I smiled despite the excruciating pain. At least the son-of-a-bitch wouldn't get the money.

I lay perfectly still; hoping Pete would assume the single shot had taken me out. My only chance was to catch him by surprise. When several seconds passed, I opened my eyes a crack and witnessed the strangest thing. Pete was lying on his chest near my feet, his right arm stretched over the side as if reaching for something below the catwalk. Turning my head I stared through the steel mesh at Murphy's Law in action. A shoulder strap of the still weighty backpack had caught on the threads of an oversized bolt. And adding insult to injury, the mutinous Velcro straps had somehow resealed themselves.

Although it felt like my chest had been hammered by Muhamed Ali in his prime, I forced myself to sit up. Pain and tears blurred my vision, but through the haze I spotted Pete's gun pressed under his left hand. When I reached for it and wrapped my fingers around the still-warm barrel, he looked up over the edge in shocked surprise. I had no time or strength to wrestle the gun away and use it against him. It was all I could do to wrench it from his grasp and pitch it backwards over my shoulder.

Both of us watched as the gun arced high into the air, ricocheted off the water tank, and bounced to a stop inches from the edge of the catwalk. I looked back at Pete who was grinning in triumph as his hand came up over the side clutching the half full backpack. With an eerie calm he refastened the Velcro, stood up and fit the bag across his shoulders.

"You're wearing Lott's Kevlar vest," he said looking down at me in reluctant respect. "I remember reading about it in the bitch's journal. Congratulations, Max. Spared for the moment. But my next shot will be upside your head. Then I'll climb down and do your old lady."

I huddled against the side of the tank as Pete went for the gun. When his back was to me, I struggled to my feet and took off in the opposite direction. I moved along at a decent clip for a man who had just been shot, and was almost halfway around the giant tank before I was forced to stop and catch my breath. Narrowing my eyes against the pain I stared in the direction I had come, expecting Pete to slip around the curve. When he didn't, I was forced to make a sucker's choice, and after flipping a mental coin, headed back the way I had come. When I found myself at the ladder with Pete nowhere in sight, I did a quick check on my mom. Surprisingly she was almost halfway down, but for some reason she had stopped moving. I would have given anything to help her but if I started down, we'd both be dead.

Ten yards to my left I spotted a succession of steel rungs welded directly to the side of the water tank. They led straight up and seemed to continue to the top of the steep, conical roof. With my options long gone, I began a climb that proved much more challenging than the ladder leading to the catwalk. The side of the tank was completely vertical, and every step made my bruised chest burn in agony.

As I neared the roof, Pete shouted at me from the catwalk. I looked down in time to watch him cock the revolver and take aim.

"Bye-bye, Maxie," Pete shouted. "See you in hell."

My fingers froze around the rung of the ladder. The howling winds slowed, and I could have sworn I heard the gun's hammer strike home. Tensing for the impact, I had the fleeting image of a super-heated lead ball with a smiley face barreling up my rear end. When that didn't happen, I looked down to see Pete struggling with the obviously uncooperative weapon. I took that as my cue and scrambled up the remaining five feet of ladder.

At the top, I heaved my upper body onto a flat, ten-inch lip of steel that circled the base of the cone-shaped roof. But before my legs could follow, a bullet tore savagely into the flesh of my right calf.

A searing pain exploded within me, almost as if the offending bullet had managed to work its way into every cell of my being. When it wound down to a dull roar I was able to pull my legs up and out of harm's way. Leaning back against the steep roof, I stared in morbid fascination as blood pooled around my shoe and dripped over the edge. My stunned brain finally registered that the flowing red river was actually my blood, and a wave of dizziness threatened to wash me over the side.

How I remained conscious I have no idea, but when I peeked over the edge and watched Pete start up the ladder a sick sort of relief washed over me. The longer it took to hunt moi, the more time Marie would have to get away.

That damn little voice in my head kept repeating "git along little doggie" and eventually I obeyed, scuttling along the narrow ledge on hands and knees, and leaving a trail of blood a blind man could follow. Not that it mattered much. There was nowhere to hide.

By the time I had made it to the Woodward side of the tower, Pete had caught up with me. He screamed an order to stop and I complied, almost gratefully, swaying toward the open rim before falling onto my side against the roof.

As the wind wailed around us, Pete approached, a deranged smile stretching his lips tight against his straight white teeth. "Look at us up here, Maxie!" he shouted, eyes ablaze with insanity. "Is this too fuckin' cool or what? Just like Jimmy Cagney in White Heat. 'Top of the world, Ma'!" he screamed and fired two rounds into the roof in imitation of the movie's demented gangster. "Top of the world!"

Pete laughed hysterically, and danced a little jig. "Maxie. Maxie. Maxie," he sang. "I am so glad you didn't buy it that night on the expressway. Stalking your ass was much more fun. My only regret is that I didn't get to see your face when I offed your fucking pussy cat."

The winds ripped at my words as I played psycho-boy for time. "Why the hell did you kill Andra? She never did anything to you."

"For the same reason I'm going to kill you," he said and broke into a joker-like grin. "You and that bitch turned Fox against me."

"Yeah, right," I said. "It didn't have anything to do with you beating the shit out of her and treating her like dirt."

Pete ignored the accusation.

"What about Andra's mother? Why kill her?"

"Because she was there, man," he sneered as spittle foamed on his lips. "What was I going to do? Ask her to leave the room while I raped her daughter? I made the old lady watch and she loved it. Made Andra watch too while I smothered her mommy and torched her bed. I wish you could have seen the bitch beg, Max. She was down on her knees. Begging. Right where that fucking cunt belonged. How about you, Maxie? You want to try begging for your life? Come on, you shit. Beg!"

It was too late in the game for his threats to intimidate me. I had already accepted the fact that it was the end, and I was far beyond any fear of death. Funny thing, that. A good portion of my life had been spent trying to Mambo with that elusive mind-state. Now that we were finally in step, it didn't seem like such a big deal.

A feeling of resignation washed over me as Pete pointed the gun and pulled the trigger. I saw his hand jerk with the recoil and a moment later a single bullet smashed into my right arm. The force of the slug rocked me onto my back, and greased by my own blood I slid steadily toward the roof's edge. I was about to lose consciousness. Strange how you know when a thing like that is going to happen. But before blacking out, I witnessed an awesome sight.

A giant black bird with wings fully extended came screaming down the side of the steep metal roof and slammed headlong into a stupefied Pete Deville. The shocked man was propelled several feet off the roof where he hung, arms and legs scrambling for a non-existent hold, his mouth open wide in a silent scream before he dropped like a stone through empty space.

Chapter 19

I awoke the next day adrift in a drug-induced haze. My first thought, when I could actually put a whole thought together, was that I might possibly be dead and suffering in hell for my sins. It sure felt like it. My entire body ached like a bad tooth. And a strong sensation of nausea coiled inside my gut. After a mental inventory of my numerous strains and pains I decided I must be wrong about the dead thing. No way could death feel as bad as this.

I lay still for several minutes, afraid to move. I didn't want to do anything that would increase the pain. The pain. The two words wormed their way through a small hole in my consciousness and started me asking questions. Why exactly was I in so much pain? What the hell had happened to me? And where was I? That last question seemed like it was the key. If I could figure out where I was, it might cue some memory about how I got there.

Afraid to open my eyes, I gave the air around me a sniff. It smelled faintly medicinal, like disinfectant and alcohol. And there was a soft beeping sound coming from my right. I decided the only way to satisfy my curiosity was to open my eyes. When I finally worked up the courage, I saw Zed and Mom looking down at me.

I gazed at my two favorite women in the world, and felt my mouth fall open with wonder. "Whoa," I groaned feebly, my throat dry as dust. "Is this heaven or what?"

"Absolutely," answered Zed as she filled a glass with ice water and put it to my lips.

I took a small sip and glanced around. When I realized I was in a hospital room, my reason for being there came flooding back.

"So where are the angels?" I croaked, shaking my head in an attempt to fight off the incessant call of Morpheus. "I thought there were supposed to be angels in heaven."

Mom folded her arms across her chest and leaned against Zed's hip. "Who do you think we are, Sonny and Cher?"

The analogy was so comical I laughed despite the pain.

"Let me guess," I said to Marie. "You're the guardian angel of motorcycle mamas. And you," I nodded at Zed. "Surely you must be the Great Mother, Lilith, first wife of Adam, defiler of the missionary position."

Zed's eyebrows rose in obvious pleasure. "Too much Demerol for you, Buster," she said and flashed a sultry smile. "But I'll accept that compliment."

She was right about the Demerol. I could almost feel the heavy meds trying to smother the worst of the pain. The drug's demand that I return to sleep was enticing, especially now that I knew Mom was alive and Zed nearby. At least I thought I knew that. Maybe seeing them was only a dream. My eyes had closed and I could have sworn I heard myself snoring.

When I awoke the following morning, the pain had localized itself in my left arm and right leg. And my chest, not to be outdone, felt like it had been used for kickboxing practice by the entire women's Olympic team. The latter complaint was the result of the .38 caliber slug smashing against my Kevlar vest from barely five feet away. That first bullet left me with a bruised lung, two cracked ribs, and powder burns on my face. The hospital night crew called the wounds to my leg and shoulder "through and throughs." They assured me several times (I guess I kept nodding out and forgetting) that neither bullet had taken out anything vital. Still. It sucks to get shot. Especially three times in the same night.

At eight the next morning a nurse came bustling in with my pain shot.

"Not this morning, thanks," I said and waved her away. I was determined to stay awake long enough to hear the story of what happened on the zoo tower after I had checked out.

My mom arrived at ten sharp and laid the whole story on me, her voice so animated with the memory, she seemed almost giddy.

"It was too bizarre, Maxie. I'm trying to get down that G.D. ladder and not doing too good, when Zed pops up beside me. Man, you should have seen her, all trussed up in some kind of black leather bodysuit. That long hair whipping behind her like a cape. Christ! She looked like a freaking super hero!"

"Hey, I'm not convinced she isn't," I said.

Mom nodded in agreement before continuing. "She had a whip coiled around her waist and..."

"A whip?" I broke in.

"Yeah," Mom laughed. "Don't you love it?"

I shook my head and smiled.

"Anyway," Marie went on, eager to tell the story. "She used the whip to form a safety harness for me and when I assured her I could manage the rest of the way, she practically flew up the ladder. I lost sight of her when she climbed on the roof but I guess she went up one side, looped a rope around that ball at the very top of the tank and shoe-skied down the other, straight into Pete."

I had a mental picture of the giant black bird soaring down the steep roofline at breakneck speed.

"I wish I could have seen Pete's face when Zed sent his ass flying," Marie said. "I'll bet he pooped his pants before he hit the ground."

"Is he dead?"

"As a doornail," Mom said with finality. "The fall broke his neck."

I must have looked thoughtful because she reached over and pinched my cheek.

"Don't waste your time feeling sorry for that asshole," Marie advised. "He was going to kill you. Christ! He was going to kill me. And he made me climb that damn water tower. I'm an old lady, you know. I can't do things like that anymore."

"It's not Pete," I said. "I was thinking about Fox and how she's going to feel when it all comes out. Does the media have the story?"

Mom reached in her bag and pulled out the Detroit Free Press. "You made the front page, baby boy." She tossed the paper on the bed.

I picked it up with my good hand and read the two-inch headline. "Tower of Terror. Accused Murderer Takes Fatal Fall."

"Tower of Terror?" I asked glancing at Marie who had rocked back on her heels, face pink with pride.

"That was mine," she bragged and gave me a toothy smile. "I said it when they interviewed me for the eleven o'clock news and the papers picked it up. Pretty cool, huh?"

"Yeah," I answered whacking myself with a mental head-slap for giving her that collection of classic disaster flicks last Christmas. "Real cool."

The news story, most of it direct quotes from my mother the media star, covered her kidnapping, my rescue attempt, and the seeding of several hundred thousand dollars in and around the zoo grounds. What the article failed to mention was the still half-full backpack that went down with Pete, and the mysterious Amazon that had saved both our butts.

I looked at my mom and raised an eyebrow.

"Wonder Woman insisted I leave her name out of it," she said lowering her voice. "She wants you to do the same. Nobody else knows what happened up there except you and Pete, and he's not going to tell anybody."

I thought about that for a moment and decided she was right.

"You were unconscious when Zed lowered you to the catwalk," Mom said winding up her story. "After she helped me make it down the support cables we worked out my story for the police."

"What about my gun?"

"Zed took it," Marie answered glancing toward the door. "She said it would only complicate things for you if it was found there."

"And the backpack?"

"She collected that too," Mom said grimly. "Took it right off Pete's body. After she left I called 911 on the cell phone she gave me."

I must have looked pensive because Marie rushed to assure me that Zed was okay. "You like her, don't you, baby boy?" she said flaunting her mother's intuition and laughing when my face flushed red. "I think she's kind of sweet on you too."

"I hope you're right, Mom" I said, thinking hard about my Amazon beauty and the fact that she didn't return my "I love you" the other night.

The hospital staff was great but what I really wanted was to get the hell out of there. All those sick people's germs hunting around for new digs. Now that was a true tower of terror. Finally my doctor, nudged along by my insurance carrier, agreed to discharge me.

While driving home Zed announced she'd be staying with me until I was stronger. For the next several weeks I was under her very personal care. She replaced my pain meds with massage and herbal teas, fed me a meatless diet to strengthen my immune system, and wrapped my wounds in some kind of sweet smelling leaves before applying new bandages. Added to these medical ministrations was a daily dose or two of sex. Does this medicine woman know how to take care of her patients or what?

"The sex is necessary," Zed explained when I teased her about it, "to keep your circulation stimulated."

"Works for me, babe. You give great circulation."

Riff came by to visit several times while I was convalescing. Her first time out she cornered me in the kitchen and read me the riot act.

"You," she said tapping a fingertip against my forehead, "are completely certifiable. Do you know that?"

I started to protest but she stopped me short with a raised palm.

"And owning a gun does not make you "James freaking Bond.""

"But..."

"But, my ass," she said. "What are you going to do next? Stop cutting hair and become a private investigator?"

"Hmmm," I said and stroked my chin for effect. "Think anyone would be interested in my services?"

Riff and Zed hit it off right from the start and it looked like they could easily become good friends. Talk about your intriguing developments. At first I was concerned they might compare notes on my sexual technique, but when I sensed the rapport building between the two exciting women, I found myself wondering if the three of us might...well, never mind. Men can be such pigs.

As my mom said, Pete had paid for his crimes when Zed knocked his sorry ass off the tower. Unfortunately he wouldn't suffer in jail like I had hoped, but at least he'd never hurt anyone again. Our man Stumpy, on the other hand, in an attempt to save himself from a sentence of life without parole, spilled the entire story of how Pete had killed Andra and her mom. Stumpy admitted being at the Martin house the night of the murders, but said that he robbed the place while Pete kept Andra and Lila in the bedroom. Claimed he wasn't aware Pete had killed the women until he bragged about torching Lila's bed and using a pint of whiskey he had in his pocket, to get it rolling. Stumpy would be charged as an accessory in all three deaths, and according to Riff, would probably wear an orange jumpsuit for the rest of his life.

A month later I was back at the salon cutting hair two days a week. It was nice to see everybody and hear what was happening at the mall. I decided after being away that I really did enjoy my work. It was fun and relatively safe as long as I didn't breathe in too much powdered bleach and hairspray. It also gave me the opportunity to get personal with a lot of great people. Most of my clients were friends and I miss them if I'm away too long.

The part I didn't like about being back was, of course, the dreaded paperwork. Fox could handle the lion's share of the business but there were some things only

I could do. Like signing checks for my hard-working employees at ten o'clock at night because they had to be paid the next day.

As I sat at my desk signing the last paycheck, there was a sharp knock on the door to the service hall. Good thing nobody could see me because the unexpected sound made me jump, and my pen went flying across the room. It was obvious the effects of the tower incident hadn't worn off entirely.

Swallowing my anxiety, I stood, moved cautiously toward the door and reached for the handle.

"Well, duh," said the ever-vigilant little voice. "Might be smart to ask who it is first."

"Who is it?"

"It's me, Bobby."

I opened the door and the office overheads threw a rectangle of light across the dim hallway. My old friend Bobby Deegan stood bathed in the soft glow. I had not seen him since that day we met on the golf course. He looked California tan. And dressed in jeans, black high-tops, a Detroit Tigers cap and warm-up jacket, he reminded me of old times together.

"Bobby. What's up?"

"Stopped by your house," he said. "You weren't around so I thought I'd try here. Read all about your adventure and the money you spread around the zoo."

"You and most of Michigan's other residents."

"So how ya feeling?"

"Healing up."

"How about your mom?" he asked.

"In better shape than me, thankfully."

"I wish I'd been there to help, Max. Sorry."

I waved away his apology and returned to the chair behind my desk.

Bobby leaned inside the doorway, both hands in his jacket pockets. He gave my office the once over before crossing the room and sitting down on the divan that faced my desk. "So this is the nerve center of your empire," he said. "And here you are, the dedicated businessman working diligently into the night. Who would have thought you were capable?"

"Don't tell anybody," I said and put a finger to my lips, "but I'm not. I know how to cut hair and sign checks. Beyond that, I rely on the good people working for me. They cover my ass."

Bobby looked straight at me, his expression unreadable. "Good thing that Pete guy didn't get Lott's four million."

I nodded in agreement. "He was a sick puppy."

"How much did you lose up on the zoo tower?"

"Close to three hundred thousand."

Bobby whistled in awe and leaned into the cushions. "That's a lot of dough."

"Yeah, well," I said and rocked back in my chair. "It wasn't mine to begin with, so it's no big deal. I told the zoo curator that whatever they found on the grounds, they could keep. He predicts the public will flock to the zoo in record numbers for a while, hunting around for stray cash. I guess it's already increased attendance."

"Didn't the G-Men want to know where all that money came from?" Bobby asked.

I rolled my eyes in acknowledgment. "Oh yeah. The Feds are still dogging the paper trail. But since I'm a bona fide lotto winner, and Johnny Lott was smart enough to put away clean money, they're having trouble disputing my story."

"What about the rest of Lott's cash?"

"Actually it's here," I said nodding at a safe in the corner. "Can't put it in the bank. And I don't want it in my house anymore."

"You could put it in a foreign bank," Bobby suggested. "I've got a friend in Florida who can get it to the Bahamas by boat."

I shook my head. "Thanks for the offer, but I'm thinking of setting up some college scholarships in Andra's name. My accountant is looking into it."

"With some smart overseas investments, you could afford to set up twice as many."

I looked at Bobby questioningly. Was it my imagination, or did he seem a bit too interested in the remaining cash?

"Too much trouble, man," I said, dismissing his suggestion. "I don't even want to deal with this but I think it's the right thing to do."

"You could turn the money over to me," Bobby joked.

At least I thought he was joking. When I looked into his flat green eyes, I wasn't sure.

"Truthfully, Max. I deserve that money."

"You deserve it?" I asked warily, not at all happy with the way the conversation was going.

"That's right," he said and his tone grew insolent. "Lott and I were partners on a deal in Europe. He screwed up and I got busted. Spent more than six years in a filthy fucking Italian prison. You have no idea what it's like being an American in a foreign prison."

So that's where he had disappeared to all those years. He never told me. "You're right about that," I said and wished suddenly that Bobby and I weren't alone in the salon.

"All the perverts want a piece of your ass," he went on, "and nobody dares to be your friend. In the beginning I'd cause trouble so they'd put me in solitary. I hated being penned in that damn cage, but it was the only place I could get any peace. The guards caught on soon enough, and after that they left me at the mercy of the other prisoners."

"Must have been hell," I said. "I'm sorry."

I watched his expression grow hard and cruel as if he was disgusted by my sympathy. The icy stare he flashed carried a whole lot of information.

"Lott agreed to pay me three million if I did the time and didn't take him down with me."

Now it was my turn to whistle. "Six years must have been tough," I said, trying to lighten things up. "But at least the pay was good."

Bobby's gaze blanked-out and I figured he was reliving memories of prison life. "Guess that depends," he said dully, "on how many dicks you can handle poking up your butt."

I squirmed in my chair.

"After I got out I showed up at Lott's house for the payoff. He was more than happy to oblige. One thing about Johnny, he took care of his debts. When he went upstairs to get the money, I followed. Saw him go inside the wall mural and come out with the cash. Couldn't help wondering how much more he had socked away in there."

And how you could get your greedy little hands on it, I thought.

"I was out of the country on business when Lott got hammered," Bobby continued. "By the time I got back, you had bought his house and moved in. I could hardly believe my luck. Figured there was a good chance you didn't know about the shrine room or the money. Thought I could slip in some night and grab whatever was there. Didn't count on you shooting me."

My eyes opened wide in surprise. "What?!" I said. "But I thought Pete…"

Bobby shook his head.

"I shot you?" I said stunned by the revelation.

"Just a scratch," he said staring at me intently. "More blood than damage."

"Sorry, man," I murmured. "I had no idea…"

"Hey, no problem," he said cutting me off. "I would have done the same thing if I had found you in there. Forget about it."

I wasn't quite sure how to respond to that, so I kept quiet.

"Look, Maxie, I deserve Lott's money more than you do. I was stuck in that cage for six years because of him. Now I need to be out on the golf course. It's the only place I can breathe."

"So who's stopping you?" I said. "Go golf."

"The courses I like to play are expensive and I'm running low on funds."

"So," I said trying to remain calm. "Because you want to live it up, you expect me to turn over three and a half million, just like that?"

He looked at me, serious as hell. "Yes."

"And if I don't?" I asked testing the already muddy waters.

"Then I'd be forced to kill you," he said. And calmly as you please, took a semiautomatic from his jacket pocket and fit a silencer on the end of the barrel.

"You wouldn't," I said. But the evil glint in his eye told me he definitely would.

With his left hand, Bobby pulled a pack of cigarettes out of his shirt pocket, shook one loose and caught it between his lips.

"So what's it going to be, Maxie?"

"What are my choices?" I said stalling for time.

"Not a hell of a lot, I'm afraid."

I glanced down at my desk for anything I could use to protect myself. There was my open check ledger, the phone, and half a dozen cans of Paul Mitchell Super Hold hairspray that had been delivered without caps. Not much defense against the very lethal handgun staring me in the face. Reaching into his pants' pocket, Bobby pulled out the lighter I had seen him use that day on the golf course. I remembered it because to fight the wind on the open fairways the flame had been set high enough to singe his eyebrows.

Bobby rambled on about something, his voice cocky, but I wasn't listening to a word. My brain was too busy trying to save my ass. Unfortunately, the only idea I could come up with was extremely risky and it involved getting even closer to my loony ex-friend. But dangerous as that was, it beat an unchallenged bullet to the brain.

It was a wonder my legs could actually support me but I rose cautiously, walked slowly around the desk and sat on the edge directly in front of Bobby.

"Easy, Maxie," he said, pointing the gun at my heart. "You're not wearing Lott's vest tonight."

"You wouldn't really shoot me," I said. "Not after a lifetime of friendship."

Bobby sneered, and when he spoke I watched the cigarette ride his lower lip like a jockey. "You don't get it yet, do you, Max? You still think of me as your childhood pal."

Yeah, right, I thought. In the proverbial pig's eye.

"Hey, man," I said trying to play the simp he expected. "That money's been nothing but a pain in the ass to me. And if you want it that bad, you can have it."

Bobby smiled.

"But what happens after that?" I asked.

His face flushed with excitement. It was hard to hide so much evil. "I'd take the cash and be on my way," he said fingering the lighter. "What else?"

"Oh I don't know. I kind of thought you might shoot me anyway. You know, to keep me quiet."

"Quiet about what?" Bobby said arrogantly, although I was sure he was shooting for innocence. "It's like you said before, man. The money wasn't yours to begin with. How could you claim it was stolen?"

We locked eyes for a beat before Bobby went on. "Nope. You give me the dough and I'm out of here."

Uh huh.

Bobby's smirk brought his cigarette to attention and as his lighter paused at the tip; my fingers encircled the nearest can of hairspray. One second ticked by…two. Bobby's thumb skimmed the flint-wheel sparking a five-inch flame that erupted like a geyser. As he touched fire to cigarette, I snatched up the spray and shot the aerosol stream directly in his face, igniting the propellant and turning the can into a mini flame-thrower. Bobby let out a blood-curdling scream and fired his gun, but I was already up and running.

Bolting through the service door, I ran wildly down the dimly lit hall, hoping I might run into a security guard. But like cops, they're usually not around when you need them. Halfway down the long hall it came to me that I was going the wrong way. All I would find in this direction is the service elevator and stairs leading to the loading dock. I screeched to a stop and turned around, but at that exact second the door to my office slammed open and Bobby staggered out into the hall.

He held a forearm above his burned eyes. I had obviously hurt him. But to prove he was still in the game, he fired off two rounds that whizzed by my ear and embedded themselves in the drywall. I didn't need a house to fall on me. I took off running in the opposite direction.

I could hear Bobby's footsteps trailing me as I skidded around a corner and headed for the stairs to the loading dock. Passing the freight elevator, I saw the doors were open, and making a quick detour, I ducked inside, hit the button for the third floor then slipped out again. It was a little bait for Bobby. And I hoped to Christ he would take it. A moment later, I was making my way down to the loading dock. At the bottom, I listened to Bobby pounding on the elevator doors one floor above me. Now he'd be forced to choose a direction. I knew it was the wrong one (for him anyway) when I heard him running up the steel stairs to the third floor.

Am I good or what?

I crept out of the stairwell and into the dimly lit loading bay, empty except for the boxcar-sized trash compactor that loomed against the far wall. The only way out of there, other than the stairway, was through the two huge loading bay doors. Unfortunately, both looked to be locked down for the night. A single security lamp far above fogged the walls in gray-black shadows and the surrounding air, rife with the smell of rotting garbage, was still and quiet.

The sound of shoes pounding down the stairs made my chest swell with panic. Remember how I said I was good because I did that elevator thing? Well forget it. Bobby had already figured out my scam and was on his way down.

I looked around for a place to hide but my choices went from limited to zip. There was nothing in the loading area except me, and the ever-hungry garbage eater. In desperation, I punched the salon's access code into the compactor's control panel and the square door on the side of the massive contraption popped open.

I had no time to consider the consequences of my rash act. Bobby would be down there any second. It was either hide in the maw of this mechanical monster or let him shoot me down like a dog. I had wounded him, conned him, and compromised his professional reputation. There was no way was he going to let me live to tell that tale to the cops or anyone else.

Bracing my foot on a curved pipe below the door, I took a deep breath and boosted myself into the compactor. It was pitch black inside with a smell that would offend Pepe Le'Pew and as the seconds passed my stomach cramped and threatened to return my dinner. But tossing my cookies, although not one of my favorite things; was low on my list of worries. Bobby had entered the loading dock.

I hooked my fingers around the bottom of the steel door and pulled it towards me making sure not to let it close all the way. If that happened, the compactor would go into action and whatever was inside, namely me, would be crushed flat.

Bobby's voice echoed in the loading bay, jarring my already frazzled nerves. "I know you're here, Maxie," he said with total conviction. "I can smell your chicken-shit fear."

A quick sniff of the surrounding air told me Bobby was bluffing. Not even a bloodhound could pick out my chicken-shit fear from the putrid smells inside that funky dumpster.

I heard footsteps and peeked out just in time to watch Bobby walk through the dim pool of light in the center in the bay. He paused long enough for me to see that his eyebrows had been singed black as coal.

I pulled back when he turned my way, thinking it never pays to piss off a guy holding a gun.

"Come on, Maxie," Bobby said his voice coaxing and conciliatory. "All I want is Lott's money. Unlock the safe and I swear I won't hurt you."

And if you believe that, I have a citrus grove on the north end of the Russian tundra I'd like to sell you.

Bobby went quiet and in that deafening silence I knew I'd been made.

"Dangerous place to be hanging, buddy," he said addressing me directly through the crack in the door. "Smells real bad too. Sure you wouldn't rather come back to the salon and open the safe?"

I didn't answer.

"I'm going to get the money either way so you might as well make it easy."

"Maybe," I said stalling for time as I felt around for something to jam into the door. The ruthless bastard was going to close it if he didn't get what he wanted, and unless I could stop him, I was going to end up a human pancake. I searched blindly until my fingers closed on a rough piece of wood about a yard long. In a quick motion, I jammed it through the opening and held tight.

Bobby snorted at my feeble attempt to save myself and slammed the steel door against the wood several times.

"I'm sick of fucking with you, Max," he seethed through the dark crack. "Do us both a favor and cave. You can't beat me."

I knew he was right. With my arm still weak from the bullet I'd taken a month ago Bobby could have easily wrenched the wood from my grasp. Maybe I should just do what he wanted and take my chances.

I released my grip on the wood and Bobby swung the door wide.

"All you have to do is open the safe, Maxie. Is that so tough? You don't want to die in there, man."

"Okay," I said feigning defeat, which wasn't very hard. But as I started to climb out the door Bobby waved me back with his gun.

"On second thought," he said shaking his head. "It will be easier without you. You're too lucky. And I can bring a guy in here tonight who will crack that safe like a piggy bank."

"But…"

"Sorry, old friend" Bobby said insolently, his face set with an ugly sneer. "But you're heading for that big hair salon in the sky. Care to trade a bullet for the safe combination? It's my last offer."

I stayed silent.

"Say hi to God for me," he said giving me a little wave. And with those final words, he slammed the door.

As metal met metal, the giant compactor shuddered to life. The high whine of hydraulic motors pierced the air and with a loud clunk, the steel plate to my right began inching slowly toward me.

Damn it! Had I been spared Pete's murderous intentions only to be flattened into pulp and buried in some nameless landfill? What the hell was that all about? And where was that damn little voice when I needed it? Why didn't it tell me Bobby was a crazy shit and to avoid him like the plague? Scrambling to my feet I scrunched against the garbage behind me, no longer caring about the bad smell. I was about to become part of it any minute.

As the steel plate crept toward me inch-by-inch I thought I heard voices calling my name. For a moment I imagined I might already be dead and they were deceased relatives urging me to let go and move into the light. But one of the voices sounded like my mom. How the hell could Marie be welcoming me to the afterlife?

I leaned sideways and pounded on the door of the compactor calling for help. My only answer was the sound of the steel plate grinding steadily toward me. Standing on tiptoes I flattened myself against the already compressed garbage behind me. The metal wall was so close it was squeezing my chest like a breastplate, causing me to gulp mouthfuls of the stale air. Just as my hip bones were being pressed into the trash, the hydraulic whine of the motor ceased and the deadly plate stopped its progression.

I was pinned tight between steel and waste, not sure what the turn of events could mean and not giving a damn. Maybe Bobby was going to ask me for the safe combination one last time, and maybe if he would promise to shoot me before restarting the compactor I might tell.

A moment later, the compactor's hydraulics reengaged and the crushing wall reversed its direction. Sixty seconds later it was back in its original position.

With a loud click, the compactor door cracked open and swung wide. A moment later a face popped through the hole. "Who rang that bell?" said a familiar voice attempting to imitate the palace guard in the Wizard of Oz. But I wasn't fooled. The Emerald City never smelled that bad and the horse-like face could only belong to my friend Kenny Dougland. "Maxie," he said grinning broadly as he reached a hand in to grasp mine, "How ya doing, buddy-boy?"

I climbed carefully out of the dumpster and gazed in wonder at the scene before me. Bobby was on his knees, disarmed and subdued by the one-and-only Zed. And standing in front of him, pointing his own gun directly at the center of his forehead was the incomparable Marie Snow. Talk about your dynamic duos.

Chapter 20

▼

The next morning Zed and I were lounging in bed when we heard the doorbell.

"Now who would want to visit us this early in the morning?" I asked lazily, sliding my arm around the woman that lay snuggled beside me.

"It's your mother bearing baked goods," Zed answered smugly as she nuzzled closer.

I looked down at her and raised an eyebrow. She brought her head up and met my gaze.

"It's nothing like that," she said in answer to my unspoken question. "Marie told me she was coming over this morning."

"That's not what I had in mind for breakfast," I said, cupping one of Zed's weighty breasts. I kissed her and she moved her mouth over mine with delicious tenderness, while at the same time trailing a hand up the inside of my thigh. When the exploring fingers reached their target my carnal senses ignited like a torch.

"Easy, big boy," Zed purred, and gave me a final squeeze. "We've got a visitor, remember?"

Twenty minutes later the coffee was brewed and the three of us sat at the kitchen table chowing down on fresh bagels and croissants. I was trying my best to get a straight story out of Marie about what went on last night, but she was having too much fun ragging on Bobby.

"I never trusted that little shit," Mom said. "Even as a kid, he had a creepy side. I don't know how many times I told you not to hang out with him."

"You didn't like anybody I hung out with, Mom."

"Hmmph!" Marie said, as she sipped her coffee. "Well I guess I was right about that one. You should always listen to your mother. Right, Zed?"

The Amazon beauty only smiled. She didn't want to mess with my mom. Who could blame her?

"And then," Mom said stabbing a finger at me for emphasis. "You just let his ass go. What was that about? Some of your Buddhist balance crap? We need the bad guys so we can tell who the good guys are? That is such a crock. I never should have taken you out of Catholic school."

I stared at her.

"All right, all right," she said, unable to hide her smile. "Maybe it's not a total crock. But do we need so many creeps? And when we meet one that tries to kill us, is there anything in the cosmic-law books that says we can't shoot him a little bit?"

I breathed out a long sigh. "Shoot him a little bit?"

"Yeah," she said impudently then winked at Zed. "Maybe only shoot one of his balls off instead of both."

"Ah, of course," I said throwing up my hands. "Why didn't I think of that? A little torture is always good for the soul."

"Max is right, Marie," Zed chimed in, a devilish smile lighting up her face. "Shooting off only one of his balls might make him even meaner. It would have to be both or nothing."

The women laughed and slapped a high five across the table.

"Men," my mom said giving me a self-satisfied look before reaching over to biff me lightly in the back of the head. "What do you know? You can't even hold on to your hair."

"It's a well known fact that men get their hair genes from their mother's side of the family," I said. Actually, I didn't know if that was true or not, but I'd heard it somewhere and it fit the situation.

Mom ignored my comment and continued her story. "Good thing I was at your house when that weird looking dude showed up. Man, what a face. His parents must be butt-ugly. Should be a crime for two ugly people to get married and produce children."

Zed and I exchanged glances.

"He was babbling on about how you were in trouble," Mom went on, "and how we had to get to the mall to save you. I thought he was nuts, until he mentioned Bobby's name. That got my attention. I asked how the hell he knew Bobby, and he said that's who was trying to kill you. Don't ask me why I believed him, but the next thing I know, we're zipping off to the mall on my bike."

"Your bike?" I asked, picturing the scene. "You and Kenny rode to the mall on your motorcycle?"

"Yeah," Mom answered as amusement flickered behind her brown eyes. "It was either that or his bicycle. And I'm too old to ride on the handlebars."

I was thinking the woman wasn't too old for anything as she continued her story.

"We got in the mall through the theatre entrance and made our way down a service hallway to the loading bay."

"Hold it," I said raising a palm. "What exactly was your plan?"

"Plan? Who had a plan? We were there to save your ass."

"But how were you going to do that?"

"Mom leaned forward in her seat and thrust out her chin. "I was armed with the power of motherhood. You don't wanna be messin' with that."

I shook my head and tried to look serious. "Not even."

Mom gave a tight nod, satisfied I knew where she was coming from. "I walked straight up to that bastard and got right in his face. Threatened to tell his mother he was up to no good."

"You threatened to tell his mother?" I said. "Ooh, that must have scared him."

"Damn right it did. Darlene Deegan is a cruel bitch and I could tell by his reaction, that he was still scared to death of the woman."

I thought back to the black eyes and bruises Bobby usually sported as a kid. Some of them came from fights around the neighborhood, but I knew most came from the regular beatings he got at home.

"Unfortunately the threat didn't work as good as I hoped."

"Well, duh," I said. "The man is a professional killer."

"Did I know that?" Mom snapped back. "Did you ever tell me little Bobby Deegan kills people for money?"

I shrugged my shoulders and flashed a cheesy grin. I guess I never had told her my suspicions about Bobby. But then again, why would I?

"He called me a pushy bitch," Marie said indignantly. "And then he stuck a gun in my face." She stopped her tale and looked questioningly at Zed and me. "Well?" she implored. "Can you believe it?"

"Believe what?" I asked.

Mom glared at me. "That he called me pushy. I'm not pushy."

"Pushy? You? Never."

Mom scrunched up her face and gave me the finger. "There's a big difference between being a forceful woman like myself, and being pushy."

"Oh, a huge difference," I said and hid my smile with a bagel.

Marie shot me a kiss-my-ass smirk and went on with her story. "I have to admit, Bobby was very scary looking with those toasted eyebrows. And for a couple of seconds there, I thought for sure he was going to shoot me and what's-his-name. That's when Zed came charging out of nowhere and knocked his sorry ass to the ground."

I turned to Zed and winked. "You da man, babe." I said, holding up a clenched fist.

Zed didn't respond. She only stared at me through half-hooded eyes, an indulgent smile playing across her beautiful lips.

"When he hit the ground," Mom said, "I snagged his gun and Zed told the weird guy…"

"His name is Kenny," I said.

"Whatever," Marie answered, annoyed at the interruption. "Zed told him to hit the emergency button on the trash compactor. He did, the door popped open and guess what we found inside?"

I didn't bother to ask Zed how she knew I was in trouble. I'm only grateful she did. Twice now, the mysterious woman had saved me from certain death and I'd been considering ways to repay her. I finally decided to offer her a million dollars out of Johnny Lott's stash. If she accepted, and I was pretty sure she would, I'd consider my debt only partially paid. For the balance, I would volunteer to become her sex slave for the rest of my life. I realized that meant spending long blissful hours trying to satisfy this incredibly gorgeous creature but hey, never let it be said that Max Snow welshed on his debts.

I glanced over at the awesome Amazon and thought about the delights hidden beneath her snug silk kimono. Zed returned my look with a knowing smile, and I watched her large eyes darken with desire. Weeks ago, she had suggested that some men might consider her ability to sense their moods a blessing. And she was absolutely right.

Mom stood up and announced she was leaving. "I better take off," she said, grabbing her beat-up Coach backpack off the table and slinging it across one shoulder. "And I won't be back for awhile. Don't think there's room in this house for me and all these hormones. Besides, I met a new man and I hope to be cooking-up some of my own real soon."

"You go, girl," said Zed and she and Mom did the secret women's handshake.

"Who is it this time?" I asked.

"His name is Davenport Davies," Marie said her voice full of amusement. "Can you believe that handle? Most people call him D.D. He puts together month-long scuba-diving trips in the Galapagos, and he asked me if I wanted to go."

"You don't dive," I said.

"Well not yet anyway," Marie answered pulling her car keys from a pocket of the backpack. "But D.D.'s volunteered to become my personal instructor. He's got the most marvelous blue eyes. I just couldn't refuse. And I'm anxious to see how he fills out his wet suit."

"Spare me the details, please," I said, hugging the tiny woman and kissing the top of her head. "And make sure you're not getting mixed up with some golddigger."

"Never mind about me," Marie said before dragging my face down to whisper in my ear. "You just take care of yourself. And try not to blow it with Wonder Woman here. She's the best thing to come your way in a long time."

After walking my mom to her car I returned to the house and locked up behind me, wishing I had a "Do Not Disturb" sign to hang on the door. I was anxious to begin that sex slave position I had been thinking about, and I didn't want any uninvited guests.

Zed stood waiting at the bottom of the stairs, and as I walked toward her, she loosened the belt of her kimono. A slight shrug of her powerful shoulders sent the silky fabric floating to the floor like a shadow, and slipping a hand under each breast, she squeezed the taunt bronze flesh.

I approached the tantalizing vision with the idea of making love to her right there on the stairs but as I neared, Zed shook her head slowly.

"If you don't mind," she said starting up the stairway. "I think we'll save that particular fantasy for another time. Today I want to luxuriate in bed, where I expect you to pamper and spoil me, and satisfy my every whim. Are you up to it?"

"Up to it?" I said, sliding out of my own robe and following a step behind. "I'll have you know, lady, that I'm licensed by the State of Michigan to perform those very functions."

"Well, yow." she said mimicking my oft-used expression. "Then give me the works, Mr. Max."

We stayed in bed most of that day and it was my pleasure to serve, and serve, and serve. Something about the incredible woman brought out the best in me, and although I'd tried to resist, it was a lost cause. I had fallen head-over-heels in love. The idea of giving my heart away was more than a little scary. But as my recent experience with two cranky killers illustrated, the end is always nearer than you think. If Zed would have me, I was going to spend whatever time I had left with the exquisite enchantress.

Zed slipped off to hit the bathroom. When she returned a few minutes later, she sat cross-legged on the bed and looked at me with a serious expression.

"We've got to talk."

"Sure," I said running my fingers through her raven locks. "What about?"

"I'm going to have to leave the country for a while."

"Leave?" The single word hit me like an unexpected punch in the face.

"Yes. I need to return home."

I sat up straight and looked at her wide-eyed. "Home? You mean Belize?"

She nodded.

"But..." I searched my dazed brain for the correct words. "I thought this was your home. I mean I want this to be your home, Zed. Right here, with me."

"There's something I need to take care of down there."

"I'll go with you."

Zed shook her head. "No. I need to do this alone."

I tried to swallow down my rising anxiety. "How long will you be gone?" I said attempting to keep my voice steady.

"It's hard to say."

"Won't it be dangerous?" I asked, thinking of the paramilitary crazies she had once fled.

"Perhaps, but I have to go."

It was a simple statement. The kind you didn't even attempt to argue with.

"When will you leave?" I asked, not really wanting to know the answer.

"Tomorrow."

"Tomorrow?" I repeated stunned by the bombshell.

We sat knee-to-knee, staring at each other. "I thought something was going on between us."

Zed gazed at me with her large black eyes. "You make it sound like I'll never return. I will."

"When? In a week? A month? A year?"

"I can't say."

"Well can you guesstimate?"

Zed shook her head.

"What am I supposed to do in the meantime?"

Zed laughed softly, leaned forward and kissed my cheek. "Live your life of course. I won't ask questions."

"I'll give it my best shot," I said and made a half-hearted attempt to return her breezy smile.

Zed uncoiled gracefully and stretched out on the bed before me. "See that you do," she said wrapping a hand around my balls and squeezing just hard enough to make me wince. "And when in doubt, wear a condom."

At three the next afternoon, I stood at the window of Metro Airport's International Terminal watching Zed's plane taxi down the runway. I already felt empty inside and wondered if I should have tried harder to convince her to stay. My attraction to independent women has always been a double-edged sword. This time it had sliced my heart in two.

Several weeks later, I was at the salon locked in my studio, feeling sorry for myself. I had spoken to Zed that morning which should have made me happy, but it didn't. The phone connection was bad so we couldn't talk freely and once again she couldn't give me any clue as to when she would return. In fact she told me it might be a while before she could even contact me again. Not exactly the news I wanted to hear.

As I considered the dismal prospect of eating dinner alone, the locked door of my private studio opened and a pair of hefty breasts poked through the doorway. They were followed by a diminutive woman in five-inch patent leather heels. In fact, Bette's entire outfit (what there was of it) was black patent leather, and the glossy fabric hugged her unbelievable form like a second skin.

"Maxie-o," she chirped, placing tiny hands on shapely hips. "I need your help."

0-595-29936-9